FOWL PLAY

THE JUNIPER JUNCTION COZY HOLIDAY MYSTERY SERIES: BOOK SIX

AMY M. READE

PAU HANA PUBLISHING

BOOKS BY AMY M. READE

THE JUNIPER JUNCTION COZY HOLIDAY MYSTERY SERIES

The Worst Noel
Dead, White, and Blue
Be My Valencrime
Ghouls' Night Out
MayDay!
Fowl Play

THE LIBRARIES OF THE WORLD MYSTERY SERIES

Trudy's Diary

THE MALICE SERIES

The House on Candlewick Lane
Highland Peril
Murder in Thistlecross

STANDALONE BOOKS

Secrets of Hallstead House
The Ghosts of Peppernell Manor
House of the Hanging Jade

BOOKS BY A.M. READE

THE CAPE MAY HISTORICAL MYSTERY COLLECTION

Cape Menace
A Traitor Among Us

ACKNOWLEDGMENTS

As always, I would like to thank my husband, John, who is always my first reader. Thanks also to Holly Bolicki and Anna Maria Tothivan for their invaluable assistance in making this a better book.

*For the members of Mystery Authors International, in grateful
appreciation of all their support*

CHAPTER 1

Thanksgiving was a week away and Lilly Carlsen was running herself ragged. Her to-do list included preparing her jewelry shop window displays for the holidays, visiting her mother, Bev, as often as possible at the assisted living facility, and getting Bev's house ready to put on the market. But Lilly was no quitter, so she was also worrying about Vanessa's future as an unwed mother, fretting about the trip to Afghanistan that Hassan was planning, and experiencing the entire spectrum of guilt over moving Bev out of the home she loved and had lived in for decades.

It had been another long day at work and she was glad to be home. She gathered her purse, her sketchbook of jewelry designs, her travel mug of coffee—left untouched since her arrival at work early that morning—and got out of the car. She started toward the house but turned around when a sudden and heavy pounding from next door echoed through the otherwise quiet neighborhood.

"Come on, Xavier!" someone yelled. It sounded like a woman's voice. Lilly set her things on the roof of her car and walked over to the neighbor's front yard. She had glimpsed the new occupant of the house from afar but not yet met him. It seemed he had an irate visitor.

"Hello?" she called into the darkness. Two sconces, one on each side of the front door, illuminated the person making all the noise. It was, indeed, a woman. She was practically buried under an armload of boxes and bags. Lilly walked a bit closer and raised her voice so the woman could hear her.

"Hello? Is everything okay?"

The woman uttered a tiny shriek of surprise, then turned her head. "Oh, yes. Everything's fine. I'm sorry if all my noise disturbed you," she called out. "I'm trying to get Xavier to open the door. I know he's in there."

"Can I help you hold that stuff?" Lilly ascended the front steps and held out her arms. The woman looked grateful as she handed Lilly two of the smaller boxes to hold.

"I'm so sorry about this." The woman reached out a mani-cured finger and pressed the doorbell three times. "Here I am with all this stuff Xavier asked me to bring him and he's not even answering the door. Oh, I'm so rude. I'm Mimi Gordon." She made an attempt to shake Lilly's hand, but the tower of boxes she was holding threatened to topple over, so she gripped the boxes more tightly and laughed. "We can shake hands some other time."

Lilly grinned. "That's okay. Why don't you just put every-thing down while you wait for him to get to the door?"

"Because if and when he opens the door, I want him to see how hard I'm working to get him settled in." She winked.

Lilly had no idea what Mimi was talking about, but she stood next to her, thinking of how ironic it was to have someone on this particular porch apologize for making so much noise.

Until just a few weeks ago, the house had belonged to Edna Laforge—or rather, to Edna Laforge's estate. Edna had died of a sudden heart attack in the spring and it had taken her sons several months to get the house cleaned out and put on the market. Once it was up for sale, it sold quickly.

Mimi knocked on the door again. "Xavier!" she yelled. She let out a loud "ugh" and turned her head toward Lilly. "You don't have to wait here. It's cold out. If you can just set those boxes down on the steps, I'll—oh!"

The tower of boxes in her arms started to sway. She over-compensated for their movement by jerking her arms and a moment later the entire pile came crashing down onto the porch. Boxes spilled open, spewing their myriad contents: pencils, pens, small memo pads, photos, empty manilla folders, cords and cables, two fake plants, several magazines, and about a million other small things that would take forever to clean up.

"I don't believe this," Mimi muttered. "I am going to kill that man when he opens that door."

"Let me help you," Lilly said. She set her boxes down and knelt next to them, reaching to pick up a pen still rolling across the floor.

"Thanks." Mimi pushed an empty box toward her. "It doesn't matter if it's neat. Just shove stuff right in there. I'll get everything straightened up and put away one of these days." She busied herself scrambling for bits of paper and small office items that were scattered everywhere.

Lilly tried to ignore the hunger pangs gnawing at her stomach and bent forward to reach a folder that had slid across the floor. As she dropped it into the box, she heard a faint *click* and the front door swung open.

CHAPTER 2

*L*illy looked up to see a man standing in the doorway, wearing only a towel around his waist and another one over his shoulders. He grinned when he saw her and Mimi on the porch floor.

Lilly scrambled to her feet as Mimi gave the man a look that could cut glass. "What gives? I've been waiting here for so long the neighbors started taking pity on me." She stood up and brushed her hands on her jeans. Lilly gaped at the man in the towel, who was extraordinarily handsome.

The man ignored Mimi and held out his hand to Lilly. "I'm Xavier Gordon. You're one of the neighbors?"

Lilly had recovered from the shock of seeing her neighbor half-naked in the frigid evening air and shook his hand, nodding. "I'm Lilly Carlsen. I live next door." She indicated her house with a nod.

"It's nice to finally meet you. I should have introduced myself to the neighbors by now, but I've been busy with ..." His voice trailed off and he waved a hand behind him. "All this."

"Are you going to help us or just stand there?" Mimi asked. She bent over and righted one of the boxes that had tipped over.

"Let me grab some clothes and I'll be right out." Xavier went inside, leaving the door open.

"Come on in," Mimi said to Lilly. She hefted one of the boxes that hadn't lost too many of its contents. Lilly picked up a box and followed her inside.

She had no sooner walked into the foyer than she was hit with the scent of Edna and the cleaning supplies the woman had used relentlessly. Lilly smiled a half-smile, wondering what Edna would think of the strapping man who was now living in the home where she had spent so many years.

"Can I get you something to drink?" Mimi asked, leading the way into the kitchen.

"No, thanks. I'll just set this box down wherever you want and then I'll go home. My daughter is going to wonder where I am."

"Oh, how old is your daughter?"

"Nineteen. I have a son, too, but he's away at college. He's twenty."

"Xavier and I never had children."

Lilly didn't know if that was a good thing or a bad thing, so she kept her mouth shut. Mimi sighed and pointed toward the kitchen table. "You can just set that box down there if you can find room. Would you look at this place? It's like he never learned to clean up after himself."

Indeed, the sink was full of unwashed dishes and there was a bottle of mustard, an open bag of sliced bread, and an empty wine bottle on the counter. There was no sign of a wine glass—Lilly wondered if Xavier had just taken swigs right from the bottle. She let out a laugh as she remembered how messy her ex-husband, Beau, had been.

"It's been so long since I had a husband, I had forgotten what a mess they can make."

Mimi laughed, too. "Well, luckily Xavier and I aren't married anymore, so I'm not touching this mess."

"Oh, sorry," Lilly said. She felt a flush of embarrassment creep up her neck.

"It's okay." Mimi waved her hand dismissively. "We are much better friends than we were spouses."

Just then a fully clothed Xavier came into the kitchen. He had slicked back his wet salt-and-pepper hair. "Meem, can you clear a spot in the office? I'll just put all the boxes from the front porch in there."

"All right."

"Let me help you," Lilly offered. She followed Xavier outside while Mimi opened the door to the room that used to be Edna's downstairs guest room.

"You sure you don't mind?" Xavier asked. "It's really nice of you." He grinned, the dimples in his cheeks deepening.

"I don't mind at all. I'll just gather up some of the things that fell out of the boxes." She knelt and began tossing all the detritus into empty boxes while Xavier took a few trips to the office with more boxes.

When Lilly had cleaned up everything on the porch floor, she stood up and carried one last handful of pens and pencils into Xavier's office.

"It was nice to meet both of you," she said. "I'm going to head home now."

Xavier stood up from placing a heavy box on the floor and extended his hand again. Lilly shook it as Mimi came to stand next to him, brushing hair away from her face. She shook Lilly's hand, too. "Thanks so much for coming over and rescuing me, Lilly. I'm sure I'll be seeing you again. I'll be visiting often."

Lilly let herself out the front door and hurried to her own house. She hoped Laurel had made something hearty for dinner.

CHAPTER 3

*B*arney met her at the door, as usual, tail wagging and feet prancing in delight at Lilly's arrival. Behind him was Fred, the newest addition to the family. Fred really belonged to Bev, but since Bev had moved to the assisted living facility, Fred had come to live with Lilly and Laurel.

Fred, an adorable and docile cocker spaniel with a weak bladder, was still finding his comfort zone in Lilly's house. He seemed to like playing with Barney (though Barney had been quite jealous of him in the beginning), but Lilly was sure he missed Bev.

"Hi, Mom." Laurel came into the kitchen wearing rubber gloves and holding a wad of squashed paper towels. She scowled. "Fred peed in the living room."

"Thanks for cleaning it up." Lilly gave Fred a pointed look. "It's a good thing you're so cute."

She set her handbag and notebook on the counter. "What a day. Harry and I were run off our feet. People have started their Christmas shopping early this year."

"That's good, isn't it?"

"It is, but I had hoped to have more time to work on some

new designs." Lilly had a flair for designing jewelry and had created some beautiful pieces in the past. She had gotten away from it in the last couple years, but was itching to return to it. It provided a creative outlet she found relaxing and stimulating. Besides that, her designs were always hot items in her shop.

"Are you hungry? Vanessa and I made chicken divan for dinner." Vanessa, Laurel's best friend, had been staying with the Carlsens for a while. She was nineteen, seven months pregnant, and unmarried. Her parents had kicked her out of the house and stopped paying for college once they found out she was pregnant, and Lilly had offered the quiet young woman a place to live. Cyrus, her boyfriend and the father of her baby, was still in college and hailed from New Mexico, so they hadn't seen each other much since summer.

"Ooh, that sounds delicious. I'm starving."

While they ate Lilly told Laurel and Vanessa about meeting Xavier and Mimi.

"They're divorced, but they seem to be good friends now. I don't know too much about them other than that."

"I've seen them. I assumed they were married. Does the inside of the house look nice?" Laurel asked.

Lilly shrugged. "It's still a mess. He's putting an office where Mrs. Laforge's downstairs guest room used to be."

"What does he do?"

"I don't know. It didn't come up."

"Where did he move here from?" Vanessa asked.

"That didn't come up, either."

"Kids?"

"That did come up. No kids."

"Where does the ex-wife live?"

Lilly laughed. "You two are nosy."

"We should make them something and take it over to welcome them to the neighborhood," Laurel said.

"You mean welcome *him*. She doesn't live there."

"Okay, whatever. How about a sweet potato pie? We can make it tomorrow and take it over after dinner."

Lilly smiled. Ever since Laurel had begun culinary classes at the community college, she had amazed Lilly with her ability, creativity, and eagerness to learn. It helped that Laurel had grown up watching Noley, Lilly's best friend and now sister-in-law, a nationally renowned chef, work her magic in the kitchen.

"Sounds good to me. Thanks for making dinner, girls. I'll do the dishes."

Lilly dialed Hassan's number and talked to him while she cleaned up from dinner.

"How was your day, love?" he asked when he answered.

She melted inside. Between the warm tone of his voice and the British accent, she could listen to him talk all day.

"Busy. How was yours?"

"Great. I had a call with my source in Afghanistan early this morning to talk about my heading over there after the snow melt in the spring. He's got some stunning lapis lazuli."

"You're really set on going back to Afghanistan, aren't you?"

"I would love to. I'm dying to see the stuff they found. It's in a cave so remote that it takes three days just to hike in."

"I know you're dying to see it. It's the actual dying I'm worried about. Springtime is when the fighting starts."

"I'll be away from the fighting, love. And these men protect me fiercely when I'm there. I'm one of the few buyers they can trust."

"I know. Let's not talk about it."

"I won't mention it again until I know more. It would take until springtime to set up the trip, anyhow."

"All right." Lilly suddenly didn't feel like talking anymore.

"Lil? You still there?"

"I'm here."

"Don't worry about anything. I've made the trip many times and I've come home safely each time."

"You said you wouldn't mention it again."

He chuckled. "I'm sorry. Hey, I talked to my parents today. They can't come for Thanksgiving, but they'll definitely be visiting before Christmas."

"I'm sorry they can't join us for Thanksgiving, but it'll be nice to see them whenever they can visit."

CHAPTER 4

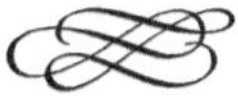

The next evening Lilly took the sweet potato pie to Xavier's house. Laurel and Vanessa had decided to stay home and watch a movie instead of going out into the cold. Lilly knocked on Xavier's door and Mimi answered it.

"Hi, Lilly. Come on in."

"Thanks." Lilly followed Mimi into the house, which had been neatened up considerably since Lilly's last visit. "I brought you and Xavier a sweet potato pie, sort of a welcome-to-the-neighborhood gift."

Mimi had taken Lilly straight through to the kitchen and now her eyes lit up. "I love sweet potato pie! What a nice thing to do. You shouldn't have." She grinned. "I'm a terrible cook, so Xavier never gets homemade pie." Then she moved toward the kitchen doorway and shouted at the ceiling, "Xavier! Come on down! Lilly brought pie!"

When Xavier came downstairs a minute later, he was dry and fully clothed. Lilly couldn't decide if she was pleased or disappointed. He smiled and glanced toward the pie. "Is that for us?"

"Yes, to welcome you to the neighborhood."

"Well, thank you! Let's have some now, shall we?"

Mimi set three plates and three forks on the counter and rummaged through a drawer, eventually holding up a pie server in triumph. "Found it. Lilly, want to do the honors?" She handed the server and a long-handled knife to Lilly.

Lilly cut three slices from the pie while Mimi clicked a button on a countertop coffeemaker. "Decaf okay for everyone?"

"Sure, thanks," Lilly said. She handed plates to Mimi and Xavier.

Xavier led the way to the living room. The walls, which had been off-white when Mrs. Laforge lived there, were painted a light gray and the molding had been spruced up with bright white paint. A low-slung, tufted black leather sofa sat against one wall, with a sleek chrome and glass coffee table in front of it. Lilly thought the room looked nice, though it seemed a little out of character with the Craftsman style of the house. Mimi pulled a clear acrylic chair up to the coffee table and gestured for Lilly to sit on the sofa. Xavier sat down at the other end and Mimi took the chair. There seemed to be a tacit agreement that no one would touch the pie until the coffee was served.

"I'm sorry everything was such a mess when you were here last night, Lilly," Xavier said. "We've been hard at work getting things spruced up, haven't we, Meem?"

Mimi nodded. "The carpet wasn't in bad shape, so we decided to just paint the walls for now and get the furniture set up. Xavier will be starting work next week and he needs the place to be presentable."

"Oh? You work from home?" Lilly asked.

Xavier crossed his legs and leaned back. "Yes."

Lilly waited for him to elaborate.

"Xavier's a psychiatrist," Mimi offered.

"But before you get concerned, Lilly, you don't need to worry about having psychiatric patients in the neighborhood,"

Xavier said. "The ones who are truly dangerous to themselves or others are either hospitalized or they don't visit doctors like me to begin with, and the others, the vast majority of psychiatric patients, are of no danger. I don't worry about having them in my home."

That was good to hear, though Lilly had noticed an alarm system control pad on the wall next to the front door. That hadn't been there when Edna was alive.

Mimi excused herself to get the coffee and returned just a minute later with a tray containing a carafe of coffee and all the necessary accoutrements. She poured Lilly a mug before pouring her own and Xavier's. Lilly added sugar and cream and sat on the edge of the sofa.

"What do you do, Lilly?" Mimi asked, settling into the acrylic chair. Lilly wondered how anyone could sit in one of those and be comfortable.

"I own a jewelry shop on Main Street. It's called Juniper Junction Jewels. I also design jewelry."

"Really? I've never met a jewelry designer before," Mimi said. "You and I are the creatives in the room, I guess. I own a florist shop."

"Oh, wow. That sounds like a great job," Lilly said. "Is it nearby?"

"Oh, no. I'm from Cheyenne, Wyoming. I'm heading back just as soon as Xavier is settled in."

"And are you from Cheyenne, too, Xavier?" Lilly asked.

Xavier nodded. "We get as much snow there as you do here, I'll bet."

"We definitely get our fair share of snow." Lilly laughed.

"Speaking of snow, I think it's supposed to snow this week at home," Mimi said. "Maybe I'll head back tomorrow instead of Monday to avoid bad weather."

"Will you be coming back for Thanksgiving, Mimi?" Lilly asked.

"Unfortunately I'm not, but I may be able to get away the next day or the day after. I promised my sister I'd spend Thanksgiving at her house this year."

"In that case, Xavier, would you like to have Thanksgiving dinner at my house?"

"I wouldn't impose like that, Lilly, but thank you."

"You should go," Mimi urged him. "Otherwise you'll be alone."

Xavier looked at Lilly. "Are you sure you don't mind?"

"Absolutely not. Dinner's at three."

"Thanks very much," Xavier said.

Mimi smiled. "That's very nice of you, Lilly."

"Listen, why don't I let you two take a look at the weather?" Lilly suggested. She had finished her pie. "I need to be getting back home and maybe seeing the forecast would help Mimi decide when she needs to leave to beat the weather."

"Oh, I didn't mean to make you leave," Mimi said.

Lilly made a dismissive gesture with her hand. "I have things to do tonight, and I'm sure you both do, too. I just wanted to officially welcome you to the neighborhood, and I didn't intend to eat the pie I brought." She grinned.

"It was delicious. Thank you, Lilly." Xavier stood with Lilly and walked her to the front door. "Don't be a stranger."

"Thanks again, Lilly!" Mimi called from the living room.

Xavier closed the door behind her and Lilly hurried back to her house, where Barney and Fred were waiting, as usual.

CHAPTER 5

*L*illy's cell phone rang the moment she had had taken off her coat and shoes. She glanced at the caller ID and smiled when she saw Noley's name.

"Hi, Nol."

"Hi. I haven't talked to you in a couple days."

"I know. You've been so busy lately, I figured you'd call when you got a chance to catch your breath."

"Catch my breath is right. I've been trying to finish up a column, test stuff for my next cookbook, and work with the magazine editors on next year's cakes issue." As recipe developer for a national cooking magazine, Noley was involved with the creation of every issue, and she also wrote a weekly syndicated cooking column. She was a sought-after interviewee for television and radio appearances, too.

"How many times have I said you need another assistant?" Lilly asked. Noley had an assistant at the magazine, but since that woman's paychecks were signed by the magazine and not Noley personally, Noley couldn't give her assignments unless they were associated with the magazine. Noley needed someone else to help with all the other things she was involved in.

"I know, I know. You've told me, Bill has told me, my mother has told me. But listen. I have news. I've actually been interviewing people in all my spare time, all ten minutes of it, and I've decided on someone."

"You're finally going to hire someone? That's great!"

"Her name is Chelsea Fortune and she just moved to Juniper Junction recently. I met her in Armand's bistro yesterday when I stopped in to grab a coffee."

"I'm so glad to hear it. When does she start?"

"The day after Thanksgiving. Bill is in the little office off the kitchen right now, making sure it's ready for her."

"I can't wait to meet her."

"Good, because I invited her for Thanksgiving. I hope that's okay. She's from Seattle and her whole family is still there. She doesn't have the money to buy a plane ticket to see them, so I told her she was welcome to join us. I hate the thought of anyone spending Thanksgiving alone."

"That's fine. The more, the merrier. In fact, I'm glad you mentioned inviting Chelsea, because I've been expanding the guest list, too."

"That's great. We'll have a whole crowd. Who's coming?"

"Mom, obviously. And I'll invite Beau and Nikki. They probably have plans, but I think it would be nice to invite them. The kids would like to celebrate the holiday with their dad. And I love Nikki. I'll also invite Harry and Alice. Harry mentioned at work the other day that Alice doesn't like to cook. His family lives in Arizona and Alice doesn't have much to do with her family, so I thought it would be nice to include them. And I invited my new neighbor—the one who bought Edna Laforge's house."

"Like you said, the more the merrier. Is Hassan's family going to be in town?"

"Unfortunately, no. But they'll visit sometime before Christmas."

"Anyone else?"

"What about your mom and dad?"

"They're going to New York City with my sister. They've been planning it for a couple years. They said they could cancel it to spend the holiday with Bill and me, since this is our first Thanksgiving as a married couple, but I told them to go ahead with their plans. I'll see them when they get back."

"Okay. I'll call Harry and Beau now. If you think of anyone else to invite, go ahead. We might as well go all out."

Harry was thrilled to get the invitation. "Really? We would love that. Let me just double-check with Alice."

Lilly only had to wait a few seconds. "We're in," Harry said when he came back on the phone. "Thank you for the invitation. I think Alice was getting nervous about us trying to cook Thanksgiving dinner on our own." He laughed.

"Great. I'm going to call Beau and Nikki and invite them, too. See you Monday." Lilly dialed Beau's number and waited for him to pick up.

"Hi, Lil."

"Hi. Listen, I was wondering if you and Nikki would like to come for Thanksgiving."

"Aw, I'm sorry. We can't. Now that we're married the deal is we spend every other Thanksgiving and Christmas with her family. Like, we'll go there for Thanksgiving this year and then we'll be here for Christmas with the kids, then vice versa next year. See?"

"Yes. That's fine, I just wanted to extend the invitation. Don't forget to call them on Thanksgiving, though."

"Lilly, what am I, six? Of course I'll call them on Thanksgiving."

Lilly bit back the retort that he hadn't called for the fifteen Thanksgivings he had missed with them. She didn't want to say something she might regret later.

"No, I don't think you're six. Have a nice Thanksgiving if I don't talk to you."

"You, too," he said in a grumpy voice.

Nikki would make sure he called the kids.

CHAPTER 6

On Sundays Lilly tried to spend as much time with her mom as she could, but on this particular Sunday, with Thanksgiving looming, Lilly only had time for a short visit.

As recently as May, a mere six months ago, Bev had been living in her home in Juniper Junction. She had the help of nurses to get around, but as spring had turned to summer, the deterioration in her physical and mental abilities due to the ravages of dementia had been rapid. By the end of the summer, Lilly and Bill had been forced to make the heart-wrenching decision to place Bev in the care of people who had access to medical and technological resources that home nurses simply did not have.

Lilly and Bill had shed more than a few tears when the time had come to discuss Bev's care arrangements with her. Of course Bev didn't want to leave her home. Of course she didn't want to lose the companionship she had enjoyed for so many months with her nurses, and Nikki in particular. Of course it was hard to leave Fred behind with Lilly. And of course she was scared about the future. Lilly had all those same feelings, and she knew Bill did, too.

But the simple fact was that no one outside a skilled care facility had the resources necessary to give Bev a high quality of life with her illness. Even in her current state, Bev understood that. Somewhere in her brain, which had once been so organized, so quick, so sharp, she had known there was no other choice.

The move to Larkspur Manor had been hard at first, but Bev had settled in nicely, all things considered. She attended physical and occupational therapy sessions several times a week, she dined with other residents, and she was encouraged to play games, watch old movies, listen to audiobooks, and spend time daily making friends with other residents. Memory care specialists were there every day to work with residents on memory retention skills.

In addition to the therapy provided, Larkspur Manor was situated on a lovely hill overlooking an evergreen forest and large blue lake. There was a courtyard surrounded by stone walls where people could sit outside and enjoy the scenery. There was a music room with regular headphones and noise cancelling headphones. Residents who preferred not to wear headphones could request music to play in their rooms. It always made Lilly smile to hear strains of swing music that were invariably playing in the halls and watch the smiles on the faces of people who might not remember a daughter or a son or a spouse, but could remember melodies and lyrics from decades earlier.

Lilly parked the car and made her way toward Larkspur Manor's formally landscaped forecourt. The snow Mimi was worried about had indeed fallen overnight and all the boxwoods, dwarf white cedars, holly bushes, and pebbled walkways were coated in a soft white blanket of snow several inches deep. Lilly wondered idly if Mimi had left for home. She continued to the large double wooden doors in front of the beautiful stone building, their chicly distressed ivory paint belying the state-of-the-art technology and modern conveniences within. The building had once housed a convent and was perfectly suited to the mobility needs of the patients and the aesthetic of the forested environment.

Lilly signed in at the registration desk, greeting the receptionist with a smile, then proceeded down the hall of Bev's wing toward her room.

She knocked on the open door before entering, then peeked around the door when there was no answer. Bev wasn't there.

Greg, the newest nurse on the floor and Bev's instant favorite, came into the room just a few moments later.

"Hi, Mrs. Carlsen." Greg smiled at her.

"Hi, Greg. Any idea where Mom is?"

"I saw her heading this way a second ago." Greg set a contraption on Bev's bedside table. "I found a portable CD player that she can use to listen to audiobooks."

"That's a great idea. Thanks, Greg."

Greg left and Lilly waited for Bev. It wasn't long before she heard Bev coming. Bev shuffled in her suede moccasins, making a *shush, shush* sound with every step. Lilly had become used to hearing that sound whenever she visited.

When Bev came into the room she gave Lilly a confused look, then her eyes brightened and Lilly knew Bev had recognized her. She had not known Lilly several times since coming to Larkspur Manor, and Lilly feared the time was coming when Bev wouldn't remember her at all.

"Hi, Mom." Lilly rose from the armchair and walked over to Bev, planting a kiss on her cheek.

Bev smiled gently. "I haven't seen you in a long time, Candace."

Lilly's heart sank. Candace was Bev's sister and had passed away when Lilly was in her teens.

"It's Lilly, Mom."

Bev's eyebrows furrowed in concentration, but she said

nothing. Lilly chided herself for correcting Bev and confusing her even more. She led Bev over to her favorite armchair.

There was a knock on the door that mercifully broke the silence. Lilly and Bev turned to see a large elderly man ambling in.

CHAPTER 7

"There you are, you sweet thing," the man said, coming closer to Bev and Lilly. Bev flushed and looked at her hands, folded in her lap.

Lilly looked up in surprise. *Sweet thing? Who is this guy and did he really just say that to my mother?* She stared at Bev, willing her to provide an explanation. But Bev only had eyes for the man advancing, however slowly, toward her chair.

"Mom?"

Bev finally turned toward Lilly. "What?"

Lilly raised her eyebrows and nodded toward the elderly man, but either Bev didn't notice or she was ignoring Lilly's silent plea for information.

"Hello, young lady," Finley said, looking at Lilly. "Who're you?"

"I'm Lilly, Bev's daughter."

"Well, nice to meet you, Lilly. I'm Finley, Bev's boyfriend."

Lilly choked on her own spit and hacked away until she could catch her breath. She finally opened her mouth as if to speak, but nothing came out.

"Are you all right?" he asked. Lilly gave one more cough and nodded.

Bev laughed. "You look like a guppy."

Lilly looked from her mother to Finley and back again. "Your boyfriend?" she finally asked.

"Yes. Is it that hard to believe?"

Lilly spluttered. "No. Of course not. I—it's just that—I mean, I didn't know."

"Dad?" came a woman's voice from the hallway. Finley grinned. "That'll be my daughter." He plodded to the door and stuck his head into the hallway. "I'm in here," he called.

A moment later a tall woman with a short platinum bob came into Bev's room. She threw Finley an exasperated look. "Dad, I turn my back for one second and you're gone."

"I wanted to visit Bev."

"Hi, Bev," the woman said.

"Hello, dear," Bev replied.

I am obviously the last to know about this, Lilly thought, suppressing a scowl.

"You could have told me," the woman said to her father. Then she held out her hand to Lilly. "Hi. I'm Mirren Balfour. I see you've met my father, Finley Balfour."

"Yes. I'm Lilly Carlsen. It's nice to meet you." Lilly's head was spinning.

Mirren put her hand on her father's shoulder. "Do you want to go back to your room? I need to head out soon."

"Why would I want to do that? I just got here," Finley said.

"Well, I need to get going soon. I have to pick up groceries before I go home."

"Let's just stay with Bev for a little while."

"All right," Mirren dragged a chair from the hallway into the room and sat down next to Finley, who had already sat in the chair next to Bev.

"How are you tonight, Bev?" Mirren asked.

"Good."

"What did you have for dinner?"

Bev shrugged.

Lilly sat forward. "How long have you known my mother?"

"Oh, I would say about a month," Mirren said. "Dad kept talking about a woman named Bev and I finally asked if I could meet her."

Lilly nodded. "I don't think I've ever seen you or Finley before."

"I guess we've just been passing each other like ships in the night." Mirren grinned.

"Isn't she pretty?" Finley asked Lilly, gazing at Bev.

Lilly smiled. "Yes, she is pretty."

"And she's got big boobs."

"Dad!" The horrified look on Mirren's face matched Lilly's.

Bev laughed aloud. "They're not that big."

Lilly closed her eyes for a moment, wishing she could evaporate. But no such luck. When she opened them, she was still sitting with the others. She wondered if it would be rude to cover her ears with her hands.

Mirren rubbed her forehead. "Dad, you can't talk about women that way."

"Why not? It's true." He winked at Bev, who blushed every shade of pink. Then his eyes widened and he looked at Lilly. "I haven't actually seen them yet, though. Her boobs, I mean. Don't think that."

Yet? "Okay." Lilly struggled to suppress the urge to hold up her palms to stop him from talking.

"Okay, Dad. I think you've caused enough trouble for one night. Come on, let's get back to your room." Mirren stood and held her hand out to her father.

"I'm staying here." Finley folded his arms across his chest.

"Okay, but I have to go. I'll see you tomorrow." Mirren stood up to leave.

"I'll walk out with you," Lilly said. She turned to Bev. "Mom, I'm going to head out, too. I have a ton of things to do before Thanksgiving."

"All right. Thank you for coming to see me."

Lilly got that familiar lump in her throat when her mom said that. She hoped that eventually she would stop feeling so guilty about having moved Bev out of her house and into Larkspur Manor. This new place was beautiful and the skilled nursing staff wonderful, but it wasn't home.

Lilly and Mirren left, heading in the same direction in the parking lot.

"I'm sorry if you were startled to meet my father," Mirren said. "And, obviously, I'm sorry for his crass comments. The man has no filter."

Lilly smiled. "It's okay. I didn't know Mom had a boyfriend, that's all. I wonder why she didn't say anything."

"Who knows?" Mirren shrugged. "There's my car," she said, pointing. "I'm sure I'll see you again, Lilly, now that we're practically related." She laughed at her own joke and Lilly couldn't help but laugh along with her.

"Nice to meet you, too." Lilly slid behind the wheel of her car. As she drove out of the parking lot, all she could think was, *if Bill knew about this and didn't tell me, I'll kill him.*

CHAPTER 8

On Sunday evening Lilly and Bill had a meeting with Isabelle Montrose, the real estate agent they had hired to put Bev's house on the market. It was the only time the three of them could meet together and in person.

Bill was waiting for Lilly outside the real estate firm where Isabelle worked. "You ready for Isabelle?" he asked.

"As ready as I'm going to be," she replied.

Lilly smirked. Isabelle was a little intense. And the purpose of this meeting was for Isabelle to try to convince Lilly and Bill to delay putting Bev's house on the market. She thought they should wait until spring.

Lilly and Bill did not agree with her.

"All right. Let's go in."

He held the door open for her and she led the way into the nondescript office with stock photos of smiling families and mountains and closeups of flowers. The furniture and carpets were a tan-gray and it looked even more gloomy on a weekend evening, when many of the lights were off.

Bill touched a silver bell on the reception desk and they waited. Presently Isabelle came striding down the hall from her office. She wore a severe blue suit with red and gold epaulettes on the padded shoulders. Her shoes were high heeled—too high. She wore blue stockings to match the suit and her hair was a short, curly mop of gray. Her eyes were an arresting green. Despite her apparent lack of a wardrobe update since the mid-1980s, she was a striking woman. Lilly wondered if she always dressed like that to work on weekends.

"Hello, Bill, Lilly," she boomed, shaking hands with each respectively. "Come on back to my little corner of the real estate industry. I was just fixing coffee. Want some?"

"No, thank you," Bill and Lilly said simultaneously.

"Well, you're better people than I am!" Isabelle said with a barking laugh. "Have a seat. I'll be right back." She waved them into her office.

Bill and Lilly sat in the two chairs across the desk from Isabelle's swivel chair and waited silently.

"So how was your weekend?" Isabelle asked as she walked into the office a minute later. Lilly jumped at the sound of Isabelle's voice.

"Sorry, didn't mean to scare you there, Lilly."

The woman's voice was a chainsaw on Lilly's nerves. "Oh, you didn't scare me. I was just in my own little world, that's all."

Isabelle sat down and held the coffee mug up to her nose. She took a long sniff and heaved a loud, contented sigh. "Is there anything better than fresh coffee?"

An indoor voice would be nice. Lilly smiled and didn't dare look at Bill. She wondered if Isabelle had ever thought of switching to decaf.

"So. My calendar here reminds me that we're meeting to discuss the timing of putting your mother's house on the market," Isabelle said.

"That's right." Bill sat forward in his chair.

"Here is my thinking: houses sell better in the spring, plain and simple. I think you should seriously consider waiting until spring to put your mother's house up for sale. I know, I know, that sounds strange coming from a realtor, but you know my job is to do right by the both of you. And I say that means waiting." She paused. "Let's discuss."

It was no wonder this woman was the highest-grossing realtor in Juniper Junction. Lilly had a feeling there was more than one person living in a house they hadn't wanted to buy simply because Isabelle scared them into signing the contract. Then she felt bad for feeling that way—they were lucky to be working with the skilled realtor, whom they had met when she sold Mrs. Laforge's house to Xavier.

"The thing is, Mom has already moved out and is living at Larkspur Manor, as you know," Lilly began.

Bill took up the conversation. "That's right. And it's hard for all of us, obviously. Mom didn't want to move out of her house, and we didn't want her to move. Circumstances dictated our course of action."

"Yes, of course. I understand that, but you're not hearing me," Isabelle said. "You're going to get more money if you wait and sell in the spring."

"It's not the money that's important," Lilly said. "What's important is that it's very painful for us to keep going to check on things at the house. I think Bill and I would simply feel better if we didn't have it hanging over us all the time."

"I can get someone to check on the house for you."

Bill shook his head. "The house is our responsibility until it's sold. We're both very busy," he continued, gesturing toward Lilly. "Between our jobs and our own families, and spending time with Mom at Larkspur, we don't have a lot of extra time to be taking care of the house."

"Yes, but I can get someone to check on it *for you*. Then you don't have to do it."

"Yes, we get that," Bill said. "But neither of us is comfortable hiring someone to look after the house. That's our job."

"What we're saying is, we don't want to wait until spring to sell the house. We want to put it on the market as soon as possible," Lilly said. She hoped her voice sounded firm enough to be convincing.

Isabelle sat back in her chair, then sat forward, grabbed her coffee, and sat back again. "So what I hear you saying is that you want to put the house on the market now."

"Yes," Bill and Lilly said together.

"I think you're making a mistake, but I can put it on the market if that's what you want. We need to discuss pricing. I'd like to go through the house again and look at some comps. Then I'll present you with my recommendation and we'll go from there." She sat forward and looked at her calendar. "Is there a time tomorrow when you can meet? I'd say we could do it tonight, but I think you should take at least twenty-four hours to think about what I've said. You don't want to leave money on the table."

Bill was silent for a long moment and Lilly was afraid he was going to erupt. But he managed to remain polite. "Actually, tonight would work very well for me. How about you, Lilly?"

"It's not great, but it's better than any other day this week," Lilly said.

Isabelle grudgingly agreed to drive over to Bev's house. "I should have you sign a waiver or something so you don't come back in the spring and tell me you could have gotten more money by waiting to sell," Isabelle said, shaking her head.

"I'll sign anything you want, but let's get the house on the market as quickly as possible," Bill said.

Isabelle laughed. "I was only joking there, Officer."

Bill pressed his lips together. Lilly could practically feel the heat emanating from him—he did not like people making light of his profession. She leapt into action before he blew his top. She stood up quickly, holding out her hand to Isabelle. "Thank you for meeting with us, Isabelle. We both really appreciate your time. We'll meet you over there in a few minutes."

After Isabelle had gotten the information she needed at Bev's house, she left with a promise to call Lilly and Bill on Wednesday to talk about pricing the house.

Great, Lilly thought. *I have nothing else to do the day before Thanksgiving.*

CHAPTER 9

When Lilly got to work Monday morning, Harry was already there, setting out displays and cleaning the glass cases. *If he keeps the house clean the way he keeps the shop clean,* Lilly often thought, *Alice really lucked out.*

"The new owner of the herb shop up the block stopped by just before you got here," Harry said.

In the days leading up to the opening of the herb shop, Lilly had visited several times to introduce herself to the new owner, but each time she stopped by the owner hadn't been there.

"Oh, darn it. I've been wanting to meet her. The couple times I've seen her outside her shop, I've been too busy to run over. What's she like? And why did she come in here?"

"Her name is Phoebe. She seems cool. She came in here just to introduce herself and get to know the neighbors."

"That was nice of her. I'll go to Armand's at lunchtime and pick up some cookies to take over. I can't wait to see the inside of her shop."

That afternoon, Lilly, holding a box of raspberry *macarons*, pushed open the door of the herbery. A bell above the door tinkled gently as she stepped across the threshold into the cool, softly lit herbery. She stood in the doorway, breathing in the beautifully earthy aroma created by the mingling of all the herbal scents. Glass apothecary jars lined the forest green built-in shelves. A gorgeous old-fashioned cash register held pride of place on the counter at the back of the shop and an antique-looking bronze mortar and pestle stood next to the cash register, completing the quaint look of the space. A woman with long brown hair and a dark blue caftan looked up from where she stood behind the counter.

"Good afternoon. Welcome to The Herbery."

"Thank you. I'm Lilly Carlsen, owner of Juniper Junction Jewels, and I'm here to finally welcome you to Main Street."

The woman smiled broadly, coming out from behind the counter and extending her hand to Lilly. They shook hands and Lilly handed her the box of macarons.

"Is this for me?"

"Yes. They're from Armand's Bistro."

"Thank you very much. I'm Phoebe Detweiler. I was in your shop just this morning to introduce myself."

"Yes, my assistant told me. I apologize for taking so long to get over here. Actually, I have been by, but I always seem to choose times when you're not around."

Phoebe gave a rueful smile. "I'm sorry about that. With a new shop opening, I should be here as much as possible. The trouble is that I'm having a house built and it has taken a crazy amount of my time. It wasn't very smart of me to open a shop and build a home at the same time."

"Are you from Juniper Junction?"

"No. I'm from Arizona. I moved here just recently. I've been renting an apartment and it was time for me to have a place to call my own."

"I can imagine. That's a lot of change in a small amount of time."

"I divorced my husband and needed a change. I studied

botany in college then spent the ensuing two decades working for my husband as his medical office manager. It was time to do something for me. And I never lost my love of herbs and plants, so this just seemed perfect."

"What do people do with the herbs you sell?"

"Well, the most obvious thing is to use them for cooking. The edible herbs I sell here are all food-grade, sourced nearby and in some cases in my own container gardens. They're fresh as can be. But more importantly, herbs are used for medicinal purposes. People don't realize how many herbs contain compounds that support and supplement a healthy lifestyle and even treat common illnesses and disease."

"That's fascinating."

"I'm going to start teaching classes here at the shop as kind of a way to introduce myself to the community—and market my wares, of course." She giggled. "You should join one sometime."

"That would be great. I'll definitely do that." Lilly smiled. "I need to be getting back to the shop, but I'm so glad I got a chance to meet you."

"Likewise. Before you go, can I ask you a quick question?"

"Sure."

"Can you recommend a great restaurant that's serving Thanksgiving dinner? I won't be able to get back to Arizona to see anyone in my family and I've told them not to bother coming here because I'll be busy with the shop. But I would like to splurge on a nice Thanksgiving dinner."

"I can tell you the names of several great restaurants serving Thanksgiving dinner, but I don't like the thought of you spending Thanksgiving alone. Why don't you join my family?" The words were out before Lilly realized what she was saying. But she couldn't take them back—she hoped no one would mind having another total stranger at dinner. But only if Phoebe said yes, of course.

Phoebe was staring at Lilly with large, round eyes. "Are you serious? You would be okay with having me—a complete stranger—at your house for Thanksgiving?"

"Of course. We've invited quite a crowd. The more the merrier," Lilly said. *At least, I hope so.*

Phoebe let her hands fall to her sides and cocked her head at Lilly. "I don't know how to thank you. Of course I accept. You are too kind."

"Oh, it's nothing. I'll write down the address for you. Dinner's at three."

"What can I bring?"

"Just yourself."

"I just can't believe this. Thank you so much."

Lilly scribbled down her address on a piece of paper from her handbag and handed it to Phoebe.

"Thanks, Lilly."

Lilly waved goodbye and returned to the jewelry shop, where Harry was waiting on a customer. When the man left, Harry faced Lilly. "How did it go with Phoebe?"

"Great. She seems very nice. I hope I'm a good judge of character because I invited her to Thanksgiving dinner."

Harry's eyebrows shot up. "Really? Wow—you're even nicer than I thought."

Lilly laughed. "Flattery will not get you out of helping with the dishes on Thanksgiving. She mentioned that she was going to eat out that day because she won't be able to visit her family, so I just suggested that she have dinner with us. I hate the thought of anyone spending Thanksgiving alone."

"That's really nice of you, Lilly. I mean it. And I'll even do all the dishes."

CHAPTER 10

*W*hen Lilly went home that night she found Laurel and Vanessa with their heads together over a notebook. "What's going on here?"

"We're making out a schedule of when each side dish has to be made so everything is ready when the turkey is carved."

Lilly glanced at the list, which included all the basics: gravy, cranberry sauce, squash, sweet potatoes, white potatoes, rolls, green bean casserole, corn pudding, and pies for dessert.

"I invited another person, too," Lilly told them. "She's an herbalist who just opened a shop on Main Street. She moved here from Arizona recently and can't go back there for Thanksgiving. I didn't want her to have to celebrate by herself."

"That's cool," Laurel said. "Do you know if Sally Anne is coming?"

Sally Anne was Tighe's girlfriend. They had been dating for about six months and Tighe was enraptured.

"I don't think so. Tighe was pretty sure her parents wanted her to spend Thanksgiving weekend with them."

"Cyrus isn't coming, either," Vanessa said, not trying to hide the sadness in her voice. "For the same reason—his parents want him to spend Thanksgiving with them."

Lilly felt sorry for Vanessa and didn't know how to respond. Vanessa rarely mentioned Cyrus's parents. Like her own parents, they were not happy with the idea of their young son becoming a father and carrying on a relationship with someone of a different race. Cyrus was of Arabic descent and Vanessa was white. But unlike Vanessa's parents, they were willing to continue helping Cyrus pay for college as much as they could. Unfortunately, that was not much, and as a result Cyrus was floundering in debt. Also unlike Vanessa's parents, they were still interested in maintaining a relationship with their son.

Luckily, Lilly didn't have to respond to Vanessa because her phone rang and a quick glance showed Isabelle calling. Maybe "luckily" was the wrong word, Lilly thought.

"Hello?" she answered.

"Yes. It's Isabelle."

"Hi, Isabelle. Calling with a price for Mom's house?"

"No. I'm calling because my shower sprang a huge leak and there's water all over my house. I know you and Bill and I were going to meet Wednesday to discuss pricing your mother's house, but I wanted to let you know that I won't be able to make it. I've contacted a cleanup company, a friend of mine who demolishes and puts up drywall, and a painter. Repairs will start tomorrow, but I expect the job won't be done by Wednesday. I can't meet with you with all this going on, too."

"Oh, I'm so sorry to hear that, Isabelle. Don't worry about Bill and me. Maybe we can meet next week."

"I'll be in touch. Now I have to call my family members to tell them the bad news. They can't come to my house for Thanksgiving because there's water everywhere."

"Oh, that's too bad. Why don't you come here and have Thanksgiving with us? We're having a crowd."

"Well, I certainly didn't say that because I was trying to wrangle an invitation."

"Of course not. I know that. But you're welcome to come over. There's no sense in you being alone for Thanksgiving when we have lots of food and people here."

"Well, that would be appreciated. Just so long as you don't think I was trying to invite myself."

"No. I would never think anything like that. Dinner's at three. We'll see you Thursday."

Lilly hung up, hoping she hadn't just extended an invitation she would regret.

CHAPTER 11

Wednesday arrived almost before Lilly realized it, and the afternoon went by in a rush of preparations for everything that could be assembled ahead of time. Noley came over to help —Laurel put her in charge of making and shaping the yeast rolls, then preparing pie crusts for filling.

"Do you hate being told what to do?" Laurel asked Noley with a worried look.

"No way. I love it. For once I'm not in charge of anything, and it's great." Noley wiggled her fingers, covered with flour. "I'm totally content to just do what I'm told."

Hassan knocked on the back door and came into the warm, busy kitchen. Lilly kissed him and handed him a vegetable peeler. "I'm glad you're here. Time to get to work." Hassan laughed and did as he was told, peeling potatoes and butternut squash.

When most of the prep work was done, Laurel and Vanessa went upstairs to Laurel's room and the rest of the adults, including Bill, who had come over to Lilly's house after getting off shift, retired to the living room for some liquid refreshment.

It had been a long day, and Lilly sat back against the sofa, sighing contentedly. "This is the calm before tomorrow's storm, I guess."

"It'll be great," Hassan said, placing his hand on her leg. "I'll come over early tomorrow morning to help set up the tables and chairs."

"Thanks. We're going to have to decide where to put everyone before we go rearranging the furniture."

"What time will Tighe be here?" Bill asked.

"He wanted one last evening with Sally Anne," Lilly said.

"Young love," Noley said.

"She's a sweetheart," Lilly said. "They're cute together. Plus, Mom loves her. Sally Anne went with Tighe the last time he visited Mom over at Larkspur during fall break."

Lilly turned to Bill. "And speaking of love and Mom, did you know she has a boyfriend?"

"What?!" Bill's chin dropped.

Noley sat forward, her eyes widening. "Bev has a boyfriend?"

Lilly nodded. "Yup. His name is Finley and he is quite taken with her, apparently. I didn't find out about it until Sunday."

"Finley … Finley … I don't remember hearing that name," Bill said.

"Me, neither. But his daughter, Mirren, knew all about the relationship. She came into Mom's room with Finley the day I met him. Mom even knew who she was."

"What's he like?" Hassan asked.

"Big, ruddy, friendly. Seems to appreciate her, um, womanly figure." Lilly shook her head. "I never would have thought Mom would fall for someone after Dad died."

"That was a long time ago, though," Bill said. "I guess it's not that unusual."

"You're right. I was just startled to learn of this romance going on right under my nose."

"It is a little shocking," Bill agreed.

Noley turned to Bill. "We should get going. Tomorrow's

going to be here before we know it." Bill stood up and reached out his hand to pull Noley up from the sofa.

"You two go on. I'll take care of your wine glasses," Lilly said. They thanked her, said their goodnights, and left.

Hassan stood up. "I'm going to get some cheese and crackers. Can I get you anything?"

"No, thanks."

When Hassan returned he put his arm around Lilly and she nestled into it. He leaned forward to kiss her just as the Laurel appeared in the doorway.

"Eww. Get a room." Laurel stood with her hands on her hips. "Mom, what time are you getting up in the morning?"

"Whatever time you tell me to."

"Okay. We need to get an early start. How about six?"

"In the morning? Tomorrow is supposed to be a holiday. A day off. Can't we make it seven? Or even eight?"

Laurel let out a belabored sigh. "All right. Vanessa and I will get up at six and get the food started. You just get up whenever you want. I'm going to bed."

CHAPTER 12

*D*espite her wishes to the contrary, Lilly was awake before six the next morning. She lay in bed, with Barney and Fred curled up next to her, petting their fur and wishing she could go back to sleep. But since that apparently wasn't going to happen, she shuffled downstairs to start the coffeemaker. Laurel and Vanessa were already in the kitchen, dressed and preparing the stuffing. Vanessa was in charge of melting an obscene amount of butter in a large pan and cubing day-old bread while Laurel chopped onions and celery.

"Happy Thanksgiving! You two were serious about getting up early, weren't you?" Lilly asked with a smile.

"Hi, Mom. Happy Thanksgiving!"

"Happy Thanksgiving, Mrs. C," Vanessa echoed.

"Put me to work," Lilly directed them.

Before long the kitchen was filled with luscious scents of Thanksgiving. Hassan arrived around mid-morning and Noley and Bill got there before noon, bearing a relish tray, cheese and crackers, and spiced nuts for lunch. Lilly kept looking at her watch, counting the minutes until Tighe arrived.

When he came in the back door, all dinner prep screeched to

a halt while everyone crowded around him, kissing him, hugging him, slapping him on the back, and generally being thrilled to have him home again.

"Hi, everyone," he said, his smile wide. "You just saw me a month ago for fall break. I haven't been gone that long!"

Lilly hugged him again. "We know that. We're just glad you're here. Now, take off your coat and have a light lunch, then get to work. You can make the cranberry sauce." She grinned.

Harry and Alice showed up shortly after Tighe arrived. They had brought a couple bottles of wine—one white and one red—and a lovely cinnamon-scented candle. "I was thinking of making cookies and bringing them over," Alice said. "But knowing how good the cooks are around here, that would be a little like giving Mozart a kazoo."

Lilly squeezed Alice around the shoulders. "Cookies would have been wonderful. But I love candles, too. And kazoos, for that matter." She laughed and opened the wine, setting it out for people to help themselves.

Shortly after Harry and Alice arrived, Bill and Noley left to pick up Bev at Larkspur Manor. Fred spotted Bev as soon as she came into the house. He was over the moon, as he proved by piddling all over Vanessa's feet. Once Bill had Bev seated in an armchair in the living room, she asked him to bring Fred to her so Fred could sit on her lap. Both she and Fred seemed to be in their own world for several minutes while numerous conversations went on around them. She stroked his fur and he leaned happily into her chest.

A short while before dinner there was a knock at the front door. Barney was exuberant at the sound. He had been stuck like glue to Tighe's side, but now he catapulted toward the front door, barking in a frenzy of excitement. Fred watched, probably a little uncertain about all the activity and people.

It was Phoebe. Lilly welcomed her inside and introduced her to everyone, knowing there was no way Phoebe would remember all the names. And as she was making introductions, there was another knock at the door. Lilly opened it to see a smiling Xavier standing there, looking especially distinguished in a tweed jacket and holding a bouquet of flowers and a bottle of wine. A beautiful young woman with a mane of auburn hair was coming up the walk behind him. Noley appeared behind Lilly.

"Oh, I thought it might be Chelsea," she said when she saw Xavier. Then she saw the woman coming up the front steps. "Oh, hi, Chelsea! Come on in and meet everyone."

Xavier stood back and motioned for Chelsea to go ahead of him. Lilly saw him glance at her bottom as she squeezed past him. When they entered the already-crowded living room, Lilly introduced them to everyone. She would have sworn she saw a look of surprise pass ever so quickly over Phoebe's features when she was introduced to Xavier. More likely it was lust.

Isabelle was the last to arrive. She swept in just before three o'clock, lugging a giant copper pumpkin.

"What's this?" Lilly asked with a grin.

"That's your hostess gift," Isabelle said, looking around at all the faces in the living room. "Hi, everyone. I'm Isabelle. I'm a realtor." She smiled at Xavier, probably happy to see another familiar face.

Eventually everyone shook hands with all the newcomers and Lilly made sure everyone had something to drink. She had been mulling cider in a slow cooker in the kitchen for hours and that was proving to be a popular beverage.

Lilly had been nursing a worry in the back of her mind that all the activity and people might be too much for Bev, but she needn't have fretted. Bev enjoyed meeting everyone and almost immediately became the center of conversation. The kids, including Vanessa, sat across from her on the sofa while everyone else stood around the living room, listening as Bev told stories, in her halting speech, of Thanksgiving when she was a child. Lilly smiled, not only because she loved to hear the old tales, but because everyone else seemed to be enjoying them, too.

Suddenly a terrific crash echoed from the kitchen. Lilly was the first one to arrive on the scene, as she was standing closest to the kitchen.

"Noo! No, no, no, no!" she shouted.

Within seconds, every guest except Bev was staring at the kitchen floor, where both dogs stood over a beautifully browned and glistening turkey. They were taking turns pawing at it, then shrinking back from the hot bird.

Laurel let out a shriek. "What? How did they get the turkey off the counter? I can't believe this!" She leapt forward and shooed the dogs away. As if sensing they had done something wrong, Barney and Fred slunk into the living room, where Lilly was pretty sure Bev would comfort them with cooing noises and a complete lack of concern over the ruined main course.

"Mom!" Laurel wailed. "What are we going to do?" Vanessa bent down to start cleaning up the mess on the floor, but Hassan took her arm and gently helped her stand up.

"Leave that to us," he told her.

"Come on, Vanessa," Tighe said, leading everyone back into the living room. "Sit down and relax. Who needs their drink topped off?" Lilly listened to him with relief and pride, knowing he had the situation in hand in the living room while she and Noley, Laurel, Bill, and Hassan cleaned up the mess on the kitchen floor.

"Does anyone know if the grocery store is open?" Lilly asked.

"I think it is, or at least it was when we drove by it earlier," Bill said.

Lilly spoke to Hassan. "Do you mind running over there to see if they have any cooked turkeys? They were running a deal for completely cooked Thanksgiving meals that people could order and pick up yesterday. Maybe they have some left."

"I don't mind at all," Hassan said. "I'll leave now, if you guys don't mind me cutting out in the middle of this mess."

"Way to get out of the kitchen, Hassan," Bill said with a grin. Hassan laughed, picked up his keys, and was gone.

The whole turkey went into the garbage, and Noley offered to take it outside while Lilly and Laurel scrubbed the grease and sticky stuff off the floor. Bill headed back to the living room, but returned a moment later.

"Ah, Lilly, there's kind of a weird vibe in the living room. Why don't you go in there and restore order? I'll help out in here."

Lilly sat back on her knees and brushed a hank of hair away from her forehead. "What's the matter?" she asked in a low voice.

"I'm no expert, but I would say there are a couple women fighting over your neighbor."

Uh-oh. I shouldn't have left Xavier unattended.

She scrambled to her feet. "Thanks. I'm on it."

It didn't take long to assess the situation. Chelsea and Isabelle, seated rigidly at either end of the sofa, scowled at each other while Xavier spoke to Bev as if nothing was amiss. Phoebe scowled, too, but wasn't looking at anyone. Her hands were clasped tightly in her lap. Lilly suspected, as Bill had, that whatever was going on had something to do with the handsome doctor who was talking to her mom, seemingly oblivious to the hostility he had spawned.

"Well! That was exciting and totally awful," Lilly said brightly, coming into the room. "Have you ever seen anything like that in real life? I mean, I've seen movies where the dogs destroy Thanksgiving dinner, but who'd have thought it would happen to us? Hassan is going to the grocery store to see if they have any cooked turkeys over there. Good thing we made tons of sides." She said everything in a rush and let out a maniacal laugh.

Isabelle and Chelsea looked away from each other and Lilly raised her eyebrows in Phoebe's direction. Phoebe looked away. Lilly locked eyes with her son, who was watching the whole scene unfold with a bewildered look. Harry and Alice both wore fake smiles while their eyes begged Lilly for guidance.

"Tighe, can you turn on the television? Maybe there's a replay of the Thanksgiving Day Parade in New York. Does anyone else want to see it?"

"I love the parade!" Harry said, nodding like a bobblehead. Alice agreed a little too heartily. There were a few other listless nods around the room. Lilly didn't even like parades, but she had to do something to lighten the atmosphere. Tighe turned on the television and looked for the parade, finally finding a channel that was replaying it.

Noley called Chelsea's name from the kitchen. Chelsea hurried out of the living room and Lilly stole a glance at Isabelle, whose shoulders relaxed. Alice smiled at the float on the television. "Don't you love the floats in the parade?" she asked.

"I do. They're the best," Harry said.

A faint chorus of "Yeah"s made their way around the room just as Lilly's phone rang. It was Hassan.

"You're not going to like this. They're sold out of cooked turkeys."

Lilly groaned. "Do they have any fresh turkeys? Or turkey breasts? We might have time to throw a small one in the oven."

"I'm afraid not. How about sliced turkey from the deli? I can see if they have any."

Lilly thought for a moment. It definitely wasn't ideal, but at least they would have turkey. Maybe they could cobble together some sandwiches with the rolls and the stuffing and cranberry sauce.

"I guess so. It's probably the only way we're going to get turkey."

"Got it. I'll be back in just a few minutes."

Lilly hung up and went into the kitchen, where Chelsea was snapping photos of Noley on her phone. Noley was still on her hands and knees cleaning up the kitchen floor.

"What are you doing?" Lilly asked.

Noley grinned. "Chelsea's taking some photos for my social media accounts. I thought it would be fun to show people that Thanksgiving isn't going to be perfect and that's completely okay." She stood up, brushing her hands on her pantlegs. "Have you heard from Hassan?"

"Yes. Not a cooked or even a fresh turkey in sight. He's going to get sliced turkey from the deli and we're going to make sandwiches."

CHAPTER 13

Not many minutes later Hassan was back at the house, laden with four pounds of deli turkey (Cajun-spiced, because that was all they had) and two pounds of provolone cheese, thinly-sliced. Everyone except Bev took turns crowding into the kitchen, making his or her own sandwich for Thanksgiving dinner. Bev sat at the table in the dining room, waiting for Lilly to make her a sandwich. All the hot and cold side dishes were on the buffet, lending a delicious aroma to the house.

Lilly had not thought about a seating arrangement before the meal, since she had assumed all her guests would behave like adults. But as the three women had proven in the living room, that was not the case. So as people filed into the dining room with their sandwiches and lined up to help themselves from the side dishes on the buffet, Lilly did some quick thinking. She pointed each person to his or her seat as they left the buffet. She divided Chelsea, Isabelle, and Phoebe among the two rectangular tables, making sure they weren't facing or beside each other. She placed Xavier next to her mother, hoping they would continue their conversation. It was a brilliant arrangement, if she did say so herself. The only problem was that two of the women would have to sit at the same table to keep females at Xavier's table to a minimum.

Lilly, Hassan, Tighe, Chelsea, and Isabelle sat at one table. "So, what brought you to Juniper Junction, Chelsea?" Lilly asked when they were seated.

"I'm from Washington State. I actually followed my boyfriend here, but we broke up. I liked it here so much that I decided to stay."

"And you met Noley at Armand's Bistro?"

Chelsea nodded. "Yeah, and it's a good thing, too. I was down to my last few dollars and I needed that job." She giggled.

"Are you a cook?" Hassan asked.

Chelsea laughed. "No way. I'm a professional takeout orderer. I can't cook anything."

"It seems like you'd want to know how to make something," Isabelle said with a sniff.

"Oh, I can probably manage a can of soup or a scrambled egg," Chelsea answered, waving her hand breezily.

"Your mother must be so proud," Isabelle muttered.

"What did you say?" Chelsea asked, leaning around Tighe so she could look at Isabelle. Lilly groaned inwardly. That wasn't supposed to happen. Why couldn't Isabelle keep her mouth shut?

"I said, 'your mother must be so proud,'" Isabelle answered, her eyes boring into Chelsea's.

"You have no idea what my mother is or isn't proud of, so you should probably shut your mouth," Chelsea said in a low voice.

Lilly threw a worried glance over to Noley's table, but Noley was busy talking to Bev about Bill's childhood. Lilly did notice, however, that Xavier was side-eyeing her table, and Chelsea in particular. She suspected she was watching the beginning of a love triangle—if not a love rectangle, with Xavier as the main character and Chelsea, Isabelle, and Phoebe petulantly vying for his attention. She briefly wondered how many women he could woo at one time.

Thankfully, dinner and dessert were over swiftly and before six o'clock the guests were putting on their coats and taking their leave from Lilly's family, Hassan, and Vanessa. Lilly was pretty sure Harry and Alice would decide on the way home, if they hadn't already, that they would do almost anything to avoid Thanksgiving at Lilly's house again.

The dishes were done and Bill had built a fire in the fireplace, so everyone sat down drowsily and chatted while they contemplated the possibility of eating more pie.

"That young man is trouble," Bev said suddenly.

"Tighe?" Lilly asked in surprise. "He's not trouble."

Bev was shaking her head. "Not Tighe," she said with the exaggerated patience of someone dealing with a simpleton. "The other one. The good-looking one."

"Thanks, Gran," Tighe said, rolling his eyes.

Lilly laughed. "She didn't mean it that way."

"She might mean me," Hassan said with a wink.

"Do you mean Xavier?" Noley asked. "He seemed nice to me."

"Xavier. That's the one. He's trouble," Bev repeated.

"What makes you say that, Mom?" Lilly asked.

"I just know. He's a ladies' man, but not in a good way." Bev spoke slowly and carefully.

"I don't know much about him, only that he moved here from Wyoming just a couple weeks ago," Lilly said.

"He was very nice to me," Vanessa said.

"He was," Laurel chimed in. "He pulled out Vanessa's chair for her and everything."

"See what you can find out about him when you talk to Chelsea," Lilly said to Noley. "There was definitely something going on there."

"I will. I'll talk to her tomorrow. It'll be her first official day as my assistant."

Bev closed her eyes and leaned her head against the back of her armchair.

"Mom, are you getting tired? Maybe we should get you back to Larkspur Manor," Bill suggested.

"Yes, I want to go. Billy, will you drive me?"

Bill nodded and Noley smiled. Lilly knew Bill hated it when their mother called him "Billy."

"Sure thing, Mom. Nol, you ready to go?"

Noley nodded and Lilly disappeared to get everyone's coats. When they were all bundled up, Lilly kissed Bev's cheek and promised to visit the next day after work. "It'll be a little later than usual because tomorrow is such a busy shopping day," Lilly said. Bev nodded, and they both knew Bev would not remember that information by the time she got back to Larkspur Manor.

After they had left, the kids trooped upstairs while Lilly and Hassan sat together on the sofa. Lilly curled her legs up and lay her head on Hassan's shoulder, closing her eyes.

"Thanks for saving the day with the sliced turkey." She grimaced. "That was a Thanksgiving meal to remember, wasn't it? And not in a good way."

She sensed Hassan smile, rather than seeing it. "Everything was delicious. Everyone knows that Thanksgiving is all about the sides, so the turkey was never going to be the star of the show, anyway, regardless of how delicious it would have been."

They were silent for several minutes. Lilly enjoyed being snuggled inside Hassan's arm.

"What do you suppose was going on with Xavier and the women?" Hassan asked.

"I don't know. I'm guessing each woman was somehow jealous of the others. I don't know how it happened so quickly. If I can think of some diplomatic phrasing, I'll ask Phoebe next time I see her. Noley is going to try to get some information out of Chelsea. It was probably a mistake to invite Isabelle because she's obnoxious, but I didn't want her to have Thanksgiving by herself."

"I think you did the right thing. Besides, you couldn't have known there would be such a strange dynamic going on."

"Hmm."

"You're exhausted. I'm going to go home and let you get some sleep. Tomorrow's going to be a long day for you," Hassan said, kissing the top of her head. "Hopefully you'll be busy from the time you open until the time you close."

Lilly held up crossed fingers. "Let's hope."

They kissed goodnight and Hassan left, his breath leaving tendrils behind him in the air.

CHAPTER 14

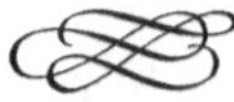

*B*lack Friday proved to be just as busy as Lilly had hoped it would be, and Lilly was not pleased to get a call from Isabelle in the middle of the day suggesting a listing price for Bev's house. She promised to talk to Bill and hung up as quickly as she could. Streams of customers came in looking for unique pieces of jewelry to give as Christmas gifts, and Lilly had almost exhausted her supply of already-made custom designs by the time she and Harry closed the shop that evening.

Lilly went to see Bev as soon as she and Harry had put away the displays and locked the doors. Greg, the new nurse, was coming out of Bev's room as Lilly walked in. When she slammed into him, he caught her elbows to steady her.

"Hey, where's the fire?" he asked with a laugh.

"Oh, I'm so sorry. I promised Mom I'd come to see her tonight, but my shop closed late." She peered around Greg, expecting to see Bev sitting in her chair.

"She's asleep already," Greg said. His eyes clouded. "I don't think you should wake her up."

"Oh, I won't wake her up. I feel so bad, though. I promised her I'd be by to see her."

"Why don't you leave her a note? The nurse on duty in the morning can make sure she sees it first thing."

"That's a great idea. Can I leave it with you?"

"Sure. I'll make sure it gets to the right person."

"Thank you."

Lilly dashed off a few lines to her mother, apologizing for not getting to Larkspur before Bev's bedtime. She handed the note to Greg and made her way toward the exit. Mirren was just leaving, too, and she hailed Lilly in the forecourt.

"Happy belated Thanksgiving," Mirren said. "Did you have a nice holiday?"

"Hi, there. Happy belated Thanksgiving to you. We had a great day. How about you?"

"It was nice. My dad came over to my house and it was just him, me, my sister, and my husband." Mirren smirked and Lilly wondered why.

"We had a whole menagerie of people. Also, the dogs ruined the turkey, so we ended up getting sliced turkey at the deli and having sandwiches for the main course."

Mirren threw her head back and laughed. "That's great! What a way to improvise! I'm sure it wasn't funny to you, but it's one of those things that'll get funnier with time, I'm sure."

"I hope you're right." Lilly grinned.

"Would you like to get coffee sometime next week?" Mirren suggested.

"Sounds great. How about early Wednesday? Is seven-thirty too early?"

"Not at all. I'll meet you at the coffee shop on Main Street at seven-thirty on Wednesday morning, then." They parted when they reached Lilly's car and Lilly went home.

After a late dinner of leftovers, Lilly sat on the sofa, her eyes closed, enjoying the quiet. A moment later, though, she opened her eyes to see Fred standing at her knee, staring at her.

"Do you need to go out, Fred?" Lilly jumped up, relishing the thought that Fred might piddle outdoors instead of on the living room rug. "Come on, boy." He trotted after her and followed her into the backyard. She shivered while she waited … and waited … for him to find the perfect spot.

While she waited a car pulled into Xavier's driveway, which was adjacent to her own. When the car door closed with a *thwack,* the sound echoed through the neighborhood, shattering the icy silence. Lilly frowned as Fred looked up, startled. He had just found The Spot where he could do his business and now he would have to find another one.

Lilly recognized Xavier's voice as soon as the car door closed. He was on the phone. It hadn't been her intent to listen to his side of the conversation, but his voice carried on the cold air and she couldn't help overhearing.

"Uh, sure. I'm free tomorrow."

"Dinner? That would be fine. Give me your address and I'll pick you up."

"Great. I'll be there at six."

Xavier went into his house and the air was silent again. Fred trotted over to Lilly and looked up at her. "Good boy, Fred. Let's go inside."

Noley called a few minutes later.

"How did Chelsea's first day of work go? And what did she have to say about Xavier and Isabelle?"

"I think today went well. She's quick and eager to help. She talked about Xavier way too much for someone she just met yesterday. She's totally smitten already."

"That's what I figured."

"She didn't mention anything about the other women, and I didn't want to pry."

"That's okay. I have a feeling we'll find out what was going on. Oh, is Bill there? I talked to the realtor today and she named the price she thinks we should put on Mom's house."

Noley put Bill on the phone and he and Lilly discussed the listing price. They agreed to go with Isabelle's suggestion. Before going to bed, Lilly texted Isabelle with the go-ahead.

CHAPTER 15

Saturday started out almost as busy as Black Friday had been, but by late afternoon the stream of customers had dried up. Harry went to the front window and looked up and down Main Street. "It's pretty empty out there. Good thing the Christmas lights are already up or it would be depressing."

"It's never too early for Christmas lights," Lilly said.

"That woman from the herb shop is out there. She must be closed already."

The door jingled a minute later and Phoebe walked in.

"Hi, Phoebe."

"Hi. Lilly, I came over to thank you again for hosting me for Thanksgiving. Everything was delicious."

"Even the Cajun turkey sandwiches?" Lilly laughed.

"Especially those. Do you know how healthy Cajun spices are? They contain vitamin A, vitamin B6, iron, magnesium, and even fiber. They also have anti-inflammatory benefits and help with constipation."

Harry raised one eyebrow. "That's a relief," he said with a laugh.

Phoebe was not amused. "There's nothing funny about constipation, I can assure you."

Lilly intervened before Harry could speak or Phoebe could continue to overshare.

"Well, I was glad you could join us, Phoebe. Did you get a lot of foot traffic in your shop yesterday?"

"I was expecting more, to be honest. I was certainly hoping for more. That rent doesn't pay itself. In fact, I was so worked up over the lack of customers that I went in the back and made a soothing pineapple-sage tisane."

It seemed best not to dwell on Phoebe's lack of business on the busiest shopping day of the year, so Lilly focused on the tisane.

"That sounds delicious." She said it to be polite, but in truth it sounded odious.

"I'd be happy to teach you how to make a tisane," Phoebe said. "It's similar to tea, but true tea comes from leaves of members of the *Camelliaensis* family. Tisanes are made with other herbs and botanicals."

Lilly smiled. She didn't want to learn how to make a tisane. She was just fine with coffee and regular tea, thanks.

"Actually, Lilly, my botanicals are the reason I stopped by."

"Oh?"

"Yes. I was watching your mother, poor dear, at Thanksgiving and I noticed she seems to be exhibiting rather pronounced symptoms of dementia."

If that had not been so true, Lilly might have resented the comment. But, she supposed, it was obvious, even if she hadn't mentioned it to Phoebe before or after Thanksgiving dinner. Harry cleared his throat and went into the back office. Lilly waited a few beats while she decided how to answer Phoebe.

"Yes, she does have dementia. She lives in Larkspur Manor in their memory care unit."

"Well, I wanted to let you know about several herbal remedies and concoctions that help with dementia."

Lilly pursed her lips and thought for a moment. "I'm not sure about that. She's on medications that her doctors have prescribed and I wouldn't want to introduce anything that could react with those meds."

"You could check with her doctors and make sure they're okay with it. Many medicines are essentially poison."

Lilly didn't appreciate the hard sell. Bev and her family were happy with the treatment she was receiving—she had been shuffling less since beginning physical therapy, and her speech had improved slightly after working closely with a therapist. Bev liked her doctors and Lilly and Bill found them honest, forthright, and compassionate. But Lilly had a feeling Phoebe wasn't going to let this go. *Maybe the best way to go forward,* Lilly thought, *is to humor her.*

"All right. If you want to give me some literature about herbal remedies for dementia symptoms, I can read them and let you know."

"Actually, I was thinking of having you over to my shop and giving you a hands-on tutorial on making them yourself. It would be my way of thanking you for inviting me to Thanksgiving dinner."

Lilly forced a smile. She supposed it would be rude to refuse.

"Okay, thank you. When would you like me to come over?"

"How about tonight?"

Lilly figured the sooner she went, the sooner it would be over. "All right. Bill's going to see Mom tonight, so I can come over after I close up the shop. Thank you again."

"It's my pleasure." Phoebe took a step toward the door, then turned around. "I was surprised to see Xavier Gordon at Thanksgiving. Did you say you two are neighbors?"

"Yes. He moved in a few weeks ago and I didn't want him to be alone for Thanksgiving. How do you know Xavier?"

"Oh, I've known him for a while. He is quite a ladies' man."

Lilly couldn't argue with that. "I don't really know him. He's good-looking *and* a doctor, so he probably has women lined up to date him."

"Hmm. It would appear that way. At least two of them were at Thanksgiving dinner." Phoebe gripped the door handle and pushed it open. "I've got to run, Lilly. I'll see you tonight."

Lilly waved goodbye and called to Harry, who was still in the office.

"Harry? Where'd you go?"

Harry appeared in the office doorway wearing a sheepish look. "I'm sorry, boss. I didn't want to be around when she started talking about your mom."

Lilly smiled. "I appreciate that, Harry. But she's right. I wanted to be offended, but I really can't. She's just speaking the truth. She even offered to teach me how to concoct some herbal mixture for my mom, and I couldn't say no because I'm a sucker. So guess what I'll be doing after work."

"You're not a sucker, just a nice person who can't say 'no.'"

"Thanks, Harry. I don't know if that's good or bad." Lilly laughed.

"I think it depends on the circumstances." Harry went to the window and looked up and down Main Street. "Not many people out tonight. I guess everyone's spent all their money."

He and Lilly started putting the jewelry away early, so by six o'clock they were ready to lock up the store.

"I'll see you Monday, Harry. I'm off to Phoebe's."

"Have fun." Harry waved goodbye, tugging his scarf more snugly around his neck. Lilly walked briskly up Main Street to Phoebe's shop.

She tried opening the front door of the herbery, but it was locked. She admired the beautiful gold etching of "The Herbery" on the plate glass window of the shop, softly lit by a nearby streetlamp and twinkling fairy lights. She peered inside. There were no lights on in the front of the shop, but Lilly could see a light coming from the office in the back. She shivered and knocked on the window. No answer.

Great. I'm freezing my pants off and I have to walk all the way around back to get in so I can learn how to make some potion that I don't even care about. Lilly breathed into her scarf and continued up the block to a quaint alley between two stores a few doors down from the herbery. She hurried to the area behind the stores where shopkeepers parked their cars and made her way to Phoebe's back door. It swung open when she tried the handle.

Lilly stepped inside and immediately felt the warmth of the shop envelop her. She took a long, deep breath in and savored the scent of herbs and spices wafting from the front of the shop. They were calming and cozy.

"Phoebe?" she called. The office was a mess, with papers piled everywhere and small jars of herbs littering the shelves and the desk. A filing cabinet sat in one corner, topped with several watering cans of varying sizes. Lilly maneuvered around the disorganized assortment of things until she came to the doorway to the back of the shop.

She peeked into the shop as a prickle of unease slithered up her arms and across the back of her neck. Something wasn't right. She reached for the light switch on the wall.

The pendant lights above the counter flickered to life, illuminating the only object on its surface, the big antique cash register. As she moved toward the counter, Lilly gasped. Phoebe Detweiler was lying face-down on the floor, her hair soaked in a puddle of blood.

CHAPTER 16

"Phoebe!" Lilly yelled.

Her heart beating a crazy rhythm, she raced over to the motionless woman and shook her. When there was no response, Lilly fumbled in her purse for her cell phone and called nine-one-one. In breathless, rapid tones she explained what she had discovered. The dispatcher said he would send help immediately.

It only took the police a few minutes to arrive, and they were followed quickly by an ambulance, its siren blaring and lights swirling incongruously against the backdrop of the Christmas fairy lights along Main Street.

Lilly waited in Phoebe's office while the EMTs did their work, and before long one of them stuck his head into the back office and addressed a police officer. "We're calling the medical examiner. The victim didn't make it."

The last thing Lilly remembered was calling feebly for an officer to catch her as she fell to the floor.

WHEN LILLY CAME TO, she was in a half-seated, half-prone position on the floor. A police officer was holding her under her armpits and an EMT was leaning back on his heels near her. She closed her eyes and swallowed hard as a wave of nausea washed over her. Someone whose voice sounded far away said the motive apparently hadn't been robbery.

"You're going to be all right," the EMT said. "You fainted. I gave you smelling salts."

Lilly nodded, her head swimming with confusion. She squinted, trying to remember what had happened just before she blacked out.

It came to her in another rush of nausea. "Phoebe? What happened?"

"We're hoping you can help us with that," the officer answered.

Lilly gave him a confused look. "What?"

"We'd like to ask you a few questions once you've got your bearings."

Another officer stepped into Lilly's visual field and looked down at her. "Feeling better?" she asked.

Lilly nodded. "I think so."

"Let's get her into the chair," the standing officer said. She produced an unopened bottle of water and held it out to Lilly as the EMT and the other officer helped her settle into Phoebe's office chair. The EMT reached for the bottle, unscrewed the cap, and handed it back to Lilly, who took a big gulp. Gradually the fog in her brain cleared and she was struck anew with the horror of what she had seen. She took another drink.

"You look like you're feeling better," the female officer said. "I'm Officer Perez and this is Officer Nutley." She nodded toward her partner.

Lilly nodded.

"What is your name?"

"Lilly Carlsen."

Officer Perez pulled up another chair and sat down. She asked for Lilly's home and work telephone numbers and addresses. Nutley wrote them down as Lilly answered.

"And what brought you here tonight?" Officer Perez asked.

"Phoebe asked me to come by after I closed my shop. She wanted to teach me how to make some kind of herbal remedy for my mother's dementia."

"So you came over here after you closed your shop? Is there anyone who can confirm where you were this afternoon?"

Lilly was confused. "Uh, yes. My assistant, Harry. He was with me all afternoon."

"And was anyone with you when you came here to the herb shop?"

Lilly shook her head. "No."

"And how do you know Phoebe Detweiler?"

"I only met her recently. I welcomed her to Main Street and then she came to Thanksgiving dinner at my house."

"You invited an almost-stranger to your house for Thanksgiving?"

"I actually invited four of them. They were all going to be alone for Thanksgiving and I hate to see people alone on Thanksgiving."

"Who were the other three you invited?"

Lilly ticked off names—Xavier Gordon, Chelsea Fortune, and Isabelle Montrose.

"Can you provide the contact information for them?"

"I'll have to check my phone for Isabelle's number. I don't know the phone numbers for Xavier or Chelsea, but Xavier just moved into the house next door to me and my best friend just hired Chelsea as an assistant. Isabelle Montrose is the realtor my brother, Bill Merriweather, and I hired to sell our mother's house." Lilly scrabbled for the phone in her handbag.

"Bill Merriweather is your brother?" Officer Perez's eyes widened in obvious surprise. "Excuse me a minute." She rose and went into the alley behind the herb shop. Lilly took the opportunity to look through her contacts for Isabelle's number. Officer Perez held a mumbled conversation which Lilly couldn't make out and then returned to the office and continued her questioning about Lilly's presence in Phoebe's shop.

"We're going to need you to come to the police station and provide a statement about what you saw here tonight," Officer Perez said.

"Okay. Right now?"

"Yes, if you're feeling up to it. If you don't feel like driving yet, one of us can drive you to the station and bring you back to get your car. Tomorrow is okay, but the sooner you do it, the better your recall is going to be."

"I think I'm okay to drive. I'll go over now."

"My partner will follow you." Officer Perez nodded toward Nutley.

"My car is behind my jewelry shop down the street."

"Then he'll drive you to your car," Perez said.

Nutley stood up and followed Lilly out the back door, where several police cruisers were parked. He walked to the closest one, opened the back door for Lilly, and closed it after she was seated. The trip only took about a minute—Nutley seemed to know exactly where the back of the jewelry shop was located. Lilly hadn't said a word. Her mind churned with thoughts of Phoebe, the things she and Lilly had talked about over the past few days, and the general humiliation of being driven anywhere in the back of a police car.

She got into her car and led the way to the police station, which, she reflected, had become a familiar drive in the past few years.

How do I get myself into these messes?

CHAPTER 17

After signing her statement at the police station, Lilly was exhausted and ready to go home and collapse. She was signing the log to leave the building when she heard her name.

"Lilly!"

Bill was jogging toward her from the hallway behind the reception desk. She waited for him to come to a stop next to her before greeting him.

"I suppose you know why I'm here," she said.

"I just heard. I was sitting in on an interrogation. I can't believe it. What happened? Are you all right?"

"I'm as good as can be expected after finding a dead body."

"What happened?" He led the way outdoors so other people in the station weren't privy to their conversation. The night sky shone inky black with a smattering of stars. Lilly led the way to her car and they sat inside to talk.

"Tell me everything," Bill directed.

Lilly repeated the story she had told Officers Perez and Nutley. Bill didn't interrupt.

"So Perez is the one you talked to," he finally said. "She's good, but she's like a dog with a bone. I don't know if that's good or bad as far as you're concerned."

"What do you mean?"

"What I mean is, if she suspects you of having anything to do with Phoebe's death, she's not going to leave you alone."

"Suspects me? Of killing Phoebe? You're kidding."

"I'm not saying she suspects you. I'm only saying that it'll be a rough road if she does suspect you."

"Can't you talk to her?"

Bill nodded. "I'll talk to her. But she's strictly by-the-book, so I'm not sure how much good it'll do me to say anything. In fact, it might do more harm than good."

"But you'll try?" Lilly frowned. She hadn't seriously thought she would be suspected of killing Phoebe, but she supposed there was a strong possibility Perez would zero in on her. After all, she found the body, she was alone when she went to Phoebe's shop, and she had invited Phoebe, practically a stranger, into her own home recently. She leaned her head back against the car seat and closed her eyes.

"Take it easy, Lil. Like I said, Perez is good. She'll leave no stone unturned. That's good for you. She's bound to find out who really killed Phoebe."

Lilly could only nod in response.

"Here's what I want to know," Bill said. "How did you get involved in something like this again? You're like a death magnet."

Lilly's eyes snapped open and she glared at her brother. "Don't call me that!"

"You know what I mean."

"There's a simple explanation. I'm the unluckiest person on Earth."

"Listen. I've got to get back in there, but go home and try to relax. I'll call you tomorrow."

When Lilly got home she went straight up to her bedroom,

where she donned the comfiest pajamas she could find. She went back downstairs, opened a can of tomato soup, and that simmered while she made a grilled cheese sandwich. Perfect comfort food. She flipped through the mail while she waited for the food to cook, inhaling sharply when she saw a handwritten thank-you note from Phoebe. She shook her head in bewilderment at the timing.

Tighe, Laurel, and Vanessa were out, so Lilly called Hassan while she ate. He was shocked to hear about Phoebe's death.

"Thank God you didn't walk in on the killer." Lilly could hear the concern in his voice. "What am I going to do with you?"

"Take me away from all this?"

"It sounds like that's exactly what I should do. Are you sure you're okay?"

"I guess. I feel terrible about Phoebe. If I had gotten to the herbery just a little earlier, maybe I could have deterred whoever it was from even coming into the shop. And if I'm honest, I'm also a little worried about myself. Bill said the officer who questioned me at the scene is, quote unquote, like a dog with a bone, and she's already asked me where I was right before I found Phoebe. Harry was at my shop and saw me leave, but no one else that I know of saw me between the time I left my shop and the time I got to Phoebe's shop."

"I wouldn't worry about it. You had no reason to want to harm Phoebe, so I'm sure the officer will back off when she realizes that."

"I hope you're right."

"Do you want me to come over?"

"All the time. But tonight I'm going straight to bed as soon as the kids get home."

"All right. Call me if you need anything or just want to talk. I love you, Lil."

"I love you, too."

Lilly was picking up the phone to call Noley when everyone got home. They were shocked to hear what had happened. They fussed and clucked over Lilly until she shooed them to their rooms, but not before warning them that the police would need to speak to them.

Finally she called Noley to tell her about finding Phoebe's body. Bill had already told her, so Noley had been waiting for Lilly's call.

"You must have been terrified!" Noley cried.

"If I hadn't been unconscious for much of it, I probably would have been."

"You're kidding. You passed out?" Noley gasped. "What if you had passed out and the killer had come back? I don't even want to think about it."

"Not to worry. By the time I passed out, the police were there."

"Thank goodness. Lilly, do you suppose the killer saw you in the back of the shop?"

Lilly hadn't thought of that. She wished Noley hadn't mentioned it.

CHAPTER 18

*B*ill called first thing the next morning. "I talked to Perez," he greeted Lilly.

"And? What did she say?"

"She's going to be in charge of the day-to-day in the case, and she definitely wants to interview you again."

"Why?"

"Just to ask more questions. She needs more information and since you're the one who found the body, you are in the best position to give her what she needs."

"Are you sure she doesn't think I did it?"

The silence was a nanosecond too long.

"She thinks I did it. Don't lie."

"I didn't actually come right out and ask her, but it doesn't sound to me like she thinks you did it."

"That's a huge comfort." Lilly didn't bother to muffle the sarcasm in her voice.

"No, seriously. I'll say something to her if it looks like she's putting pressure on you, but I don't think it'll come to that."

"Can't you just say something to her before she even thinks I might be involved somehow?"

"I already told you, I don't think that'll help. But I can try to find out what she's thinking. And before you ask, I'm not on the case at all. And now that I've been promoted, I have to watch myself. I can't get involved much more than I have."

Lilly sighed. "All right. If I had known this promotion would mean you can't help me get out of a possible murder rap, I'm sorry you got it."

She could hear the grin in Bill's voice. "Don't worry, Lil. Everything is going to be fine."

Lilly figured she'd better start phoning people to tell them to expect to be contacted by the police. The first person she called was Harry.

"I can't believe it," he said when she had told him what happened.

"I hate to say it, Harry, but I'm sure the police are going to want to question you and Alice, since you were both at Thanksgiving and you were the last one to see me before I went to Phoebe's shop yesterday evening."

"Don't worry about it, boss. I'm sure it's just a formality."

Lilly was getting tired of being told not to worry about it.

No sooner had she hung up with Harry than Isabelle called. The woman's voice set Lilly's nerves jangling.

"Good morning, Isabelle," Lilly said.

"Not so far. What the heck have you gotten me into?"

"What do you mean?" Lilly didn't bother to suppress the note of annoyance in her voice.

"The police paid me a visit this morning. At home. Do you know how bad that looks to my neighbors?"

"I'm sorry, Isabelle, but I couldn't very well pretend you weren't at Thanksgiving dinner. The police asked me who was there and I had to give them everyone's name."

"Well, I wish you could have kept me out of it, or at least told me to expect a visit from the authorities."

"I was going to call you this morning. I had no idea they would be asking questions so soon."

"What happened?"

"Phoebe was killed."

Isabelle spoke as if Lilly were a simpleton. "I know that. Obviously. I mean, how did it happen?"

"I don't know. I only found her body."

"Eww." Isabelle shuddered.

"I have to call everyone else who was at Thanksgiving dinner, Isabelle, so I really should get going."

"Fine. Bye."

Lilly shook her head in resignation, hoping her mother's house would sell soon so she wouldn't have to deal with Isabelle much longer.

The time had come for Tighe to head back to school. "Are you sure you're going to be all right?" he asked. "I don't like to leave in the middle of all this, but I need to get back."

"Don't worry about me. Try to get this all out of your head and concentrate on school. When the police want to talk to you, they're just going to have to do it over the phone." She hugged him and watched him pull out of the driveway with a wistful look in her eye. She always missed him the most right after he left for school.

As she was watching Tighe reach the end of the block and turn out of sight, she saw Xavier and Mimi come out of his house. Xavier was carrying a bouquet of flowers and they waved to her. She waved back and turned to go inside, but Mimi called, "Lilly! Wait a sec!"

She waited, shivering, while Xavier and Mimi hurried up her front walk. "Hi," she greeted them. "Did you have a nice Thanksgiving, Mimi?"

"I did, thanks. And you?"

Lilly didn't know how to answer that truthfully, so she merely nodded and smiled. Xavier handed her the bouquet.

"Are these for me?" she asked. "They're gorgeous! Thank you. You didn't have to do that—you brought flowers for Thanksgiving."

"Mimi arranged them and brought them from her shop. She told me a bottle of wine and a grocery store bouquet weren't good enough to thank you for inviting me for Thanksgiving, so she brought you this bouquet all the way from Wyoming."

Lilly smiled. "You didn't have to do that. The flowers and wine were perfect. But these are just beautiful. Thank you, Mimi. Would you two like to come in?"

They shook their heads. "We can't stay, but thank you anyway. We're going to brunch," Mimi explained.

"Sounds nice. Listen, I was just on my way into the house to call you, Xavier. I need to talk to you about something."

Xavier looked at her expectantly. "Yes?"

She took a deep breath and told them all about Phoebe's death. They both wore looks of shock at the news.

"I saw something online early this morning about a woman being killed in town, but there were no details," Xavier said. "I'm sure Phoebe's the one they were talking about. That's terrible."

Lilly nodded. "It was pretty awful. The reason I'm telling you about it is because the police are going to want to talk to you because you were at Thanksgiving dinner."

"Okay. I'm not sure how much I can tell them, but I'll answer their questions. Thanks for the heads-up, Lilly."

Lilly thanked them again for the flowers and they were off. Back inside, Lilly texted Noley and asked her to tell Chelsea to expect a visit from Perez. She didn't feel like telling the whole story again to Chelsea. Noley wouldn't mind.

Luckily, it was Sunday, which meant Lilly had the day off. She was grateful to be able to spend the entire afternoon visiting Bev—and Finley—because she didn't want to discuss Phoebe's death with anyone else, but instead she ended up wondering the whole time if she needed to remind them about the birds and the bees. She didn't, but the effort to refrain from doing so was exhausting.

CHAPTER 19

On Monday night Laurel and Vanessa planned to have dinner out. Lilly visited Bev, ate dinner by herself, and was sitting on the sofa checking her email when the girls came home.

"Come on in. Sit down. Everything's going to be okay, Vanessa, I promise." Laurel was talking in a quiet, soothing tone.

"What's wrong?" Lilly jumped up and was halfway to the kitchen when the first racking sob reached her ears. Her first thought was *the baby*. She covered the rest of the distance to the kitchen in two hurried steps and stopped short at what she saw.

Vanessa sat at the table, moaning, her head in her hands. She looked up at Lilly, who was shocked to see the tears and other goo running down Vanessa's face. She pulled out the chair next to the young woman.

"What happened?"

Vanessa was beginning to hyperventilate, so Lilly directed Laurel to get a paper bag from the pantry. When Laurel raced back to the table with it, Lilly fashioned a hole, put it against Vanessa's mouth, and told her to inhale and exhale.

Vanessa did as she was told, and within a minute or two, her breathing slowed. She finally took the bag away from her face and covered her eyes with her trembling hands. Lilly looked at Laurel over Vanessa's head, her eyes full of questions. Laurel met Lilly's gaze and shook her head sadly.

"Vanessa, what's wrong? Is it the baby? Are you sick? Do we need to get you to the emergency room?" Lilly wanted to scream. "Can you tell me what happened?"

Vanessa swallowed and tried composing herself. She had the hiccups and looked at Laurel, nodding.

"You want me to tell her?" Laurel asked.

Vanessa nodded, the tears seeping out again.

"Cyrus broke up with her."

Vanessa let out a loud wail and her shoulders shook as the tears began afresh. Lilly was momentarily speechless, her mouth hanging open as she stared from Laurel to Vanessa and back again. She leaned into Vanessa and wrapped her arms around the poor girl's shoulders while Laurel went for tissues.

"It's all right, Vanessa. It's all right." She cradled Vanessa in her arms for several minutes, until the crying abated and Vanessa was able to sit up, dry her eyes, and blow her nose.

Laurel sat down with them and reached for Vanessa's hand. "Do you want me to tell her what happened?"

Vanessa stared at her hands. She nodded.

"Cyrus was supposed to come up and visit next weekend, but he called Vanessa to say that he couldn't come," Laurel began. "She felt bad, but she told him that was okay and that maybe he could visit after his exams. Then he said he probably couldn't come up then, either."

Vanessa looked up. "I knew something was wrong the second he said that." She gestured for Laurel to continue.

"He told her they needed to talk, and Mom, I swear she turned as white as a sheet. She sat down and just listened, and I knew what he was saying."

Lilly tilted her head and gazed at Vanessa with sympathy and affection. "Vanessa, we're going to get you through this."

"I thought we were going to get married!" Vanessa wailed.

"Maybe you still can," Laurel said. "Maybe he just needs space."

Lilly suspected in that direction lay heartbreak and pain. She shook her head at Laurel almost imperceptibly and turned her attention back to Vanessa.

"Listen, honey. We love you. I know that's not enough right now, but you remember it. You're not alone. And that baby of yours is going to be surrounded by love when he or she is born."

Vanessa took a shaky breath and let it out slowly. "I know. I can't tell you how much I appreciate you letting me stay here. Especially now that the baby's father is going to be out of the picture. And my parents …" Her voice trailed off as she shut her eyes tightly and grimaced.

"I'm so tired," she finally said. "I wish I could take something to help me sleep. The doctor said no medicine until the baby's born. I know I'm going to be awake all night."

"How about some warm milk?" Lilly suggested. "Laurel can get some for you and add some cinnamon and nutmeg. I drink that sometimes to relax. And it tastes good, too."

"Okay," Vanessa mumbled. It was clear her thoughts were far away. Laurel got up and prepared the milk for Vanessa while Lilly let Barney out to do his business before bedtime. Before going upstairs she enveloped Vanessa in a warm hug.

"You wake me up if you need anything. Even if you just need to talk or someone to stay in your room with you."

"Same with me," Laurel said.

"Thanks." Vanessa blinked away tears that were forming again in the corners of her eyes. Then the trio made their way to their rooms.

Lilly awoke the next morning with a feeling of dread in her

chest before remembering the cause: Vanessa and Cyrus. She wondered if Vanessa had been able to sleep at all.

She peeked into Laurel's room before going downstairs to make coffee, and noted that the bed hadn't been slept in. She listened at the door of the guest bedroom, but didn't hear anything. After she turned on the coffeemaker, she went into the living room to tidy the pillows and put the dogs' toys away.

She smiled when she saw both girls asleep on the pullout bed, both dogs lounging at their feet. Barney looked up and cocked his ears. Lilly put a finger to her lips, smiling at her furry friend.

CHAPTER 20

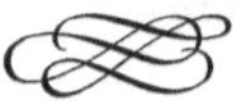

On Tuesday, Harry was already at the shop by the time Lilly arrived.

"Any news from the police?" he asked.

"I'm afraid not. I wish they would make an arrest or announce a person of interest or something—besides me, that is." Lilly sighed. She looked out the window at Main Street, where the Christmas lights lent a soft, cozy glow to the gray morning light. "There's a killer out there somewhere."

Harry was silent, and she turned around. He was gazing at something that she couldn't see, something in the distance. "You all right, Harry?"

"I just remembered something," he replied in an excited voice. "Remember how deserted it was on Main Street on Saturday evening? It was so deserted we started taking the displays down early."

"Yeah, I remember that."

"I saw someone peering in the front window of the herbery."

"Who was it?" Lilly hadn't meant to scare him with the force of her question, but he blinked and looked taken aback. "Sorry. I didn't mean to startle you."

"That's okay." Harry closed his eyes and crinkled his face. "I don't know who it was."

"Could you tell if it was a man or a woman?"

"I'm pretty sure it was a woman."

"Could you tell how tall she was?"

Harry shook his head. "No. At that distance it was hard to tell."

"Have the police talked to you yet?"

"Not yet. They haven't contacted Alice, either."

"I wonder when they're going to question you. Maybe we should call them with this information."

But they didn't have to call the police. Shortly after the shop opened, an officer came in. The door jingled, signaling his arrival, and Lilly greeted him cordially.

"I'm here to see Harry Hobart. Is he available?" he asked.

"I'm Harry." Harry stepped forward and extended his hand in greeting.

"Is there a place where we can speak privately?"

Harry glanced at Lilly. "Can we use the office?"

"Sure." Lilly gestured toward the office and Harry and the policeman disappeared inside, closing the door behind them.

Lilly drummed her fingers on the counter until her first customer came in. Thankfully, the woman wanted to see every watch in the shop before choosing one to give her husband for Christmas, so Lilly managed to keep busy while Harry was talking to the officer. If no customer had come in, Lilly thought she would have gone mad.

Finally Harry and the officer emerged. The officer thanked Harry, nodded to Lilly, then left. Lilly was still helping the woman who wanted to buy a watch, but as soon as the woman left, with a watch wrapped and placed in a fancy bag, Lilly turned to Harry with a mixture of trepidation and urgency.

"Did the officer say anything? What did he want to know? Are they any closer to figuring out who did it?"

"He started with how I met Phoebe, what the atmosphere was like on Thanksgiving, how Phoebe behaved when she was there, what I know about your relationship with Phoebe, and what I did for practically every minute from the day before Thanksgiving until the night Phoebe died." Harry sat down on a stool and ran his hands down his face. "I'm exhausted from thinking so hard."

Lilly hated to ask the next question. "Did you get a sense of who he thinks killed Phoebe?"

"I hate to say it, but I think he thinks you did it."

Lilly's insides went cold. "That's what I was afraid of. I assume you told him about the person you saw looking in the herbery window before I went over there that night?"

"You bet I did. Maybe they can get some security camera footage from other places on Main Street and identify the person."

"I hope so."

Another customer came in, followed quickly by someone else, and Lilly and Harry had to pause their conversation. Lilly's fingers were itching to text Bill and find out what was going on, but she would have to wait until later.

Laurel called during the afternoon to give Lilly an update on Vanessa.

"She's been crying off and on today, but nothing like last night," Laurel said.

"I expect that will continue for a while," Lilly said. "Not only is she going through something that is traumatic for anyone, but she's doing it while pregnant, so she has the baby to worry about. And besides that, her hormones are going crazy right now, so that's making her even more emotional than she normally would be. I feel terrible for her, poor thing."

"I'm going to try to get her to go out somewhere with me this afternoon," Laurel said.

"That's a good idea. Let me know if things go downhill."

"I will. Bye, Mom."

Lilly didn't hear from Laurel again that day, which was a good sign. At closing time, Lilly and Harry hurried to put the jewelry in the vaults, triple-checked the locks, and left. Lilly headed to Larkspur Manor to see Bev. She was just getting out of the car when the phone rang. It was Noley.

"What are you doing for dinner?" Noley asked.

"Probably leftovers. Why?"

"Want to meet me and Bill at the diner?"

"Sure. I'm just going in to see Mom right now."

"That's fine. We'll meet you at the diner in about forty-five minutes."

"Can I invite Hassan?"

"Of course!"

Lilly texted Hassan and invited him to the diner. He responded with a thumbs-up.

CHAPTER 21

When Lilly walked down Bev's hallway at Larkspur Manor, she heard the voice before she saw the person singing. It was a deep, rich baritone and it sounded like it was coming from Bev's room. Lilly quickened her steps, eager to see if her mom had finally shown some interest in playing some of the CDs she and Bill had bought for her. But when she walked into Bev's room, she stopped and stared in astonishment.

Finley stood by Bev's armchair, serenading her with an old Irish folk tune Lilly recognized from her own childhood. Her mother used to sing that same song to her and Bill. Bev was facing Finley, but her eyes had a faraway look in them and she wore a wistful smile. Lilly watched, entranced by Finley's voice, until the song came to an end and Finley glanced toward her, noticing her for the first time. He grinned.

Lilly gave a start when she heard another voice just behind her. It was Mirren.

"My dad used to sing with a theater company in the town where I grew up," she said. "Sorry if I scared you. I just went back to his room to get my phone. I wanted to record him singing again. He hasn't sung in a long time."

"It's all for Bev," Finley said. The singing seemed to have wiped him out. He sagged in a chair next to Bev and reached for her hand. She allowed him to take it and he kissed it gently. Lilly wished Bill could be there to see it.

Bev finally noticed Lilly, who was still standing in the doorway.

"Hello, Lilly, dear."

Lilly's heart gave a leap. Bev had recognized her. "Hi, Mom. Finley, that was beautiful."

"Thank you. I used to love to sing."

"It sounds like you still do," Lilly said.

"Dad, I wanted to take a video. Can you sing some more?" Mirren asked.

Finley shook his head. "I can't sing anymore tonight. Too tired."

Mirren nodded. "Are you ready to go back to your room?"

Finley nodded and allowed Mirren to take his arm and lead him down the hall. He didn't even turn around to bid Bev good-night before he left.

"He sings to me sometimes," Bev said in answer to Lilly's bemused look. "It makes him tired."

There were so many questions Lilly wanted to ask, but she had a hunch she needed to choose her words carefully or her mother would clam up and refuse to talk about Finley. Lilly was still unsure how she felt about Bev seeing Finley romantically. It seemed like a revolt against her father's memory.

"You're thinking about your father." Bev's words did not come out like an accusation, but as a matter of fact. *How does she know this stuff?* Lilly wondered.

"I guess I am."

"I miss him, but I'm not dead yet." Bev actually winked.

"Mom!"

"I have needs, Lilly."

"Mom, please—"

The conversation was blessedly interrupted by Greg, who came in to give Bev a tiny paper cup of medication.

"Good evening, Bev!" He smiled when he saw Lilly. "Was that the first time you've heard Finley sing? He's pretty good, isn't he?"

"Pretty good? He's incredible," Lilly said.

Greg busied himself with distributing Bev's medication while Lilly sat down next to Bev. They talked—well, mostly Lilly talked—about little things, like what Bev had for dinner (she couldn't recall, but it was good), the weather, and whether Bev would attend a singalong in the music room (she would not).

Lilly gathered her coat and purse. "I'm afraid I can't stay, Mom. I'm supposed to meet Bill and Noley and Hassan for dinner at the diner in just a little while."

"When is Bill coming to visit?"

Lilly ground her teeth to avoid blurting out a snarky reply. This was typical Bev—always wondering where her son was when Lilly was sitting right in front of her. Lilly had to remind herself that Bev didn't mean to hurt her feelings, that she couldn't help herself, that it was entirely possible her mother didn't actually have a favorite child.

Lilly had to hurry if she was going to get to the diner on time, so it was a good time to bid her mother goodnight before she could say anything else that might get Lilly's dander up.

"I'll see you soon, Mom." Lilly kissed Bev goodbye and left.

When she arrived at the diner, Hassan was waiting for her in the parking lot. Bill and Noley were already inside.

"Sorry I'm late."

"You're not late. We were all early. How's your mom?"

"She's wondering when Bill will be over to visit." Lilly rolled her eyes.

Hassan chuckled as he linked his arm through hers. "You know your mom loves you just as much as she loves Bill."

"Hmm. Sometimes I wonder."

"She probably asks about you every time he visits her."

"I would ask him, but I'm not sure I want to know the answer."

Hassan squeezed her arm closer and opened the diner door for her. Noley waved to them from a booth in the back of the restaurant and they joined her and Bill.

"How's Mom?" Bill asked.

"Fine. Finley was serenading her when I showed up. That man has an amazing voice!"

Bill shook his head. "I still can't believe Mom has a boyfriend."

Lilly held up her hand to keep Bill from saying any more. "Please. She told me she has 'needs.' I can't even … not right now."

Over dinners of Salisbury steak, meatloaf, and chicken and biscuits, they discussed Phoebe's death and the resulting chaos it was creating for Lilly.

"You know I can't say very much about this," Bill cautioned them. "Though the truth is, I don't know very much. Perez knows you're my sister, so I'm being effectively kept out of the loop."

"Is there anything you know that you haven't shared?"

"I don't think so. I know someone questioned Xavier and Chelsea today, that's about it. I don't even know what they said."

"Have the police talked to Laurel and Vanessa yet?" Hassan asked.

"No. And believe it or not, other news has superseded talk of Phoebe." Lilly leaned back with a sigh.

CHAPTER 22

"What other news?" Noley asked.

"I haven't even had time to tell you about it," Lilly replied. "Cyrus broke up with Vanessa."

Bill and Noley wore faces of shock. Hassan closed his eyes and shook his head.

"Oh, no!" Noley said. "What's going to happen now?"

Lilly shrugged. "I don't know. I've told her she can stay at our house as long as she wants to, even after the baby's born."

Hassan covered Lilly's hand with his own. "Well, if she and Cyrus are through for good, you're probably the best person to be helping her through this. You know all about being a single mom."

"I guess so, but my experience was a little different. I had my mom's support and Vanessa doesn't."

"But she has you and Laurel," Bill said.

"That's true. But it's not the same thing as your own mom, you know? I wish her parents weren't so pig-headed. She could really use their support."

"Is Cyrus going to stay in the picture at all?" Noley asked.

"Vanessa said he wouldn't, but maybe that was her grief talking. I don't even know if they've spoken since he broke it off with her. It's not like a normal teenage relationship where they can just go their separate ways. They have a lifelong connection now because of this baby."

"They're going to have to talk at some point," Hassan said.

"I'm sure they will. Just not right away. Vanessa is too fragile to talk to him right now," Lilly said.

"I wonder why Cyrus broke up with her," Noley mused.

"Maybe he's being pressured by his parents," Hassan suggested.

"I thought of that," Lilly said. "But why wouldn't he tell her that? It would at least soften the blow a little bit. And to think I really liked that guy." Lilly made a sound of disgust. "Who leaves a pregnant girlfriend three months before the baby comes?"

On Wednesday morning Mirren was already at the coffee shop when Lilly arrived. She was seated and had a cup of coffee in front of her, so Lilly went directly to the barista and ordered a latte.

"Good morning." Lilly dropped into the chair across from her new friend.

"Hi. You look tired this morning."

Lilly took a sip of her latte. "I am. I've had a rough week so far." She paused, then changed the subject. "Hey, I loved hearing your dad sing last night."

"Thank you. He loves to sing. He worked in construction his whole life, but the theater company was his creative outlet. He's been singing since I can remember."

"My mother loves it."

"He thinks the world of her."

Lilly smiled. "It's weird, you know? She hasn't dated since my father died. It's been decades since then. It's strange to see her interested in another man."

"I know what you mean. My father hasn't dated since my

mother died, either. And now all of a sudden he's head over heels for your mom."

Both women were quiet for several moments, enjoying the warmth and the aromas and the quiet background hum of early morning conversation in the coffee shop.

"What do you think of Larkspur Manor?" Mirren asked after several moments.

"My brother and I are very happy with the care Mom's getting," Lilly said. "And Mom says she likes it there. It took her some time to get used to it, but she seems to be doing very well."

"When my father was diagnosed with dementia, we thought it was the end of the world," Mirren said. "I have a sister, but she lives a couple hours away. My father was living with my husband and me at the time."

"How wonderful that he could live with you."

"I'm very grateful for that time. Unfortunately, my husband thinks we've done our duty by him and he's ready to get outta Dodge."

Lilly furrowed her brow.

"Basil has a job offer from a big accounting firm in Chicago. He's furious that I'm refusing to leave Dad. He says it's my sister's turn to care for him."

"Is he going to take the job?"

Mirren shrugged "Who knows? Honestly, at this point I couldn't care less. We fight about it all the time."

Lilly could hear the anger and stress in Mirren's voice. She leaned forward and put her hand over Mirren's. "Look, if anyone knows how hard it can be to deal with a parent's illness while juggling ten thousand other worries, it's me. Anytime you want to let off some steam, give me a call and we can grab dinner or something. At any given moment I'm ready to let off some steam of my own."

"Will do. Thanks." Mirren raised her coffee mug in salute.

CHAPTER 23

*N*oley called that night.

"Talk to me about something other than my mother or Phoebe," Lilly said. "How's it going with Chelsea?"

"She's pretty good. She's been organizing some of my older recipes and that's been a big help. Honestly, though, I don't know how she gets anything done with all the energy she devotes to talking about Xavier, thinking about Xavier, going out with Xavier, and generally mooning over Xavier."

"She's got it bad, huh?"

"To say the least. He seems to feel that way about her, too. They spend every spare minute together. And they only met a week ago!"

"Ah, to be that young again. Just kidding." When Lilly was Chelsea's age she was married and the mother of two very young children. "I wonder how he has so much time to spend with Chelsea when he's trying to start up a new business."

"It makes me wonder how hard he's really working on that practice. Seriously, Lil, they've been out almost every day."

"I've seen cars parked in the street in front of his house. I assume those are clients," Lilly said. "He must arrange his calendar so he has time to relax each day. That actually sounds like a pretty good idea."

"All I know is, Chelsea is over the moon for him."

"There's a pretty big difference in their ages."

"She says he's a distinguished older man."

"Or a cradle-robber. It all depends on one's perspective. Doesn't it bother her at all?"

"If it does, she's good at hiding it. Don't tell anyone I said this, but she even mentioned the M word."

"The M word?"

"Marriage."

"You're kidding. They just met!"

"Chelsea says she's found The One."

Lilly could practically hear Noley rolling her eyes—Noley, who had known Bill for years and years before their first date, would not be one to believe in finding The One at first sight.

"I wonder if Xavier shares those feelings," Lilly said.

"I can't imagine he does. He's been around the block, you know? He's got an ex-wife, a medical practice, and I'm guessing a mortgage. He's a grown-up. Chelsea is still so young."

"Well, Mother Hen, I've got to get going. Don't worry about Chelsea. She may seem young to you, but she's a grown-up, too."

"You wouldn't feel that way if it were Laurel," Noley said.

Lilly shuddered. "Don't even go there," she said with a laugh.

Lilly liked to wait until she was tucked into bed before calling Hassan because she liked his voice to be the last one she heard every day. The girls were upstairs, so after letting Barney and Fred outside one last time, she shut off all the lights downstairs and made sure the front door was locked. Looking out the side panel of the door, she noticed movement at Xavier's house. She wondered for a second if a patient was having an emergency until she recognized the figure climbing the front steps.

Isabelle Montrose.

Lilly would have recognized the woman's fluffy head

anywhere. Isabelle knocked twice on Xavier's door, then waited only a moment before he opened it and ushered her inside. Lilly was glad the lights were off in her house so they didn't notice her standing there, spying like she was ten years old.

"Hmm. I wonder what that's all about." Lilly bent down and scratched the dogs' ears. "And I wonder if Chelsea knows about it. Or if Isabelle knows about Chelsea."

She and Hassan discussed it before she fell asleep.

"Do you think I should say something to Noley? Maybe she should hint to Chelsea that Xavier is not dating her exclusively."

"I don't think you should say anything," Hassan said. "For all we know, Xavier and Chelsea have an open relationship."

"I guess you're right. But I would bet my last dollar that Chelsea thinks Xavier is only seeing her right now."

"I agree with you, but I'm not sure you should be the person to break the bad news to her."

"Technically, it would be Noley breaking the bad news."

"You're splitting hairs, love." She could hear the smile in his voice.

"I know. I just feel bad for her. She seems like a nice young woman. Funny how I don't feel bad for Isabelle, isn't it?"

Hassan chuckled. "It would take a pretty strong man to withstand her forceful nature."

"From what I just saw, Xavier may lack that strength."

CHAPTER 24

aurel accompanied Vanessa to the obstetrician the next morning. She called Lilly after the appointment.

"Mom, it was awful. Vanessa started to cry when the doctor asked her how she's been. She couldn't stop. And then I started crying, and then the nurse started crying. It couldn't have been worse."

"Poor Vanessa. She is going to have a hard time of it, I'm afraid."

"She decided to call Cyrus after the appointment. She just wanted to tell him how it went, since it's his baby, too. His mother answered and wouldn't let her talk to him."

"You're kidding. Why not?"

"She told Vanessa that Cyrus is trying to make a clean break with her because he needs to think about his future. Vanessa lost it and accused the mother of breaking them up." Laurel paused to take a deep breath.

"And then what?"

"Cyrus's mom finally put him on the phone and he told Vanessa that he's seeing someone else and to please not call him again."

"Oh, no." Lilly squeezed her eyes shut.

"So she asked him 'what about the baby? Don't you want anything to do with the baby?' and he told her he wants nothing to do with it."

"I can't believe it. He seemed like such a nice guy."

"If you ask me, I think his parents have a lot to do with it. They were supportive at first, but I'll bet the more they thought about it, the more they thought he was ruining his future by having a baby."

"You might be right. I wonder if there's anything we can do to cheer up Vanessa."

"I don't think there is. I offered to take her for coffee—decaf, of course—or for cupcakes, to the library, to Juniper Lake. She doesn't want to do anything. Right now she's just crying in her room. I can hear her."

Lilly's heart constricted. She couldn't imagine how the vulnerable young woman must be feeling. There had been moments when Vanessa seemed okay, but Lilly had a hunch this would cause great pain for a long time to come.

"I'm afraid the best course of action may be to let her grieve and give her the time and space she needs to get over Cyrus. It is not going to be easy, especially with a baby on the way, but we can be there for her and support her in whatever ways she needs."

"Yeah." Laurel's voice was distant and sad.

"Do you think she'd like to go shopping for a layette?" Lilly asked. "We could take her out as a treat."

"What's a layette?"

"The baby's first set of clothes. He—or she—will grow out of them quickly, but Vanessa will have to have them before the baby gets here, obviously. We could do that tonight if she's up to it."

"She might like that. I'll ask her."

"We can go after I close up shop tonight if she wants to."

"Okay. I'll let you know."

Laurel texted Lilly a bit later. She'll go. She finally smiled.

It was after lunch when Isabelle came through the front door. Lilly was surprised to see her during business hours.

"Hello, Lilly," she boomed. The other shoppers in the quiet store side-eyed her.

"Hi, Isabelle. What brings you in today?"

"Just browsing. I thought I'd take a look at your wares."

"That's fine. Let me know if you have any questions and I'll be happy to help you as soon as I've helped these other customers."

"Will do."

As Lilly and Harry helped the other customers, Lilly's eyes strayed to Isabelle every so often. Isabelle was obviously trying to look nonchalant, but she was hovering near the engagement rings. There was an unmistakable hunger in her eyes when she surveyed the gorgeous diamond rings Lilly had on display.

When Isabelle was the only shopper left in Juniper Junction Jewels, Lilly walked over to where she was admiring the men's watches.

"See anything that catches your eye?" Lilly asked.

"Oh, plenty. Tell me. Just out of idle curiosity, how much do you charge for an engagement ring?"

She couldn't be more obvious. A pang of pity shot through Lilly. There was no way Xavier was ever going to be buying a ring for Isabelle. "That depends on the ring. Show me which one and I'll tell you the price."

Isabelle strode over to the display of diamond rings again. "Well, just for kicks and giggles, let's say this one." She pointed to a ring featuring a marquise cut diamond surrounded by a semicircle of tiny diamonds on each side of it.

When Lilly told her the price, Isabelle let out a loud whistle. "That's a lot of money! Anything more reasonable? Do you give discounts to your friends?"

"I sell to personal friends at the wholesale price," Lilly said.

"And what would the wholesale price be for that ring?"

Lilly named a price and Isabelle's eyebrows disappeared into her curly bangs. "You don't make much on this stuff, do you?"

It's really none of your business how much I make on each piece, Lilly thought uncharitably. By now she was ready for Isabelle to leave. "Some products have a tight profit margin, yes. Do you want to see something less expensive?"

Isabelle shrugged, her wide shoulders coming up to her ears. "Might as well."

Lilly moved down the display case until she came to much smaller rings. She pointed to a half-carat ring in a gold setting. "How about that one?"

"It's kind of small."

"That's true. But it has a more reasonable price point." Lilly told Isabelle the price and Isabelle nodded.

"That price is more like it. Still, the ring is pretty small."

Lilly wanted to tell Isabelle that she was never going to find a large, high-quality diamond ring at a bargain basement price, but she kept her lips closed and waited for Isabelle to say something.

"Well, this has been an eye opener." Isabelle's laugh sounded like a bark. "Thanks for the info, Lilly. I'll let you know when I hear something about your mom's house. With the profit margins you have here, now I *know* you should have taken my advice to sell her house when you could get more money for it." She yanked the front door open and was gone.

"She's really something." Harry stared at Isabelle's back retreating down Main Street.

"She sure is."

"I wonder why she was looking at engagement rings."

"Who knows? The woman is inexplicable." Lilly didn't share her conviction that Isabelle was doing a little pre-shopping in anticipation of Xavier eventually popping the question.

Lilly hurried to lock up the store that night. She changed her clothes as soon as she got home, then she and the girls ate a quick dinner and headed out. According to Laurel, Vanessa's mood had improved when she heard about going shopping for baby clothes.

Lilly drove them to Lupine, where the shops were open later in the evening. There were several baby stores in the town, which was larger than Juniper Junction. The three had fun browsing the shops and picking out bags of adorable unisex baby clothes. Vanessa had opted not to learn the baby's gender before the big day, so they contented themselves with clothes and accessories, such as hats, booties, and blankets, in pastel shades of green and yellow.

It cost Lilly a fortune, but she couldn't complain about that when she saw the smiles that lit up Vanessa's face. It seemed Cyrus had moved to the back of her mind, at least for a couple hours.

They stopped for hot chocolate and shortbread at a dessert bistro in Lupine, then headed home. The girls chattered the whole way back to Juniper Junction about the baby, wondering whether Vanessa would have a boy or a girl. Lilly smiled, recalling those same conversations she and Beau used to have, a lifetime ago.

CHAPTER 25

*B*arney came racing into the kitchen upon their arrival back at home, his nails sliding on the floor until he crashed into Lilly.

She laughed as she bent down to rub his ears. "You're a crazy one, Barn. Where's Fred?" She looked into the living room, since Fred usually wasn't far from Barney, but didn't see him. She shrugged and turned her attention to Vanessa and Laurel, who were unpacking the shopping bags and looking again at all Vanessa's loot.

"Isn't this adorable?" Laurel squealed. She held up a long-sleeved onesie that came with a matching beanie and tiny sweatpants festooned with ducklings.

Vanessa giggled. She pointed to the softest blanket they had seen all evening, a pale yellow one with a satin border. "I wish I could use that blanket. It's so soft."

There was a knock at the back door. Lilly hurried to open it, thinking it might be Hassan making a surprise visit, but it was Mimi Gordon. And she was holding a shivering Fred.

"Fred! What—? Come on in, Mimi. What happened? Why is Fred with you?"

Mimi smiled and set Fred on the floor, whereupon Barney immediately commenced sniffing his friend for new and unusual scents. Fred wagged his tail and he and Barney went around in circles, sniffing each other, for several moments. Lilly watched for a second, then turned to Mimi with a questioning look on her face.

"He must have dug under the fence between your house and Xavier's," Mimi explained. "I could hear him whimpering and I found him under one of the shrubs in Xavier's backyard. Poor little guy."

"Mom, I must have forgotten to let him back in when I let Barney in earlier, before we went shopping." Laurel covered her mouth with her hand and bent down to stroke Fred's fur. "I'm so sorry, Fred. What would Gran say if she knew I did that?" She picked him up and carried him into the living room, with Barney and Vanessa in tow.

"Thank you so much for bringing him back, Mimi." Lilly gestured to one of the kitchen chairs. "I was just going to make some decaf coffee. Want to join me?"

"I'd love some. Thank you."

Lilly hadn't really been planning to make coffee, but she figured she should offer Mimi something in exchange for bringing Fred back home.

"You know, the woman who lived in that house before Xavier moved in brought Barney home once, too. He got out during a blizzard and she fought blinding snow to bring him home."

"That was so nice of her."

"It was, and I was surprised when she did it. She was a kind-hearted soul, but she didn't like other people to know that." Lilly smiled, remembering Mrs. Laforge more fondly than she recalled liking her while she was alive.

She poured two coffees and sat down across from Mimi. "I hear from the kids that they see patients coming and going from Xavier's house during the day. He must be building up his practice."

"He is, but it's a slow process. Building up an entirely new customer base is not an easy thing."

"It can't be easy to leave his business behind in Wyoming and start fresh someplace far away."

Mimi waved her hand dismissively. "Look at him. He's handsome, he's smart. He doesn't have any trouble with opening a new business. It's just a matter of getting his name out there so people know he's here and ready to accept clients. That's the part that takes a little time. It's all in the marketing."

"Does he have someone marketing for him, or does he do that himself?"

"You're looking at his marketing staff." Mimi smiled proudly. "Mostly the marketing is online, so I can do it from my home. When a personal appearance is necessary, I schedule him and he goes. I don't need to be part of it at all. Plus, he pays me a little bit under the table, so it helps supplement my income from the flower shop."

"You must love having a flower shop."

Mimi shrugged. "It's okay, though no one ever got rich owning a flower shop. It started out as a hobby for me when Xavier and I were still married, then of course when we divorced it became a necessity for me to make a living. And thank God for alimony, as I'm sure you know." She gave a wry chuckle.

I wouldn't know much about that, Lilly thought darkly. After Beau disappeared, leaving Lilly with the kids, alimony had been a pipe dream.

Mimi drained her coffee mug daintily. "I should get going, Lilly. Thanks so much for the coffee and the conversation. I'm sure I'll see you again. Maybe we can get drinks together sometime."

"I'd like that. I can't thank you enough for bringing Fred

back. He's my mom's dog, and if she ever knew we'd lost him, even temporarily, she'd flip."

"I'm happy to help. See you soon." Mimi waved and disappeared into the gloom. Lilly stood on the back landing until she heard the gate close between her house and Xavier's.

She went inside and found Fred sitting on the kitchen floor, his tail thumping. Lilly knelt down and stroked his soft fur. "Don't tell Mom about this, Fred."

It was late. Lilly was getting ready for bed, looking forward to talking to Hassan, when Noley called. "I had to go to the bookstore downtown today and I stopped at Ruby Red's for a new scarf. You'll never guess who I saw in there."

"Who?"

"Isabelle. And you should have seen the dress she was buying."

"Is it pretty?"

"Not on her. It's a dress for someone in her 20s. It's a leopard print and the black parts are all sparkly and it's got a long slit up the leg and a neckline that goes to her navel."

Lilly could picture Isabelle in a dress that was years too young for her and she smiled, shaking her head.

"I wonder where she's going in such a fancy dress."

"I don't know, but she's going to be the talk of the party, and not for a good reason."

CHAPTER 26

Hassan called before closing time on Friday. "How does dinner at The Water Wheel sound? I've made reservations for seven o'clock."

"Really? Sure! What a surprise. I'll run home and change and meet you there."

"You don't have to change. I'm sure whatever you wore to work is perfect. We could meet in the bar and have a drink before our reservation."

"What's the occasion?"

"No occasion. I just wanted to have dinner with you."

"You're so sweet. I'll head over there right from work. See you tonight."

"Love you, Lil."

"I love you, too."

She hung up with a dreamy smile. Harry walked by carrying a watch case. "You look like you're on cloud nine," he said.

"I am."

HASSAN'S FACE lit up when Lilly arrived. She slipped her hand in his and they made their way to the dim bar area, with its polished mahogany and burnished gold fixtures. Sparkling glasses lined up behind the bar and soft lights gave the room a warm ambience.

Lilly ordered white wine and Hassan ordered red. There were two leather armchairs in the corner of the bar, angled toward each other but facing the bar area. There was a low table between them and a brass wall sconce behind them. Hassan led Lilly to the armchairs and they sat down. Lilly breathed a contented sigh. "This is exactly what I needed to unwind," she said. Hassan nodded, leaning back into his chair and crossing his legs.

A loud voice at the doorway of the bar attracted Lilly's attention. She glanced up to find Isabelle Montrose coming into the room, teetering on heels that were too high for her and laughing at something her companion had said.

The companion followed her through the door. Xavier Gordon.

Lilly's eyes widened as she took in Isabelle's dress. Sure enough, it was an animal print with black sparkles, a long slit down one side of the skirt and a plunging neckline. Worse, though, was the matching animal print headband that kept Isabelle's unruly gray curls away from her face with a wide swath of sparkling fabric.

"Isn't that—?" Hassan began.

"Yes, that's Isabelle. And Xavier." Lilly leaned toward Hassan. "I knew she and Xavier had some type of relationship. I'm just surprised to see them out. You know, because he's also dating Chelsea."

"The two women couldn't be more different," Hassan said.

"You can say that again. Maybe Xavier is trying to decide which one suits him better." She touched Hassan's hand with her own. "Let's move these chairs so we're facing each other, not the room. Isabelle has a way of monopolizing every conversation with that loud voice of hers, and I don't want her to see me here. It's so nice with just the two of us."

Hassan smiled and shifted his chair so he was facing Lilly while she moved her chair, too, so that it didn't face the rest of the room.

But their efforts were in vain. Moments later, Isabelle walked over to them, a tumbler of amber liquid in her hand. Xavier followed her, holding an identical tumbler.

"I see you two lovebirds are wine drinkers," Isabelle said in greeting. She looked around. "Mind if we join you?" She pointed to two empty chairs nearby. "Xavier, why don't you drag those two chairs over and we'll chat with Lilly and Hassan for a while?"

Xavier did Isabelle's bidding while she watched, beaming from ear to ear. She leaned down at an uncomfortably revealing angle and spoke to Lilly in a shockingly loud whisper. "I could watch those muscles of his rippling under that suit jacket all night, couldn't you? Well, at least until dinner is over, if you catch my drift." She winked and laughed at her own innuendo and Lilly squirmed, shooting a *help me* glance toward Hassan.

Hassan was obviously trying to keep a straight face. He pursed his lips together and glanced in another direction, then stood up and helped Xavier by dragging one of the chairs over to where he and Lilly had been enjoying their drinks in peace.

"Lilly, I'm taking someone over to see your mother's house tomorrow," Isabelle said.

"Oh, that's good."

"I still say you and your brother should wait to sell that beauty."

Not this again. "Well, Bill and I decided that we'd like to sell the house as soon as possible. So I'm glad to hear that someone wants to see it."

"You know I—" Isabelle was cut off by another woman's voice.

"Xavier?"

It was Chelsea.

CHAPTER 27

Lilly hadn't seen Chelsea coming because her attention had been on Isabelle. Lilly, Hassan, Xavier, and Isabelle looked up at her in surprise. Xavier squirmed, a sensation Lilly suspected he did not feel very often.

"Hi, Chelsea," he said.

"What's going on?" Chelsea tilted her head to one side.

Xavier looked to Isabelle, then Lilly, then Hassan before answering. Lilly figured he was making a silent plea for someone to help him, but no one spoke up. Lilly was surprised Isabelle didn't say anything.

"Just having drinks," he finally said, holding up his tumbler as if to provide proof.

"So, like, just a casual get-together?" Chelsea asked.

Xavier shrugged and nodded at the same time. Chelsea's eyes narrowed as she took in the spectacle of Isabelle and her inappropriate dinner attire. "I'll talk to you later." She walked away with a female companion who had remained silent through the entire uncomfortable exchange. She looked over her shoulder once, giving Xavier a dark look.

"Who was that?" Isabelle asked brightly, as if she didn't know.

When Xavier didn't answer right away, Lilly jumped in to save him further embarrassment. "That was Chelsea Fortune. She was at Thanksgiving, too. Remember?"

"Ah, yes. I think I do. She's not terribly memorable. An intern or something, isn't she?"

"Personal assistant," Lilly corrected her.

Isabelle took a long swig of her drink and tilted her head back. "Ah, that hits the spot," she said loudly.

Thankfully, a waiter appeared at Hassan's elbow. "Mister Ashraf, party of two?"

"Yes, that's us." Hassan stood up and offered his hand to Lilly, who rocketed out of her chair.

"Enjoy your evening." She addressed both Isabelle and Xavier, but she had a feeling Xavier's evening was about to go downhill.

Her hunch was right. She and Hassan had ordered their entrées and were enjoying their wine and a small loaf of warm bread in a quiet corner of the restaurant, chatting about their days, when the waiter seated Xavier and Isabelle a mere ten feet away. Lilly closed her eyes and gritted her teeth. The last thing she wanted was to be trying to have a romantic dinner for two with her realtor and her neighbor just steps away.

"It's all right, Lil," Hassan said, covering her hand with his. "I know what you're thinking. We can enjoy ourselves no matter who sits near us." He gave her that warm smile that always made her stomach flutter.

"I know. I'm just being a baby."

When the waiter brought their food, Lilly was about to take her first bite when she heard a *psst.* She looked around, wondering where the sound came from.

Isabelle, of course. Lilly raised her eyebrows and pointed to herself as if to say *Who, me?*

Isabelle nodded. "What did you order? It looks great."

"The scallops."

"Thanks." Isabelle turned back to her menu. "I think that's what I'll get," she said in a voice loud enough for the kitchen staff to hear.

Lilly looked at Hassan, who chuckled. "Your scallops *do* look good."

Lilly couldn't help laughing. Why should she care who sat near them and what Isabelle wanted for dinner? She was at The Water Wheel to enjoy Hassan's company and undivided attention, and she intended to do just that.

Presently the server delivered food to Isabelle and Xavier. Isabelle asked for mayonnaise and ketchup to put on her potatoes.

"I don't know how Xavier stands it," Lilly said, *sotto voce*.

Hassan shrugged. "To each his own, as they say."

"I suppose you're right."

Lilly and Hassan shared dessert, a decadent pumpkin panna cotta. Lilly was heaving an internal sigh of relief that dinner was almost over and they could go back to her house or Hassan's house for a nightcap, when disaster struck.

"Are you kidding me?" Isabelle shrieked. Lilly and Hassan, along with every other patron in the dining room, turned to stare at the realtor, who was rising from her seat. Chelsea Fortune stood next to Xavier, looking confused. Isabelle was holding another tumbler, this time full of a greenish-yellow liquid. A second later, she threw the contents of the glass at Xavier's face.

CHAPTER 28

*A*ll conversation in the restaurant stopped and the place was silent. Chelsea shot a glance around and stepped gingerly backward, away from the table. When she reached the doorway of the dining room, she turned and fled. Meanwhile, Xavier was calmly wiping the liquid from his eyes with a napkin provided by the server, who was now standing next to the table, slack jawed. Isabelle staggered forward on her high heels and lurched from the room in Chelsea's wake.

"Excuse me," Lilly said to Hassan. She walked over to where Xavier still sat, now dabbing the front of his shirt in a futile attempt to get the chartreuse-hued stain out. People around the room were still staring, but now that the commotion had ended, many of them were returning to their meals.

"Xavier, can I do anything for you?"

He looked at Lilly, surprise in his eyes, probably having forgotten she was in the room after his encounter with Isabelle. "No, thank you. I think I'll just pay the bill and get out of here. I've caused enough of a scene for one night."

Lilly was dying to ask what had caused the furor, but her parents hadn't raised an idiot. She figured she would hear about it soon enough, anyway, provided Chelsea told Noley the whole story. Lilly had a hunch that would happen first thing in the morning.

Xavier left the restaurant with his head held high, as if being the target of a woman's ire was something he experienced every day and not a big deal. Lilly was impressed. *I would have crawled out of here and gone to live under a rock*, she thought.

"That was something, wasn't it?" Lilly said to Hassan. "I can't wait to hear what caused it."

"I'm sure Noley will get the low-down for you," he replied with a grin. "Let's finish dessert and get out of here. I've had enough drama."

They went back to Hassan's house after they left the restaurant. They had just snuggled up on the couch when Lilly's phone rang. She groaned. "I don't want to answer it."

"Then don't answer it."

She stole a glance at the caller ID. "It's Larkspur Manor. I have to take it." She could feel her heartrate ratchet up as she hit the Talk button.

"Hello?"

"Hi. Is this Mrs. Carlsen? This is Greg from Larkspur Manor."

"Hi, Greg. Is anything wrong?"

"I don't think so, but I thought I should give you a call to let you know that your mother is refusing to come to her room. She went to Finley's room after dinner tonight and we can't get her to leave. Do you think you could talk to her?"

"Sure. Is she right there?"

"Give me a sec and I'll put her on."

"Hello?" came Bev's voice a moment later.

"Hi, Mom. It's Lilly." There was no response, so Lilly continued. "Greg tells me you don't want to go back to your room tonight."

"That's right."

"Why not?"

"I want to sleep in here, with Finley."

Oh, boy. "Mom, there's no room for you in Finley's room. You have your own bed."

"Finley will make room. He said he would."

"Mom, the rules are that you have to sleep in your own room, in your own bed."

"Rules. Bah."

"Mom, please. Just go with Greg back to your room. Do you want me to come over?" Lilly gave Hassan an apologetic smile, and he squeezed her hand.

"My room is lonely."

Lilly's throat constricted. She closed her eyes and took a deep breath. "I'm sorry, Mom. I'll be right there. Can I bring Hassan?"

"Who?"

Lilly grimaced, wishing she could take her words back. She didn't want Hassan to know that Bev didn't recognize his name. But it was too late for that, so she forged ahead. This wasn't the first time Bev had forgotten Hassan, and he always took it in stride.

"Hassan. I've been dating Hassan for a long time. Do you remember he was there on Thanksgiving?"

Bev was silent for a moment. "No, I don't know anyone by that name. I would remember that."

"Okay. Maybe I'll bring him with me and you and he can get to know each other."

"If you say so."

"Can you give the phone back to Greg? I'll be there in just a little while. Love you, Mom."

There was no response, but a few moments later Greg's voice was back on the phone. "Thanks, Lilly. I had a feeling your mom would listen to you."

"She did. At least, I think she did. I'm going to drop by to see her in a just a bit. Thanks, Greg."

They hung up and Lilly sank back into the circle of Hassan's arm. "Do you mind going with me? I should have asked before volunteering you," she said.

"You know I'd love to. We'll have our nightcap some other night."

More than anything, Lilly wanted Hassan to move into her house or vice versa, so they could spend all their spare time together. With his business and her busy life and jewelry shop, they often had to work to schedule time together. Lilly wondered to herself for the thousandth time why they didn't just move in together—but she knew if she was honest with herself, it was an old-fashioned desire to be married before living together. She wanted to set that example for her kids.

Right now, though, there were more pressing things to think about. Like her mother's loneliness and the boyfriend down the hall.

CHAPTER 29

"Hi, Mom. Hi, Finley." Lilly, followed by Hassan, walked into Finley's room after knocking softly on the open door to announce their arrival.

"Shh," came Bev's reply. She sat in a chair next to Finley's bed. Finley lay sound asleep under the covers, oblivious to anyone else's presence in the room. Bev glanced at Hassan without the slightest hint of recognition, but didn't say anything.

"Mom, let's go back to your room."

Bev sighed and gave Finley a caring gaze. Lilly's whole body softened at the sight. She would have given anything to take Bev's loneliness away, but there wasn't much more she could do. Bev was getting the best of care in Larkspur, she was surrounded by other people with dementia and the physical decline that went hand-in-hand with it, and Lilly and Bill visited her often, just as they had when she had lived in her own house.

After several minutes back in her own room, Bev started to show signs of being tired. Her eyelids drooped when Lilly or Hassan spoke, and she stopped speaking mid-sentence if and when she found the energy to say anything at all. Lilly called for Greg and the two of them helped Bev into her nightie. By the time Lilly and Hassan left Larkspur, Bev was sound asleep. Lilly hoped she was dreaming of better days.

Lilly had driven Hassan to Larkspur on purpose so they could have a few more minutes alone together while she drove him back to her house. She smiled at him when he got in the car. "Thanks for coming. I know it's not easy for you, but it makes the whole situation easier for me when you can be there with me."

"You know I would do anything for you, love. I'm just sorry your family, and especially your mom, has to go through this."

"You know, at first I thought it would be a nightmare for Mom to have a boyfriend, but I'm beginning to think it's actually a good thing. Finley might be just what she needs to stop feeling lonely at Larkspur."

"I think it's a good thing. People need companionship at every age."

Lilly's heart was a bit lighter as she pulled up into Hassan's driveway. He kissed her goodnight, and she gave him a big hug. "Thanks for dinner, and for going to see Mom with me."

"Like I said, anything for you, love."

Saturday evening Lilly was having dinner with Laurel and Vanessa when there was a knock at the front door. Barney, with Fred in his wake, tripped over himself racing to see who was there. Lilly gently pushed both frenzied dogs out of the way and opened the door. Mimi stood there, a smile on her face.

"Hi, Mimi. Come on in."

"Thanks." Mimi followed Lilly inside, blowing on her hands to warm them.

"What can I do for you?" Lilly asked.

"I just came over to chat. Xavier is out tonight and I was bored. Are you having dinner?"

"We are, but you're welcome to join us. Have you eaten?"

"I have eaten, thanks. I should go."

"No, no. That's fine. Come have a seat with us." Lilly led Mimi into the kitchen, where Laurel jumped up and offered to fix a plate of food for her. Mimi declined the food, but accepted a glass of water. She settled down into the chair across from Lilly.

"What's new in the neighborhood?" Mimi asked. "Since I don't live here, I feel like I miss a lot."

The only thing Lilly could think to tell her was about the disastrous date between Isabelle and Xavier at The Water Wheel, and she figured that wasn't what Mimi meant. "Nothing that I can think of," she said. She looked at Laurel and Vanessa. They shook their heads.

"I hear you witnessed quite a scene at a local restaurant, Lilly," Mimi said.

Lilly almost choked on her food. Was Mimi referring to the incident Lilly thought she was referring to? She couldn't be. Lilly decided to play dumb.

She pursed her lips. "Um, I don't know..." She trailed off. No one was that dumb.

"It's okay. Obviously, Xavier told me all about it." Mimi chuckled. "That man. It's a good thing I find him so endearing."

Lilly realized, too late, that her mouth was hanging open. Mimi saw the expression on her face and hastened to explain. "He and I don't have secrets from each other. He told me all about the date with that woman." She put air quotes around the word 'date.' "And I also know about his relationship with that young redhead he met here on Thanksgiving."

Lilly put a forkful of potatoes in her mouth to avoid having to answer. She needed a second to think about what to say next.

She chewed slowly as the girls glanced from her to their plates and Mimi took a sip of water and spoke into the momentary silence.

CHAPTER 30

"I know, you're probably wondering why I left him in the first place if we get along so well. The truth is that Xavier has itchy feet. You know, he likes to move around. I'm more of a stay-put type of person. Do you know, we lived in three states during our eight years of marriage?"

This was something Lilly didn't mind talking about. "Really? It must be hard for a doctor to do that."

"Oh, you mean because he's always on the hunt for new patients? I would agree if I didn't know him so well. He's so charismatic—people tend to gravitate to him. I think I mentioned before that I do his online marketing, so it's actually not too hard for him to set up a new practice whenever he gets the urge to live in a new place."

"Where did you two live while you were married?"

"Wyoming was the last place, which you already knew. Before that it was Utah, and before that it was Arizona. He likes cold weather, so moving here to the mountains was perfect for him."

"I've known people who like to move around a lot," Lilly

mused. "They all seem to have one thing in common: a love for the unknown. For adventure."

Mimi laughed through her nose. "He's definitely a lover of adventure and the unknown. I'm not as much, so that was the one way we were incompatible. It's hard to make friends when you're moving around a lot."

"I know I would have a hard time relocating my business, even to another place in Colorado," Lilly said. "I admire him for having the courage to uproot himself in pursuit of the unknown."

"Mom, we'll do the dishes," Laurel said. Vanessa nodded.

"Thanks, girls." Lilly led Mimi into the living room and gestured for her to sit down.

"What do you know about the woman who was with Xavier at that restaurant?" Mimi asked, settling into an armchair.

Lilly wondered why Mimi was asking, if were really true she and Xavier shared everything. At least now she knew the real reason Mimi had appeared at her door tonight. She thought for a moment before answering.

"Isabelle is a realtor. I only met her recently. She was Xavier's realtor, and my brother and I listed our mother's house with her. I'm surprised you didn't meet her when Xavier was house hunting."

"Oh, Xavier insisted on tackling that responsibility himself. What I meant was, what's she really like? As a person. I already knew she's a realtor."

"I don't know her well. I suppose you could say she has a very confident personality."

Mimi laughed. "You're trying to find something nice to say, aren't you? It's okay. Xavier told me she's a barracuda."

Then why did you ask me? Lilly thought with annoyance.

"She asked Xavier out, not the other way around, just so you understand," Mimi continued. "He couldn't think of a polite way to decline, so he went. Boy, is he sorry he did." She smiled and shook her head ruefully.

Lilly could sense her face flushing. She suddenly felt something for Isabelle she hadn't before: pity. The woman obviously liked Xavier—or *had* liked him—and their date at The Water Wheel had been a disaster. And there was that awful dress, and the thing she wore around her head … for the first time, Lilly pondered whether Isabelle was just a little desperate for companionship. She wondered how many friends Isabelle really had, for all the self-confidence she seemed to exude. Maybe that projected self-confidence hid a dearth of self-esteem.

Mimi seemed to notice the sudden change in Lilly's demeanor.

"Are you all right?" she asked.

"I'm fine." Lilly mentally shook herself back into the present, in her living room with her neighbor's ex-wife. She gave Mimi a small smile. "Just thinking, that's all."

"I've probably stayed too long." Mimi stood up and waved off Lilly's half-hearted insistence that she stay. "I need to get back to Xavier's house. I left a kitchen full of dishes to wash."

After Mimi left Lilly chatted with the girls for a little while, then went upstairs and got ready for bed. Once she was under the covers and Barney and Fred were snuggled at her feet, she called Hassan. She told him about Mimi's visit and her guilt over not seeing what might be hiding behind Isabelle's rough exterior.

"That's one of the things that makes you so wonderful," Hassan said. "You're always looking for the good in people."

"I think I'm going to call Isabelle and see if she wants to get coffee with me. Maybe if I get to know her a little better, I wouldn't find her so abrasive."

"I think it's a great idea."

CHAPTER 31

First thing Monday morning, Lilly phoned Isabelle.

"Hello?"

"Hi, Isabelle. It's Lilly Carlsen."

"Good morning, Lilly," Isabelle boomed. "What can I do for you?"

"Nothing, really. I just called to see if you wanted to get coffee with me."

There was a silence as Isabelle no doubt wondered why Lilly was proposing a social outing when she had previously shown no interest in getting together.

"I guess I can do that. When and where?"

"How about this morning, at Beans on Main? Say, eight o'clock?"

"Okay. I'll see you there." There was a pause. "Thanks." Isabelle hung up. Lilly stared at the phone in her hand for a moment, wondering if she was going to regret this.

At her shop, Lilly dashed off a note for Harry, asking him to set out the jewelry displays if she wasn't in before it was time to open. She hurried to the coffee shop to meet Isabelle on time.

Isabelle was already there, sitting with her back to the wall and keeping an eagle eye on the front door. When she saw Lilly walk in, she grinned and waved heartily, attracting the attention of several people nearby. Lilly bustled over to the table so Isabelle would stop waving.

"Good morning," she said, unwrapping her scarf.

"Hi, Lilly. I hope it's okay to sit here."

"It's fine. Have you ordered yet?"

"No. I was waiting for you."

"Okay. What'll you have? It's my treat."

Isabelle's eyes widened in surprise. "Really? Thanks. I'll have a small maple cinnamon latte."

"Ooh, that sounds good. Maybe I'll have the same thing." Lilly went to the counter, placed the order, and waited the few minutes it took for the lattes to be ready. She carried the steaming mugs to the table.

Isabelle took a tiny sip of hers and nodded. "This is fabulous. Listen, Lilly, I know why you invited me here."

"You do?"

"Yes. It's to talk about your neighbor."

"Actually, Isabelle, I didn't invite you here for any reason other than getting coffee. But if you want to talk about Xavier, I'm happy to listen."

Isabelle made no attempt to hide her suspicion at Lilly's remark. "So you're not mining for gossip?"

"Of course not. I felt terrible that something obviously went wrong on your date, but I'm not into gossiping about it."

"Good. Because it's no one else's business."

"You're absolutely right." *Rats*, thought Lilly.

"Just so we're clear." Isabelle fixed Lilly with an intense gaze.

"For sure. Hey, this latte is delicious."

"Yup. I always get that in the fall when I come here." Isabelle cast a fond glance around the coffee shop. "So. I think I told you I showed your mom's house. The woman seemed interested."

"That's good to hear. Bill and I will be glad to have it off our hands."

"Mm-hmm. Selling a house is stressful. That's why I try so hard to make it painless for my clients. You and Bill are lucky because I might be moving soon."

Lilly was raising her mug to her lips, but she stopped. "Oh, really? Where are you going?"

"I don't know yet. Somewhere far away."

"Don't you like Juniper Junction?"

"Oh, yeah. I like it fine. I'm just ready for something new, that's all. You know, a bigger challenge. Maybe a city somewhere."

"How about Denver?"

Isabelle shrugged. "I dunno. Maybe. I was thinking about maybe somewhere further west. Like maybe California. I think I would like it there."

"I give you a lot of credit, Isabelle. I don't know that I would have the courage to pack up and leave my home."

"You're different because you have family here. I don't. Like I told you on Thanksgiving, my family doesn't live around here. I'm basically alone."

Lilly couldn't help the pang of pity that touched her heart.

"I'm sure you have friends, Isabelle."

Isabelle stared at Lilly for a moment. "You'd be surprised. You know that date I had the other night? The one that ended with me pouring my drink all over that rodent?"

Lilly nodded. "Yeah."

"That was the second date I've had in three years."

"Dating is hard. I'm a single mom, so I definitely know what you're talking about."

"But you're obviously in a serious relationship with that handsome guy of yours. It's different for me. I used to be married, too, but after I caught my husband cheating on me—in our own house—I left him and it's been hard for me to trust people ever since. I throw myself into my work, which is why I'm so good at what I do for a living."

Lilly didn't know what to say. She hadn't expected Isabelle to open up that way. But she figured this was something Isabelle wanted to get off her chest, so she waited for her to continue talking.

CHAPTER 32

"**I** had a few dates after I left my husband, but they didn't work out. I think a lot of men are intimidated by successful women."

Lots of people are intimidated by anyone who comes across with such force and noise, thought Lilly. She suppressed the urge to smirk.

"Xavier contacted me about buying a home in Juniper Junction, and the minute I met him I knew he was The One. At least, I thought he was. But I didn't make a move. Then when I saw him again at your house on Thanksgiving, I figured it was the universe's way of telling me to go for it. So I asked him out. He seemed surprised, but agreed to go out with me."

Lilly recalled the night she had seen Isabelle going into Xavier's house.

It seemed Isabelle was reading her mind. She had the grace to blush. "I did spend the night at his house once, but nothing happened. In fact, I slept downstairs and he slept upstairs. I had hoped he would have the guts to invite me upstairs, but he didn't. Too shy."

Lilly had a hunch shyness did not play the slightest role in

Xavier's failure to invite Isabelle to spend the night in his room, but she remained silent, only nodding her head now and then.

"And his ex-wife." Isabelle shook her head, setting her curls bouncing. "Xavier has allowed her way too much control over his life, if you ask me. I mean, I know they're friends, but she has her own set of keys to his house, she can keep track of him on her cell phone, and she calls him several times a day. Talk about controlling."

"But he wouldn't allow those things, would he, if they were unacceptable to him, do you think?" Lilly couldn't help blurting out the question, at least in part because she thought the concept of a recently divorced couple being good friends was refreshing.

"I don't think he has much of a choice," Isabelle said with an unattractive snort.

It seemed to Lilly that Xavier didn't mind having Mimi around and even welcomed it. The divorce had been friendly, according to them, so there was no reason for dislike and hurt feelings. As Mimi had said, it was all because of her unwilling-ness to leave Wyoming and uproot herself and her business. Besides that, she was obviously a huge help to him when it came to finding clients for his own psychiatry practice.

"I've met Mimi several times and she seems nice," Lilly said. She couldn't sit by and listen to Mimi being bashed by Isabelle without defending her somehow.

"Sure she does. Why shouldn't she? She's got all the perks of marriage and none of the downsides. Well, most of the perks, if you know what I mean. They sleep in separate bedrooms. She still has a significant role in his life, but he doesn't get to boss her around. Who wouldn't like that?"

Lilly had to admit to herself that Isabelle had a point, tenuous though it was. She wondered how she could steer the conversation to the incident at The Water Wheel. Since Isabelle was being so forthcoming, maybe she would open up about what happened.

Lilly sneaked a look at her watch. She didn't have much time before she had to be back at the jewelry shop.

"So tell me about Chelsea," Isabelle said, toying with the handle of her coffee mug.

Aah, here it comes.

CHAPTER 33

"Idon't know her very well at all. She came to Thanksgiving at my house because she had just moved to town and begun working with Bill's wife. Chelsea's good at her job, I know that."

"Did you also know she and Xavier are dating?" Isabelle asked with a slight sneer.

"I guess I knew they had some kind of relationship, but I don't know a lot about it."

"Well, when she stopped by our table the other night, Xavier told me she was his 'girlfriend.' Can you believe it? He's out on a date with me and he has the gall to introduce another woman as his girlfriend." Isabelle heaved a loud sigh. "So now you have the whole story, even though I didn't mean to tell you."

Lilly was struck anew with a deep feeling of pity for Isabelle. The woman apparently had little in the way of a social life, and when she made the effort, she was rewarded with public humiliation.

"I'm really sorry that happened, Isabelle. I don't know what else to say."

"There's nothing to say. It's time for me to get outta here and start fresh somewhere else."

"When do you think you'll be leaving?"

"I'm the listing agent on a number of properties, including your mother's, and I'm going to see those through to the end. As soon as they're all sold, I'm gone."

"I'm glad you'll be staying for a little while, at least."

"Thanks for the coffee, Lilly." Isabelle looked at her phone and grimaced. "I didn't realize how long we've sat here gabbing. I need to get going." She pushed herself away from the table, wrapped an impossibly long and garish scarf around her neck, and was gone with a quick wave.

Lilly walked back to the jewelry shop lost in thought. Harry greeted her with a smile when she arrived.

"Hi, boss. You look preoccupied today. Everything all right?"

"Hi, Harry. I'm fine. I just had coffee with Mom's realtor and my mind is reeling, that's all."

"Is there a lot of interest in the house?"

"I don't know. This was a more get-to-know-you type of meeting, so we didn't talk about Mom's house too much. All I know is that she's shown the place at least once."

Just before lunch a woman came into the shop looking for a custom necklace. Lilly introduced herself to the woman and spent the next hour discussing stones, settings, and chains while Harry waited on other customers. Her cell phone buzzed in her pocket several times while they spoke, so Lilly hurriedly checked her messages when the woman left.

The first one was from Noley, who had left a whispered message stating only, "Trouble in paradise." Lilly listened to the rest of the messages before calling Noley to see what was going on.

The most interesting message was from Bill, informing her of Phoebe's official cause of death—blunt force trauma to the head—and warning her not to go off half-cocked with that information. Lilly rolled her eyes on hearing Bill's cautionary tone and made a mental note to call him as soon as she got off the phone with Noley. Finally, there was a message from Isabelle, thanking her again for coffee that morning and telling her she would be showing Bev's house for the second time later to the woman she had mentioned earlier.

She dialed Noley's number, hoping her friend wasn't busy. Noley picked up the phone on the first ring. She was still whispering.

"Hi."

"What's up? Why are you whispering? What's 'trouble in paradise' mean?"

"Chelsea. She's in the next room, so I have to be quiet."

"What happened?"

"She's a mess. Something about Xavier."

"You can't tell what she's upset about?"

"As far as I can tell, it might be something about another woman."

"Is Isabelle the other woman?"

"I don't know. I'm trying to give her some space, but I actually have work that I need her to do, so I can't let her just sit at her desk and cry much longer."

"It'll probably be good for her to get to work. Maybe it'll take her mind off her troubles."

"If she tells me what's going on, I'll let you know asap."

"Thanks."

After work Lilly drove out to Larkspur Manor. She found Bev standing by her window, looking out over the trees surrounding the Larkspur Manor property.

"Hi, Mom." Lilly took off her coat and placed it across the foot of Bev's bed. Bev turned toward Lilly with a vacant look, her brows furrowed. She remained silent.

"Mom? You okay?"

Bev's eyes narrowed. "Hello," she said in a hesitant voice.

Lilly knew with ruthless clarity that her mother didn't know who she was. She swallowed hard and forced herself to smile.

CHAPTER 34

"What have you been doing today?" Lilly asked. Bev shrugged lightly and shook her head. Lilly didn't press. She didn't know if Bev's day had been boring or if Bev didn't remember what she had done all day. Maybe Bev really didn't trust the person standing in front of her. Lilly needed some air.

She gently pushed past Bev and opened a window. A brisk gust of wind blew through the room, making Bev shiver.

"I'm sorry, Mom. I was just so hot all of a sudden. I'll close the window."

Bev still hadn't said more than two words, and Lilly didn't know what to do or what to talk about. She cleared her throat. "Want to go for a walk?"

"Where?"

"Just around the floor. We can see what's going on in the community room."

Bev didn't answer, but allowed Lilly to take her arm and lead the way into the hall outside her room.

They walked slowly, not speaking. Lilly could feel Bev's arm tremble ever so slightly under her own hand. Was Bev actually afraid of her?

"Are you feeling all right?" Lilly asked.

Bev nodded and gave her daughter a benign smile.

"How's Finley?"

That finally elicited a big grin. The skin around Bev's eyes crinkled as she answered, "Such a gentleman. He and I are quite close, you know." Then she sobered. "But he has had a headache today."

"I'm sorry you can't spend time with him tonight. He's a very nice man."

"He is very different from my husband. Daniel was quiet. Finley likes to sing."

Daniel, of course, was Lilly's father. He had died years before. Lilly knew the moment Bev referred to Daniel as "my husband" instead of "your father" that Bev still didn't know who Lilly was.

Lilly's response was visceral. She fought the urge to bend over and throw up, and instead kept walking, looking straight ahead while keeping a gentle hand on Bev's arm. They continued their slow walk and suddenly the quiet was rent by a shout.

"You!"

Lilly turned in the direction of the voice and saw a woman in a wheelchair just behind them. She wore a frown and was pointing a knobby finger right at Lilly.

"Me?"

"Yes, you. Who else? I want you to push me over to her." She moved her finger like a laser, zeroing in on a woman sitting by herself in the large anteroom outside the community room, facing the wall.

"Just a minute." Lilly guided her mother to a semicircle of armchairs and Bev sat down. Lilly returned to the ornery woman in the wheelchair and grasped the handles. She moved the wheelchair forward slowly so the lady wouldn't complain about a bumpy ride.

"I want to poke her," the woman said, pointing again to the woman facing the wall.

"What?"

"Hurry up. I want to poke her."

"I am not pushing you over there so you can poke someone. That's mean." Lilly jerked the wheelchair to a stop and walked over to Bev.

"Come back here!" the old woman yelled after her.

"Come on, Mom. Let's see what's going on in there." Lilly pointed to the all-purpose room and helped her mother to her feet.

A nurse who had obviously heard the yelling hurried up the corridor toward them as Lilly ushered Bev into the large community room. Lilly looked back to see the nurse bending down level with the woman in the wheelchair. She was speaking in soothing tones, putting her hand on the woman's arm and rubbing it gently. A feeling of guilt washed over Lilly, engulfing her in shame for the way she had spoken to the woman.

It wasn't long before Lilly's emotions started to get the better of her. She could feel her breath coming faster and she was sweating. A quick glance in a large mirror that hung on one wall of the room confirmed her fear that her face had turned a sickly shade of white. She brushed her hand over her forehead and turned to her mother, who clearly was not enjoying the outing to the community room. She sat in a chair away from the other people, looking down at her hands and keeping her eyes closed.

I have to get out of here. "Mom, let's get you back to your room."

Bev obeyed without complaint, allowing Lilly to lead her back down the hall. They didn't speak on the long walk, which was fine with Lilly. She feared she would burst into tears if she had to make conversation with this woman who didn't recognize her while trying to fight off waves of emotion stemming from her encounter with the woman in the wheelchair. The saddest part? The woman facing the wall seemed not to know what had transpired and that Lilly had saved her from a vicious act by a mean old lady.

Lilly didn't kiss her mother's cheek that night. She was afraid she would scare Bev if she leaned in too close. Bev wouldn't want a stranger kissing her.

CHAPTER 35

$\mathcal{B}$y the time Lilly got to her car, she was barely holding on to the last wisp of her dignity. She slid into the driver's seat, closed and locked her door, and let loose with racking sobs that threatened to drown her in tears.

The phone rang. It was Hassan. She declined the call, not wanting him to witness this breakdown in real time.

But he called back, and each time she declined the call he called again.

Finally she managed to stem the flow of tears and summon the courage to answer the phone.

"I was worried about you." He launched into a greeting without waiting for her to say anything. "But I needed to talk to you."

"What's the matter?" she asked.

It was undoubtedly her nasal, stuffed-up voice that alerted him to a problem. "I—wait. What's wrong? Are you okay?"

Lilly didn't know if it was his concerned tone or his kind words or just knowing that he cared that caused her to well up anew. But she started sobbing again and he waited to speak until she could hear him above the sound of her own crying.

"Lilly, where are you? I'm coming to get you."

"I'm in the parking lot of Larkspur Manor. Mom didn't know me. There was this awful old lady and I was mean to her and now I'm wondering if I should be trying to take care of Mom at home and take her out of that place. Everything is wrong."

"I'll be right there. You stay where you are. Promise me."

"I will," she sniffed.

Hassan hung up and not ten minutes later he had parked next to her and was sitting in the passenger seat of her car. He took both her hands in his.

"Lilly, I'm so, so sorry. I wish I had been here with you."

"It's okay. I just wanted to see her before I went home tonight."

"You haven't eaten yet?"

She shook her head.

"Let's switch seats. I'm going to drive you over to the diner and get something for dinner." She slid out of her seat and walked around the back of the car, where he met her and held her in a long, warm hug. When he was in the driver's seat and she was next to him, she rifled through her glove compartment for tissues while he started the car and pulled out of the parking lot.

They sat across from each other at a booth in the back of the diner and Lilly stared dully at the menu.

"What do you feel like having?" Hassan asked.

Lilly shrugged. "Maybe a turkey sandwich."

"Two turkey sandwiches and two decafs," Hassan told the server.

Lilly sat back against the booth and Hassan leaned forward. He pressed his lips together and looked at her sadly. "I'm sorry you've had such a rough evening. I wish I had been there with you."

"If you had been, I would never have been able to hold it together," Lilly said.

"But I would have been there when you fell apart."

Lilly didn't have an answer to that.

"Lilly, we need to talk."

She groaned. "Please, not now. Whatever bad news you have for me, don't tell me tonight. I can't take it."

"It's not bad news. At least, I don't think it is."

"What is it, then?"

Hassan placed his hands on the table, palms up. She put her hands in his and he closed his fingers around hers.

"I think it's time for us to start talking seriously about getting married."

Whatever Lilly had been expecting to hear, that wasn't it. She stared at him for a moment, while thoughts of her mother, her mother's disease, and Larkspur Manor faded, at least temporarily.

"Really?"

Hassan laughed. "Yes, really. Do you agree?"

Lilly squeezed his hands. She didn't have to think about it at all. "I do agree. I think we're ready to start talking about it."

"Then let's talk."

"Where do we start?" Lilly felt suddenly shy. She looked down at their hands, intertwined.

"Let's start with Tighe and Laurel."

Her heart skipped a beat. Of course that was the right place to start. He had known it even before she had.

"They love you," she said, tilting her head and smiling at him.

"And I love them. They're great kids. Do you think they would be okay with us getting married? I mean, because I would be their stepdad? I don't want them to think I'm trying to take Beau's place."

Lilly was shaking her head before he could finish talking. "They wouldn't think that. They have a good relationship with

Beau now, but they have a good relationship with you, too. They met you and Beau at about the same time. They didn't remember him from when they were little, so there was no history there when they met him as teenagers."

Hassan nodded slowly. "Okay. What about Bill? And Noley? And your mom?"

Lilly snorted. "Well, since my mom doesn't even know me, I think she won't have a problem with it. And you know she loves you—or at least she did when she remembered you—and would be thrilled if we got married. And as for Noley and Bill, I think you know the answer to that. They love you *almost* as much as I do."

Hassan grinned.

"But now I have some questions for you," Lilly said. She took her hands from under Hassan's and propped her chin in them. "How do you know you'll want to stay married to me? Because I would be for keeps and I've already driven one husband away."

"You could never drive me away. I promise you that. I wouldn't be having this conversation with you if I thought you could drive me away."

"Okay, then what about my neuroses? You know, like my all-consuming anxiety about my mother and my children? What about my uncanny ability to become involved with people who are crime victims or crime perpetrators? Hmm?"

Hassan laughed, though Lilly was only half joking. "First of all, I don't think your anxiety about your mother and your kids qualifies as neurosis. It's perfectly healthy to be concerned about people you love. And as for that uncanny ability of yours, sometimes I chalk it up to bad luck and sometimes I chalk it up to life experience. Either way you look at it, I want to be part of it with you."

Lilly's gaze softened. "You have to ask me properly, you know."

"Of course. I wouldn't have it any other way. The only thing is, I don't know when it'll be because I have to find the perfect ring for you."

"I'll wait." Lilly grinned.

She put her hands back on the table and Hassan held them again. They only separated when the server brought their sandwiches and coffee.

By the time Lilly drove home, she was smiling and relaxed.

Unfortunately, it didn't last long.

CHAPTER 36

*V*anessa wasn't home when Lilly got back to the house. Laurel was there, though, and she was beside herself with worry over Vanessa's whereabouts.

"She hasn't answered her phone and I'm worried about her. She had an appointment with the nurse practitioner for blood-work and I haven't heard from her since then." Then Laurel froze. "You don't suppose there's something wrong, do you?"

"I think if something was wrong, you'd be the first to hear about it. But I do wonder where she is. Do you think she could have gone to see her parents?"

Laurel shook her head. "She can't stand the thought of them right now. She wouldn't go there."

"Try calling her one more time. She can't stay out all night." Lilly paced in a slow circle around the kitchen while Laurel phoned Vanessa.

After several moments Laurel pushed a button on her phone and set it on the counter. "No answer."

"Have you left her a message?"

"Yes. Three, in fact."

"I think—" Lilly began.

The back door opened and Vanessa walked in. She looked exhausted. There were gray circles around her sunken eyes and her cheeks were hollow.

"Vanessa!" Lilly exclaimed. "Are you all right?"

"Where have you been?" Laurel scolded. "I've been trying to get in touch with you all afternoon. How did the appointment go? Is everything all right?"

Vanessa sat down heavily at the kitchen table. Laurel went to the fridge and pulled out a plate she had set in there for Vanessa's dinner. Lilly offered to warm it up in the microwave, so Laurel pulled out the chair next to Vanessa. "Tell me everything," she instructed.

Vanessa leaned her head back and sighed. Then she fixed Laurel with a long stare.

"I'm going to have a boy."

Lilly's jaw dropped, exactly matching the expression on Laurel's face. She didn't know why this news was so shocking. After all, both she and Laurel were fully aware that the baby was going to be either a girl or a boy. But the news that Vanessa had decided to ask about the baby's gender was completely unexpected.

Laurel didn't say anything for a moment, then she broke into a wide grin. "Why didn't you tell us you were going to learn the baby's gender? I'm so excited! A baby boy! What are you going to name him?"

Vanessa smiled, but her smile was tinged with a faraway sadness that Lilly could only imagine. Here was a young woman bringing a baby into the world, without a partner, without the support of her family, without an education, and without a job. *The poor thing must be overwhelmed*, Lilly thought.

"I didn't tell you about learning the baby's gender because I didn't realize it myself. I was in with the nurse and all of a sudden I just decided that I needed to know. So I asked. She asked me if I really, really wanted to know, and I told her that I did." Vanessa shrugged. "And she told me I'm going to have a boy. I haven't thought about names at all."

"I wish I had gone with you. Then we could have celebrated," Laurel said.

Vanessa turned her sad smile on her best friend. "I'm sorry, Laur. I wasn't in the mood to celebrate."

Laurel wisely changed the subject. "So where have you been all this time?"

Vanessa shrugged. "Around. I went to the library. But mostly I was just walking around."

"You should have answered your phone, at least. We were worried about you." Laurel took in herself and Lilly with a sweeping gesture.

"My phone was dead. Sorry about that. I didn't mean to worry you."

Lilly figured it was the combination of hormones, baby gender news, exhaustion, and worry that caused the tears to start seeping from Vanessa's weary eyes.

Laurel leaned toward her friend and hugged her. "Everything is going to be okay. You'll see."

Vanessa nodded, sniffling. "I think it would help if I got a job."

"A part-time job. That's a great idea," Laurel said.

"Maybe a full-time job," Vanessa said.

"Start out with part-time and see how it goes," Laurel advised. "Want me to see if there are any job openings at the school?"

Vanessa brightened a little and nodded. "Would you? Thanks."

"I'll ask around tomorrow. Maybe there's something in the library."

Lilly had been about to offer to ask some of her fellow Main Street merchants if they needed any part-time help, but she was glad she kept her mouth shut. The girls didn't need any help solving this problem.

Part of her wanted to tell someone about the conversation she had had with Hassan, but she decided to keep that to herself. That was probably the last thing Vanessa wanted to talk about. When the time came, it would be a surprise to everyone. And there was something exciting about keeping the secret in her heart. Besides, he hadn't even asked her properly yet.

CHAPTER 37

Thoughts of Phoebe kept Lilly tossing and turning all night long. Who could have killed her? The motive hadn't been robbery, as one of the police officers at the scene had said the night of her murder. What were the usual motives for murder? The ones she came up with in the night, besides money, were love, hate, and revenge. She didn't know anything about Phoebe's love life except that she was divorced and seemed content with that. Lilly crossed "love" off her mental list. But what about hate? And was hate the same thing as revenge? Probably so, at least in some cases, thought Lilly.

She needed more information about anyone who might have hated Phoebe. And how was she going to figure it out without alerting the police, and especially Bill, to her inquiries?

And frankly, the term "inquiries" was a stretch, since Lilly didn't have any idea what to ask or of whom.

She was up long before the sun. The house was still. Barney and Fred remained sleeping on her bed, so she went downstairs, settled herself on the sofa, and booted up her laptop. She opened a tab and searched Phoebe's name. There were several articles—from the Juniper Junction online newspaper, the

Lupine newspaper, and other online sources—about the new herbery. Lilly read each one. There was nothing she hadn't already known—where Phoebe had moved from, how she became interested in the study and business of herbs, and her plans for expanding her reach in the community with classes and workshops.

Next Lilly looked at some of the other hits she had gotten with the search of Phoebe's name. There were the usual offers to find out her net worth, her criminal history, her family connections, and the list of all the places she had ever lived, but Lilly didn't trust those sites. She declined to click on any of them and searched the second page of hits.

Two items caught her eye. The first was a legal notice of the final divorce decree. The second was a mention of Phoebe's first husband. At least, it appeared to be. According to the article, written several months previously, Albert Detweiler, M.D., had been arrested in Flagstaff for driving while intoxicated.

How embarrassing, Lilly thought. *Good thing she got rid of him.*

"Mom? What are you doing?"

It was Laurel, standing in the doorway and rubbing her eyes.

"Hi. What are you doing up so early?"

"I asked you first." Laurel grinned sleepily.

"I couldn't sleep, so I thought I'd try to find out something—anything—about Phoebe Detweiler. Why are you up?"

"I couldn't sleep, either, because of Vanessa. I'm worried about her."

Lilly patted the seat next to her on the sofa. "I think Vanessa's going to be okay. But it can't be easy to be in her position."

Laurel sat down and curled her feet under her legs. "Her mother texted her yesterday to tell her that if she gives the baby up, they'll let her live at home."

"Wow. How did she react to that?"

"She doesn't want anything to do with her parents. She

didn't answer the text. She didn't tell you about it because she doesn't want you to hate them."

"That ship has sailed. I disliked her parents from the moment they decided they didn't like Cyrus because his skin is brown. Their treatment of her now that she's pregnant only confirms what I already thought of them."

"I feel bad for her."

"So do I. She's welcome to stay as long as she wants, even after the baby's born. But I agree that she'll have to get a job at some point. And the sooner, the better, at least for her mental health. She needs something to do every day besides stew about her predicament."

"I'm going to ask around today." Laurel stood up and stretched. "Did you find out anything about Phoebe?"

"Only that she was lucky to be rid of her ex-husband," Lilly said ruefully. "There wasn't much about her online. I'll have to dig a little deeper, I guess."

CHAPTER 38

That evening Lilly was walking up to the front door of Larkspur Manor when she saw Mirren coming around the side of the building. She waited for Mirren to catch up with her.

"Hi, Lilly. How is everything?"

Lilly thought for an instant about saying "fine" and going on her way, but something made her decide to talk openly to Mirren.

"Everything is okay, I suppose. Listen, Mirren, can I ask you a question?"

"Sure. We can sit over there if you want." Mirren gestured to a grouping of chairs in a corner of the spacious lobby. Lilly followed her over and sat down.

"What's up?"

Lilly took a deep breath. "I feel like I'm on a roller coaster. I love this place and think it's good for her, then I hate myself for putting her here and want to take her home with me … I want her to get to know other people, but when I try to get her out of her room I learn that the other people aren't all nice … I just never know what to expect when I visit. Do you ever feel that way?"

Mirren looked at Lilly with sympathy and concern, nodding "Yes. It's not easy, I'll say that much. The first time Dad didn't recognize me, I went home and cried for hours."

"I can't tell you how many times I've done that."

Mirren reached out and patted Lilly's hand. "All we can do is love them through it. It's not about us. What's important is that your mom feels loved and cared for."

Tears pricked the back of Lilly's eyelids. She swallowed around the lump in her throat and nodded. "I know you're right. But it is *really* hard."

"Want me to go with you to see her?"

Lilly shook her head and wiped her eyes. "Thanks, but I'd better go in there by myself. I just have to start getting used to feeling like this all the time."

"It sounds to me like you're feeling guilty. I'm afraid that comes with the territory. And if it makes you feel any better, most of the people here *are* gentle and nice. Occasionally you'll find someone who's crotchety—and it sounds like you did—but mostly, they're not like that."

"Thanks. That makes me feel a little better, I guess."

"Hey, why don't you and Hassan have dinner with my husband and me tomorrow evening? We've called a temporary truce to the fighting about his job offer and I have a feeling you could use a night out. I know I could. And besides, I'd like to have more people at dinner than just me and him."

Lilly smiled. "That would be nice. Thank you. I'll make sure Hassan is free and I'll text you.

The two women parted and Lilly headed toward Bev's room, her hands sweating and her heart beating rapidly. She knocked on the door jamb and peeked inside. Her mother was sitting in the armchair next to the window, looking outside. The lights in the room were off, allowing Bev to see the snow falling.

Lilly knocked again and Bev turned her head to face the door. "Come in."

"Hi, Mom." Lilly walked slowly toward Bev. Bev didn't answer, but stared at Lilly as she approached.

"Hello."

"How are you tonight?"

Bev shrugged. "I'm watching it snow. It must be cold outside."

"It is. How's Finley?"

Bev's face clouded for a moment, then she smiled. "Good."

"I'm glad to hear it."

The stilted conversation was driving Lilly mad. "Want to go for a walk?"

"No, I want to stay here." Bev folded her hands in her lap.

Finally Lilly couldn't stand it any longer. "Do you know who I am?"

Bev stared out the window. "Yes."

Lilly knew she would curse herself later for being so cruel, but she couldn't help herself. "Who am I?"

There was a long silence, then Bev spoke. "My nurse."

In the silence that followed, Lilly could hear a snippet of the tv show playing in the next room, someone coughing down the hall, the clack of computer keys at the nurses' station, and the low hum of the heating system.

She was beating herself up already. How dare she ask her mother to prove she knew who Lilly was? And what had she really expected? If Bev had known her, she would have greeted her by name, would have registered recognition, would have … Lilly took a deep breath. Mirren's words came back to her: *All we can do is love them through it.*

"Want to play cards?"

Bev brightened a bit and pointed to her nightstand. Lilly opened the top drawer and pulled out a deck of children's playing cards.

She pulled a chair opposite Bev and placed the cards on the small table in front of Bev's chair. She dealt the cards at Bev's request and they played Old Maid—more or less—for the next half hour. Bev didn't say much, but she smiled often and Lilly knew she was content.

When she got home that night, she was exhausted. Laurel had had no luck yet finding a job opening for Vanessa, which added to the flood of emotions she was feeling. She bade the girls an early goodnight, called Hassan to make sure he was free to go out to dinner with Mirren and her husband, texted Mirren to confirm, and fell into a dreamless sleep.

CHAPTER 39

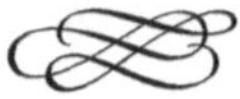

On Wednesday evening Lilly hurried home to change for dinner with Hassan, Mirren, and Mirren's husband, Basil. Hassan picked her up at her house so they could drive to the restaurant together.

They met Mirren and Basil at a restaurant in Lupine. Lilly hadn't been to the Gold Rush Brew Pub before, but one look at the dark wooden interior with its old-fashioned lighting, high-backed booths, bartender and wait staff in starched white shirts with black arm cuffs, and swinging wooden saloon doors between the kitchen and the dining room, and she knew she would be able to relax.

They sat at a small round table in the corner, under black and white photos of grizzled men from the late nineteenth century who had come to make their fortune in the Colorado Rockies. There were photos, too, of dusty streets and clapboard buildings, a showgirl in a fancy outfit, and a horse's muzzle. At Mirren's suggestion, they each ordered a Gold Rush, the restaurant's signature cocktail, and sat back to get to know each other better.

All Lilly knew about Basil was that he worked for an

accounting firm and wanted to move to Chicago. She had tried not to form a negative opinion of him based on what little she knew, so she listened closely to what he said and how he treated Mirren.

He seemed nice enough, but she noticed that he did tend to cut off Mirren when she was speaking. In fact, he did the same to Lilly. The third time he did it, Lilly pressed her foot on Hassan's and he reached for her hand under the table and squeezed it. Lilly suspected, at least momentarily, that Mirren had noticed. She felt a flush creep into her cheeks.

Before everyone ordered dessert, the ladies excused themselves to go to the restroom.

"I'm sorry if Basil offended you by cutting you off every time you opened your mouth," Mirren said when they squeezed into the restroom. "It drives me nuts when he does that."

Lilly's first instinct was to wave it off, but now she was positive Mirren had seen Hassan reach for Lilly's hand when Basil interrupted her. So instead she waved her hand dismissively. "It's no big deal. He just has opinions and he wants to share them." She grinned, hoping Mirren would drop the subject. She didn't.

"That's the problem," Mirren said wryly. "Hassan seems like such a nice person. You're lucky."

I am lucky, Lilly thought with a surge of feeling. Aloud she said, "Thank you. He's great."

On their way back to the table, Lilly was surprised to see Xavier and Mimi sliding into the booth behind theirs. They hadn't noticed Hassan and he didn't appear to have seen them. They weren't looking around, so they hadn't seen Lilly, either.

Lilly and her dining companions lingered over Irish coffee and a sumptuous bread pudding. Mirren was fascinated by the jewelry business and especially by Hassan's work as a gem hunter. Basil seemed interested, too, though it looked to Lilly like he was taking pains not to act *too* interested. She imagined he didn't want anyone to think accounting wasn't every bit as thrilling as gem hunting in Central Asia.

Lilly was content to let Mirren and Hassan talk, with the occasional remark by Basil, so she concentrated instead on trying to hear the conversation in the next booth. Mimi was speaking in low tones, but Lilly could hear her quite well.

"Xavier, I just think you're making a fool of yourself with that girl."

"She's not a girl—she's a woman. A young woman, granted, but not a girl."

"You'll be a doddering old man by the time she reaches her prime. You can't do that to her."

"Mimi, I'm not marrying her. I'm just dating her."

"Well, you and I both know what that can lead to."

Xavier chuckled. "I'm through with marriage. You spoiled me for all the others."

"Spare me, Xavier. Chelsea's a gold digger. You and I know your financial situation, but she obviously thinks you have more money than you do."

"I haven't discussed my finances with her."

"You just need to make sure a pretty little twenty-two year old doesn't end up with half your income."

"My dear, you don't have to worry about a thing. Your alimony payments are secure. I will not be marrying Chelsea or anyone else. I'm just looking for a friend, a companion."

"Yeah, well, make sure you keep it that way."

A server must have walked up to the table just then, because they made their dinner choices. Lilly had almost forgotten about her own dinner companions, so she turned her attention back to them. Before long they paid the bill and got up to leave. Lilly stayed out of sight of the booth next to them and exited the dining room in a way that, though convoluted and quite a journey, kept them invisible from Xavier and Mimi.

"Where are we going?" Hassan asked with a chuckle.

Lilly squeezed his hand. "I'll tell you in the car."

They said goodbye to Mirren and Basil in the parking lot. When they slid into Hassan's car, he turned toward Lilly.

"What's up?"

"Did you know Mimi and Xavier were sitting in the booth behind us?"

Hassan shook his head. "No."

"Well, I could hear them talking. She doesn't think he should be dating Chelsea, Noley's new assistant. She thinks Chelsea is too young for Xavier."

"Is she wrong?"

"Personally, I agree with her. But it's none of my business. Xavier has got to be, what, thirty years older than Chelsea?"

"How did he react?"

"He didn't seem mad. He said he's not looking to get married again. He just wants a companion. That just has a creepy ring to it, as far as I'm concerned."

"No doubt. I wonder if Chelsea knows he's just looking for a plaything. Er, a companion." Hassan smiled.

"I can't believe we're talking about Xavier like this. He seems like a nice enough person. But he does strike me as a bit of a player," Lilly said. "I know from talking to Isabelle that he introduced Chelsea to her as his girlfriend that night we saw them at The Water Wheel. That's what eventually led to Isabelle throwing her drink all over him."

"That's not cool," Hassan said.

"Do you think I should ask Noley to say something to Chelsea?"

"I don't know. What if Chelsea is well aware of Xavier's intentions? Or rather, his lack of intentions."

"I thought about that. But what if she's sitting at home, thinking they're going to get married, only to find out he's not interested in a long-term commitment? Noley said Chelsea mentioned the word 'marriage' in connection with Xavier."

"You could ask Noley to hint around at it, I suppose, and see how Chelsea reacts."

"I am such a buttinski."

Hassan smiled. "I wouldn't say that. You're just concerned about the feelings of a young woman."

"You make butting in sound so nice."

CHAPTER 40

When they got home Lilly called Noley. She told her about the conversation she had overheard between Mimi and Xavier.

"What do you think?" she asked when her tale had concluded.

"I feel terrible for Chelsea. Lil, she thinks they're getting married. I told you, she thought he was The One from the moment she laid eyes on him. This will devastate her."

"After you told me there's trouble in paradise, you never mentioned what Chelsea said about Xavier and possibly another woman. Has she said anything about finding him on a date with Isabelle Montrose at The Water Wheel?"

"She calmed down. I guess he explained it to her and said he had only gone out with Isabelle because he felt sorry for her."

"Yikes. Not only is that a mean thing to say, but it sort of leads Chelsea to believe there's more to their relationship than there really is."

"My thoughts exactly."

"Maybe there's a way we can let her know about Xavier's

intentions—or lack of intentions—gently. You know, sort of ease her into realizing it for herself," Lilly suggested.

"I'll think of something," Noley said. "Listen, Bill and I wanted to see if you and Hassan want to come over for dinner tomorrow night."

"After working with food all day, you want to cook for us?"

"I'm taking a mental health day tomorrow. I'm not planning to do any work at all. I thought a little dinner party would be fun."

"It does sound fun, but only if you're sure. What do you want me to bring?"

"Just yourselves. I've got the menu all planned. Come on over around seven."

"That sounds great. Thank you!"

Lilly called Hassan and told him about Noley's dinner plans. He had no plans for the next night, so he told Lilly he would be over a little before seven and they could head over to Bill and Noley's together.

HASSAN WAS RIGHT ON TIME. Lilly had already let the dogs out, so she hurried down the back steps and slid into the passenger side of his car. He leaned over and kissed her.

"I'm starving," she said.

"Me, too. Whatever Noley made, I hope there's a lot of it." Hassan grinned.

As they pulled away from the curb, Lilly noticed Chelsea walking up Xavier's front steps. Chelsea turned around when she heard Hassan's car. Lilly waved, but Chelsea obviously didn't recognize her or even see her in the darkness because she turned back to the door without returning the greeting. Xavier opened the door, kissed Chelsea's cheek, and Lilly and Hassan turned the corner.

"Did you talk to Noley about Chelsea and Xavier?" Hassan asked.

"Yes. She was going to subtly hint to Chelsea that Xavier might not want anything long-term."

At Noley and Bill's house, it was obvious Noley had spent her day off cooking. There was *boeuf Bourguignon, Lyonnaise* potatoes, *haricots verts*, and for dessert, an apple *jalousie*.

"I thought the deal was that we would have dinner with you guys as long as you didn't spend your whole day off cooking." Lilly gave Noley a stern look across the table.

Noley laughed. "Cooking all day for my family and friends is different from cooking all day for work. It's always enjoyable, but I can relax more when it's for you and Hassan."

Lilly was never happier than when she and Hassan were hanging out with Noley and Bill. Dinner had gone on for two relaxing and thoroughly enjoyable hours when Bill's phone buzzed. He glanced at it and excused himself, then walked into another room.

Noley was talking about her parents' trip to New York City for Thanksgiving when Bill came back into the room, a grim look on his face.

"Xavier Gordon is dead."

CHAPTER 41

*L*illy could only stare at her brother, dumbfounded. It was Noley who found her voice first.

"Xavier Gordon? As in, Lilly's next-door neighbor?"

"That's the one. Someone from the station called me. They want me to come into work to coordinate the staffing on this one. Perez is busy with the Phoebe Detweiler case, so I need someone else." Bill started toward the coat closet.

"Who found her?" Lilly called to him.

"The ex-wife." Bill was thrusting his arms into his overcoat when he came back into the dining room. "An ugly scene, from what I hear." He leaned down and kissed Noley, then bid Lilly and Hassan goodbye and left.

"We should go home." Lilly shot a worried glance at Hassan. "Laurel and Vanessa and the dogs must be beside themselves with the activity in the neighborhood. And Mimi doesn't know anyone else around here. She might appreciate a friendly face."

"I'll get our coats," Hassan offered. While he did that, Lilly texted Laurel to make sure she and Vanessa were okay. They had seen the police cars, Laurel said, but they had no idea what was going on. Lilly promised to be home shortly and told them she would explain everything then.

Noley stood up and began to clear the table. "Call me when you know something. I won't hear from Bill until he's on his way home."

"Will do. Thanks for dinner. Sorry we can't stay to help clean up."

"Don't give it a thought."

When they turned down Lilly's block, Lilly wasn't surprised to see the street teeming with police cars, the medical examiner's van, and two ambulances. "Pull over here," she instructed Hassan. "That way you don't have to fight your way through the emergency vehicles. I'll just walk home."

"Are you sure? I hate letting you off when there's been a killing right next door to you."

Lilly waved off his concern. "I'm probably safer tonight than I've ever been. Look at all these police officers."

"All right, if you insist. Text me when you get inside, though."

She leaned over and kissed him quickly. "I will. Promise."

When she arrived at home, having explained three times who she was, why she needed to get to the house, and where she had been, she dashed off a quick text to Hassan before going inside, where Laurel and Vanessa were waiting for her in the kitchen.

"What's going on next door?" Laurel asked.

"Doctor Gordon was killed."

Laurel and Vanessa gasped. "I can't believe it," Laurel said finally. "He seemed like such a nice man."

"Do they know who did it?" Vanessa asked.

"I haven't heard. Apparently Mimi found him."

Laurel closed her eyes. "Oh, my gosh. That's horrible."

"Did either of you see anyone over there?" Lilly asked.

Both girls shook their heads. That was when Lilly remembered having seen Chelsea go into Xavier's house a couple hours before Bill got the call. She frowned.

"What is it, Mom?"

"I just remembered something. I saw Chelsea Fortune go into his house as Hassan and I were leaving for Bill and Noley's. I need to call Bill." She pulled out her phone and dialed Bill's number, but he didn't answer. She sent him a text telling him what she had seen.

"Do you think Chelsea killed him?" Laurel's eyes were as big as dinner plates.

"I have no idea. That's an awful thought."

"Isn't he some kind of psychiatrist?" Vanessa asked.

Lilly nodded absently, thinking about Mimi finding Xavier's body.

"Maybe one of his patients killed him," Laurel said.

"It's possible," Lilly said. "But he said he didn't worry about his patients. Probably very few of them, if any, are dangerous. They're just people who need help."

"I wonder who could have killed him," Vanessa wondered aloud.

"I'm sure Mimi is still over there. I'm going to go see if she's okay. She could use some moral support right about now," Lilly said.

"You shouldn't go over there while the police are still there," Laurel said.

"You're right. I'll text her and invite her to come over here as soon as they let her go."

She texted Mimi and received a response about ninety minutes later.

Thanks. I'll be over. They're letting me leave soon.

Lilly made a pot of decaf coffee and set out a small tray with sugar and cream. When there was a knock at the back door about twenty minutes later, Lilly was ready. She opened the door and Mimi stood there.

CHAPTER 42

"*L*illy," Mimi said with a broken sob.

"Come on in." Lilly drew Mimi indoors and enveloped her in a hug. "I'm so sorry."

After a few seconds Mimi pulled away from Lilly's embrace and wiped her puffy eyes with her sleeve. "I've cried more tonight than all the other times in my life combined," she sniffled. "I called the police as soon as I saw his body, but I think I was in shock for a little while. Then once I started crying, I couldn't stop."

Lilly poured two mugs of coffee, set them on the tray, and said, "C'mon." She led the way into the living room. Mimi followed as if in a trance and sat down on the sofa. Lilly set the tray down, prepared Mimi's coffee the way she remembered Mimi liked it, and pressed the mug gently into Mimi's hands before sitting down next to her.

"Do you want to tell me about it?" Lilly asked.

Mimi took a sip of the coffee and leaned her head against the back of the sofa. "Lilly, as long as I live I'll never get the sight out of my head. He was just lying there on the floor, surrounded by his own blood." She squeezed her eyes shut as she shook her head vehemently.

"Do they know how he died?" Lilly asked softly.

"He was stabbed." Mimi started crying afresh. "He had his faults, but basically he was a decent person. I can't imagine anyone wanting to stab him."

"Was the alarm system on?"

"They don't know yet. It wasn't on when I got there. The police are checking with the alarm company." Mimi paused. "Anyone could have gone into that house and killed Xavier if the alarm wasn't set. I mean, he's a doctor. Doctors are common targets for thieves and criminals." She sniffed and sighed, her shoulders slumping.

"Do you want to stay here tonight? I'm sure the police are going to be in Xavier's house throughout the night and well into tomorrow, if not longer, so you'll need a place to stay."

Mimi's face crumpled. "That's so generous of you, Lilly. I hate to impose, but it would be nice if I didn't have to find a hotel for the night."

Lilly waved dismissively. "Don't be silly. Of course you're not imposing. You're welcome to stay here as long as you need to."

"Thank you. I think I'll take you up on that."

"Good. We have everything that you'll need—pjs, a new toothbrush, that kind of thing—but do you want me to go over to get some of your own things from next door?' Lilly offered.

Mimi shook her head. "That's okay. I'll run over. Maybe the police have found out something by now."

They sat in silence until Mimi finished her coffee and stood up. "Thanks for the coffee and for listening, Lilly. I'll go over and see if they'll let me take an overnight bag and I'll be right back."

She left. Lilly cleaned up the coffee things, then called Laurel and Vanessa into the kitchen.

"Mimi is going to spend the night, girls. Vanessa, would you mind sleeping in Laurel's room tonight? I'd like to give Mimi the guest room. I think she would appreciate a little privacy."

"That's no problem at all," Vanessa said. Laurel nodded.

"Vanessa can stay in my room as long as Mimi needs the guest room."

"Thank you. She's taking this pretty hard, as you would expect." Lilly hugged both girls and bid them goodnight.

It didn't take long for Mimi to return. When she knocked on the back door again, Lilly opened it to find her empty-handed and crying.

"They wouldn't even let me in the door to get my stuff," she wailed. "And they refused to get it for me."

"Don't worry about that at all. I told you—we have everything you could possibly need right here. Come on, I'll show you the guest room and I'll get you a new toothbrush and a set of pjs from my room."

Lilly led the way to Vanessa's room which, thankfully, Vanessa kept spotless.

"I'm just going to change these sheets quickly and then this room is yours," Lilly said. Mimi nodded mutely. Lilly busied herself with her task, then ran upstairs and returned with the items Mimi needed.

"I'm just up the stairs if you want to talk." Lilly hugged Mimi. "Let me know if you need anything."

"Thank you for everything," Mimi said.

Lilly could hear the sobbing from the guest room until the wee hours of the morning, when Mimi must have finally cried herself to sleep.

CHAPTER 43

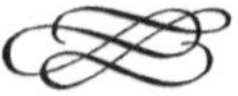

$\mathcal{L}$illy's phone rang before anyone else was up the next morning. It was Bill.

"Any news?" she asked.

"First tell me what you know about Chelsea visiting Xavier last night."

"I don't know much. I saw her going into his house as Hassan and I were leaving to have dinner with you and Noley."

"All right. I'll pass that info along."

"Do you know anything?" Lilly asked.

"Not much. Only that the alarm system hadn't been armed, so the killer wasn't necessarily someone who knew the alarm code. It could have been anyone." He sighed. He sounded tired.

"Mimi spent the night here. She was in bad shape, as you'd expect."

"That's what I heard. They questioned her pretty hard, since she's the one who found him. Just like Perez did to you when you found Phoebe's body."

"Do you think Xavier's death is related to Phoebe's death at all?"

"I don't know. Frankly, the first thing that comes to mind is that they both spent Thanksgiving at your house."

Lilly frowned. "Don't think I haven't thought of that. And speaking of Perez, has she turned her attention to someone else? Someone who might actually have killed Phoebe?"

"I wouldn't say that. She's still looking at every angle. The only people she'll cross off her suspect list are people with rock-solid alibis. I think the only person with a solid alibi so far is Phoebe's ex-husband, but don't quote me on that."

Lilly groaned. "So I should expect to hear from Perez again?"

"I'm afraid so. Don't worry about it. Perez is just doing her job and she's good at it. She'll get to the bottom of it. I have no doubt of that. Listen, I'm headed home. I worked all night. I'll talk to you later."

"Thanks for the update."

Mimi dragged herself into the kitchen a couple hours later. The girls both had things to do that morning, so they had left quietly to let Mimi sleep.

Mimi's hair was sticking up in every direction and the bags under her eyes were so big they looked like an extra set of cheeks. Her nose was still swollen from crying. Lilly had texted Harry to ask him to open the shop so she could stay home for a little while to make sure Mimi was going to be okay. When she saw Mimi, she jumped up from the kitchen table and poured her a large mug of coffee.

"How are you doing this morning?"

Mimi took a deep breath and sighed it out. "Okay, I guess. I think it's starting to sink in. I suppose I have a lot to do today, but I don't even know where to start."

"When I looked out front earlier, there was only one police car in the street. I haven't looked again, so maybe it's gone now. You might be allowed to get back into the house."

"I definitely have a lot of cleaning up to do in there."

Lilly knew the police would have searched the place to find

clues the killer may have left. They wouldn't have taken the time to clean up after themselves, so she was pretty sure the cleaning job ahead of Mimi was much bigger than Mimi realized.

"Did Xavier have a lawyer?" Lilly asked.

Mimi nodded. "I'll call him today. Xavier's will is in his office."

"I was actually thinking about his medical practice. I assume there are things that have to happen immediately. Maybe the lawyer can get started on whatever needs to be done with it."

"Oh. I guess you're right."

The phone rang and Lilly glanced at the caller ID. It was Hassan. Mimi gestured toward the phone. "You answer that and I'll go get dressed. I need to start my day." She pushed herself away from the table and Lilly answered Hassan's call.

"How's it going, love?"

"Okay. I'm still at home. Harry opened the shop for me today so I could stay here and make sure Mimi's all right. She just went in to get dressed. As soon as she's ready to leave, I'll go to work."

"How did it go last night?"

"Not well, as you'd expect. She was extremely upset. She seems a little better this morning, but she has a long road ahead of her."

"That's too bad. Anything I can do to help?"

"Not that I can think of. Why don't you come over for dinner tonight? If Mimi is still here, it might be nice for her to see a new face and talk about something other than Xavier. And if she's not, then bonus for me. Come on over around eight. That way I can stop and see Mom."

"Consider it done. See you tonight, love."

Lilly smiled as she hung up the phone. Every so often she was overwhelmed by her good fortune in finding Hassan, and today was one of those times.

CHAPTER 44

$\mathcal{M}$imi texted Lilly during the day to ask if she could spend one more night at Lilly's house. She had been cleared to go back to Xavier's house, she said, but she wasn't ready yet. Lilly quickly replied that she was welcome to stay as long as she needed.

That evening before she went home, Lilly stopped at Larkspur Manor. She went into Bev's room after taking a deep breath and crossing her fingers that Bev would recognize her.

"Hi, Mom."

Bev, who had been sitting in her chair looking out the window into the darkness, turned to look at her. She gazed at Lilly in confusion for several seconds before saying, "Hello."

Lilly's heart sank. It was the way Bev said it—Lilly knew Bev didn't recognize her. It stung, but what surprised Lilly was that she didn't feel she was going to melt down as she had just a couple days previously. It was as if somewhere in the back of her mind she was beginning to accept this new relationship with her mother. She fervently hoped she would recognize her own children until the day she died.

Lilly pulled a chair over and sat down facing her mom. "Do you mind if I sit here?" she asked.

Bev shook her head and turned back to the window. Only their reflections were visible against the darkness outside.

"If I turn off your light, you might be able to see it snowing lightly out there," Lilly said. "Want me to do that?"

"Yes, thank you."

Lilly turned off the light and sat down again. There were snowflakes falling outside and the scene was peaceful, like something from a Christmas card.

"What did you do today?" Lilly asked.

There was no answer from Bev.

"Want to play cards?"

No answer.

Lilly wanted to say something about Tighe and Laurel, but she didn't want to overwhelm Bev with a lot of questions, especially if she couldn't remember her grandchildren. She tried another tack.

"How's Finley?"

Finally, a reaction. Bev turned to her with a gentle smile. "He's very nice. He sings to me."

Lilly clenched her teeth so she wouldn't say anything she would regret. How could Bev completely forget her own daughter, yet know Finley, whom she had only known for a little while? It didn't seem fair.

Nothing about this was fair, she thought miserably. Aloud she said, "That's wonderful. He must be a good singer."

Bev nodded. "Mm, hmm. He has a lovely voice."

Those were the only words Lilly could elicit from Bev for the rest of her visit. In the accumulating snow, she trudged to her car with a heavy heart. She wished she had realized a while ago that Bev probably would not recognize her again. She tried to remember her last words to the Bev who recognized her own daughter, but couldn't. She hated to be petty, but she longed to hear that Bev didn't recognize Bill, either. She was afraid to ask because she dreaded the answer.

She was still in a funk when she arrived at home. Hassan's car was out front, and the thought of him made her smile. Mimi came over from Xavier's house right about the time she pulled into the driveway. Her shoulders were slumped and even in the darkness Lilly could see she looked defeated and exhausted. The sight brought Lilly out of her own funk in a hurry.

"How are you doing, Mimi?" Lilly asked as Mimi approached.

"I'm exhausted."

"I'm sure you are. Have you been over there all day?" Lilly nodded toward Xavier's house.

"Most of the day. I called the lawyer this morning and went over to his office for a little while, but the rest of the time I was in the house. You know, trying to make sense of things, trying to clean up the mess left by the police."

"I'm sure it would be okay if you waited a few days before going back to the house if it's too upsetting."

"I know. But I feel like it's sort of ripping off the Band-Aid. The quicker I do it now, the easier it will be in the long run."

"Come on. Let's go have dinner." Lilly motioned for Mimi to go first and they ascended the back steps. Laurel had seen them coming, likely because Barney was setting up such a hue and cry. He rushed over to Lilly the moment she stepped into the kitchen, skidding into her legs and making everyone laugh.

"I missed you, too, Barn." Lilly bent over to scratch his ears. Fred came up and waited in line, flopping onto his back for a belly rub when Lilly turned her attention to him. Mimi watched the scene unfold with a wistful smile.

"You don't have a dog, do you, Mimi?" Lilly asked.

"No, though watching you and your dogs makes me wonder why I've never gotten one."

"You should think about getting a puppy," Laurel said to Mimi. "They're so much fun."

"Now that I won't be coming to Juniper Junction anymore, I'll have to think about it."

Hassan had walked into the kitchen when he heard the ruckus the dogs were creating. He kissed Lilly's cheek. "What's this I hear about a puppy?"

CHAPTER 45

"Not us—Mimi," Laurel explained.

Hassan chucked. "Too bad. I thought maybe you were thinking about getting another dog."

"Three dogs?" Lilly asked. "I need another dog like a need I hole in my head."

"Mom, Vanessa and I made dinner."

"Ooh, that sounds delicious. I'm starving."

Everyone tried hard to keep the talk light over dinner, which consisted of chicken bundles and mashed butternut squash. Lilly figured Mimi could use the distraction and she was grateful to Hassan and the girls for providing lots of funny anecdotes and stories over the course of the meal.

After dinner Lilly shooed the girls upstairs. "You girls made dinner. I'll clean up."

"I'll help," Mimi offered.

At Lilly's request, Hassan retired to the living room with a glass of wine while Lilly and Mimi washed the dishes.

"Did the lawyer say anything about dissolving Xavier's business?" Lilly asked. "What happens to his clients?"

"Xavier used a virtual assistant for scheduling, billing, and other administrative things. I contacted the company where the assistant works so she can get to work notifying his clients what happened. That is, if they don't already know. I mean, one of them may actually have killed him."

"I'd hate to think that happened."

"Is the alternative any better? Either a home invasion or by someone he knew? Like a friend?" Her eyes widened. "Or a girlfriend?"

Lilly gave Mimi a wary glance. If Mimi knew Chelsea had been at Xavier's house, she surely would have mentioned it. *She must not know,* Lilly thought. It seemed unwise to tell her. Truth be told, Mimi's words gave Lilly pause. She had been assuming the killer was someone Xavier knew. What if there were a crazed maniac running around? One who committed random acts of violence? *Get a grip, Lilly.* She was grateful for the dogs. At least they would alert everyone in the neighborhood if someone tried getting into the house.

Mimi's thoughts seemed to be on a similar trajectory. "The police told me the alarm had not been set," Mimi said. "So anyone could have killed him. I've been assuming it was a patient, but what if it wasn't? What if it was a stranger? Or even that pretty young thing he's been stringing along?" She asked the question as if the words contained venom.

"My brother is a police officer, so I've seen up close how these investigations work. It's easy to jump to conclusions, but sometimes that's a jump in the wrong direction."

"That girl is nothing but a gold digger. I've told Xavier that a dozen times. But all he sees is the lustrous red hair and the perfect figure." Mimi shook her head in disgust. "And he didn't have as much money as you'd think, so she wouldn't have gotten anywhere if a sugar daddy was what she was after."

"It sometimes helps to take a step back and just let the police do their jobs," Lilly cautioned. Hmm. Hadn't Bill told her that a thousand times? She almost smiled at the irony, but managed not to. "Like you said, it could have been anyone. Maybe Chelsea had nothing to do with it."

"How well do you know Chelsea? I mean, I know she was at your house for Thanksgiving because that's where Xavier met her. Is she a friend of yours or something?" Something almost accusatory in Mimi's voice set off warning bells in Lilly's brain.

"Actually, I met Chelsea the same day Xavier did. She works for my sister-in-law and she was going to be by herself for Thanksgiving. So I invited her, along with several other people who were otherwise going to spend the holiday alone."

Mimi nodded slowly. "That's right. I forgot he also met that other woman here. The one with the loud voice and the weird taste in clothes. What's her name?"

"Isabelle."

"Yeah. Isabelle. What's her angle? Is she just strange, or lonely, or what? I know you said she's confident, but there are plenty of confident people who aren't weirdos."

Again, Lilly felt that pang of pity for Isabelle. How sad to be referred to as "strange" or "lonely" or a "weirdo." She felt a sudden need to stick up for Isabelle.

"She's confident and self-assured, but she can come across as pushy sometimes." Lilly cringed inwardly, wondering if that was diplomatic enough.

"She's a freak."

Lilly frowned. She had listened to enough woman-bashing from Mimi. Regardless of the friendship she had shared with her ex-husband, she had no right to put down other women who, for all she knew, might be good friends with Lilly. Lilly knew Mimi was grieving and looking for someone to blame, but enough was enough.

"Well, don't let us keep you up, Mimi. You didn't get much sleep last night, so if you want to go to bed early, we'll certainly understand. Hassan is just going to stay for a little while, then I'm going to bed early, too."

Mimi seemed to take the hint. "Okay, I'll do that. Thanks for letting me stay here again tonight."

"No problem." Lilly poured herself a glass of wine and walked out of the kitchen as Mimi went into the guest room and closed the door.

She set her wine down on the coffee table and plopped next to Hassan. He put his arm around her and she nuzzled against him. "I'm ready for Mimi to go back to Xavier's house," she whispered.

He squeezed her closer. "I know. She's hurting, though, and probably needs a friend."

Lilly sat up and reached for her glass of wine just as her phone rang. She glanced at her phone. "It's Bill."

"Hi," she answered.

"Hi. Just calling with a heads-up that Perez is planning to contact to you tomorrow."

Lilly groaned. "What for?"

"More questions."

"Is this a bad sign?"

"I don't think so. I haven't talked to her. I just heard her mention it to her partner. She didn't know I was nearby. I suspect she wants to talk to you because now two people who attended Thanksgiving dinner at your house are dead."

"Yeah, but that doesn't mean I killed them."

"Lil, you don't need to convince me of anything. I know you didn't do it. Just answer the questions Perez has and hopefully she'll leave you alone after this."

"Has anyone spoken to Chelsea about being at Xavier's house just before he died? And to Isabelle, since she had such a disastrous date with Xavier?"

"I'm sure Chelsea has been questioned pretty hard, but I don't have any details. As for Isabelle, I don't know, but I assume so. You could ask Perez, but I wouldn't recommend it. She won't appreciate being told how to do her job."

"Oh, all right."

Lilly hung up with an aggressive stab at her "End Call" button. "Officer Perez is breathing down my neck again," she told Hassan.

"I'm sorry, love. I'm sure she'll want to talk to everyone who was at Thanksgiving dinner again. I assume she'll need to talk to me, Harry and Alice, and Laurel and Vanessa, too."

"I wonder if she's talked to Bill and Noley. I never even thought to ask him." She whipped out her phone and texted Bill her question.

He responded just five seconds later with "Of course we've talked to her. We were at dinner, remember? SHE'S JUST DOING HER JOB."

"Okay, okay," Lilly muttered. "No need to get nasty about it, Bill."

Hassan chuckled and put his finger under her chin. "I'm sure Officer Perez is not trying to zero in on you. She just needs information and you are in the best position to give it to her because you organized the dinner and invited everyone with the exception of Chelsea. Cheer up, love. Come on, it's time for you to get some sleep." He stood up and pulled her up next to him. He took both wine glasses to the kitchen, washed them, and took Barney and Fred out while Lilly sat at the kitchen table, her chin in her hands.

When the dogs had come back inside, Hassan kissed Lilly goodnight. "All you have to do is go to bed," he said. "I'll talk to you in the morning."

CHAPTER 46

*L*illy and Harry spent their lunch breaks on Saturday talking to Perez and Nutley. They took turns in the hot seat in Lilly's office. Lilly went first. She folded her hands on her desk to keep them from shaking with nerves. Nutley whipped out a notebook while Perez did all the talking, and she wasted no time getting to the point.

"Now that *two* people who were at your house for Thanksgiving have died, I'm going to need more information about that day. Tell me again: who was there?"

Lilly recounted the names of all the guests.

"And how did you know each of them? Start with Phoebe Detweiler."

"I had only met Phoebe a few days before Thanksgiving. You already know she owned the herb shop up the block. I went over to introduce myself. When I heard that she was going to be alone for Thanksgiving, I invited her to my house. I don't like the thought of people being alone for the holidays."

Nutley scribbled furiously while Perez stared at Lilly.

"I still can't believe you invited a total stranger into your house for a family meal," Perez said.

"I wouldn't say she was a total stranger. It wasn't like I pulled someone off the street and demanded they come for dinner. I had met her, she seemed nice, and as I mentioned, I didn't like to think of her spending Thanksgiving alone. And it wasn't strictly a family dinner. It was a … sort of a … Friendsgiving." Lilly cringed. She hated that word.

"But Phoebe wasn't your friend."

"No. But I was thinking she might be at some point."

"Do you know where she lived?"

"No. I only knew that she was renting somewhere while she was having a house built."

Perez nodded thoughtfully. "Tell me about Isabelle Montrose."

"Isabelle is the realtor Bill and I hired to sell our mom's house."

"And you're referring to your brother, Bill Merriweather."

"Yes."

"How long have you known Isabelle?"

"Not long. We hired her because we were impressed by the job she did selling the house next door to me."

"And why did you invite Isabelle?"

"Same reason as Phoebe. She was going to be alone for Thanksgiving, so I asked her to join us."

"And Chelsea Fortune? Same reason? Taking in strays?"

Lilly frowned. "I wouldn't call it that, but yes, Chelsea was invited because she couldn't afford to go see her family. Actually, Bill's wife, Noley, invited her."

"How did Isabelle and Chelsea act around Phoebe?"

"The three women did not interact much, but there was definitely tension in the air. Isabelle and Chelsea had a bit of a confrontation at dinner because Isabelle said something snide about Chelsea's cooking."

Perez raised her eyebrows. "And the tension began with that remark?"

"No. It began soon after everyone arrived."

"And what was the source of the tension?"

"I don't know."

"What did Isabelle say about Chelsea's cooking?"

"It wasn't a big deal. Chelsea indicated she wasn't much of a cook and Isabelle remarked that her parents must be really proud of her. You know, in a snarky kind of way."

Perez nodded. "And? Anything else?"

Lilly thought for a moment. She recalled thinking something was unusual on Thanksgiving, but she couldn't put her finger on it.

She looked up suddenly. "I remember now. It looked to me like Phoebe was surprised to see Xavier there. Like maybe they had met before."

"Did you ask either one of them if they knew the other?"

"I think so. I remember Phoebe saying she had known Xavier for a while, but I didn't ask her for any details."

Perez frowned. "Okay. I'd like to ask your assistant a few questions, too. Can we talk to him in here?"

"Sure. Want me to get him?"

"I'll get him." Perez stood up and beckoned to Harry from the doorway to the office as Lilly went behind the counter.

Harry's interview didn't take long, and the officers left immediately afterward with a "thank you" to Lilly and Harry.

"That Officer Perez is scary," Harry said. "I felt like she was trying to see into my soul."

"I know, right? She's like that. It must be something they teach in the police academy. Bill has that same ability." Lilly shook her head. "I just wish they'd figure out who killed Phoebe. I don't like being in their crosshairs."

"The two deaths must be related. There must have been some common thread between Xavier and Phoebe," Harry mused.

"Yeah—they both came to my house for Thanksgiving."

"I mean besides that. I wonder if she was a patient of his."

Lilly raised her eyebrows. "That's an interesting point. I wonder if the police have checked into that. I'm sure they have."

"Probably. But they couldn't possibly have killed each other, so even if Xavier killed Phoebe, there's still a killer out there."

"I wonder if there's anyone who had a reason to kill both of them," Lilly said.

"Bill can't give you any information about what the police have found?"

"He's not supposed to. That doesn't mean I never get anything out of him, but since he was promoted he's been spending less time on the street and more time behind a desk. He has sort of a managerial position now, so he doesn't know a lot of the details he used to know. But I can work on him. Or I can get Noley to do it." Lilly grinned.

CHAPTER 47

$\mathcal{I}$t was Bill's turn to visit Bev that evening, so Lilly looked forward to getting home and relaxing with a good book for a little while. But when she answered her cell phone as she was getting into her car after work and heard Mirren's voice on the other end, crying, her dreams of relaxation evaporated like wisps of fog.

"Mirren, what's wrong?" She slid into the driver's seat and set her handbag on the seat next to her.

"I just left my dad and he's not doing well." She blew her nose, deafening Lilly.

"Oh, I'm so sorry."

"I don't even know you that well, but I thought of calling you first."

"I'm glad you called me. Where are you? I can meet you."

Mirren sniffled. "Right now I'm in the parking lot of Larkspur Manor."

"Do you want me to meet you there?"

"No. Do you want to get a drink somewhere?"

"Sure. Just tell me where to meet you and I can be there."

"How about the little Irish pub on Main Street?"

"The Randy Hare?"

"Yeah."

"I can be there in three minutes." Lilly hung up the phone and contemplated walking to the pub, but decided to drive. She found a parking spot not far from the front door of The Randy Hare and waited for Mirren to show up.

They sat across from each other in a booth near the front window of the warm, cozy pub. As soon as they ordered drinks, Lilly folded her hands on the tabletop. "Tell me what's wrong with your dad."

Mirren closed her eyes and rubbed one eyebrow with her finger. "I went to see him after dinner I knew right away that he wasn't himself. He was just sitting there in his room, staring at his feet. I couldn't get him to look up or talk to me or anything. I talked to Greg and he said Dad was like that all afternoon. The doctor saw him a little while before I got there and she said it's depression."

Lilly groaned. "I'm so sorry."

"He's suffered from it in the past. I think they'll give him an increased dose of antidepressant and he'll be okay. It's just that I don't need that on top of everything else."

"What's everything else?"

Mirren sighed. "My truce with Basil is over. He is constantly on my case about moving and leaving Dad behind. As if I would ever leave Dad, especially now that he's struggling."

The drinks arrived and Lilly took the opportunity to order something for dinner, too. She texted Laurel to say she would be a little while and not to wait for her for dinner, then turned her attention back to Mirren.

"My father is totally smitten with your mom." Mirren smiled. "She's a sweet lady."

Lilly gazed into her drink. "She is. I wish she could identify me, but I think those days are gone."

"It happens. It's a terrible disease." Mirren drained her drink and signaled the server for another. "Want one?" she asked Lilly.

"No, thanks."

They chatted while Mirren continued to down her drinks and call for more. After five or six, Lilly had lost count, Mirren was slurring her speech and listing to one side.

"I think it's time we get you home," Lilly said. "I'll drive. You can pick up your car tomorrow." The server came by with the check, which Lilly paid. She helped Mirren stand up and wrangle her arms into her coat sleeves. Mirren leaned on her a little bit as they slowly made their way to the car.

"Do you remember your address?" Lilly asked with a smile.

"Shoor do." Mirren rattled off a number and street name and Lilly headed there, keeping her fingers crossed that Mirren was right.

When they pulled up in front of a spacious stone house, the front door opened and Lilly could see Basil standing in the pool of light cast by a chandelier in the foyer. He had his hands on his hips and a scowl on his face. He didn't move to help Lilly as she maneuvered Mirren toward the front steps.

"What is going on?" he demanded.

"Nun'a yer beeswax," Mirren said.

He glared at Lilly. "I wish I could say it's good to see you again, Lilly, but it's not under these circumstances."

"She's just had a long evening, Basil."

"I can see that."

"A good night's sleep ought to help," she offered.

"I'll take her from here." Basil reached for Mirren's arm and made sure she didn't trip getting into the house. "Thanks, Lilly." He shut the door in her face.

I wouldn't want to be Mirren, she thought.

When Lilly got home, she noticed Laurel's car was not in the driveway. She let herself into the house and was surprised to find Vanessa sitting at the kitchen table. Lilly noticed the dark gray circles under Vanessa's eyes and the hollows in her cheeks. It looked like the poor girl needed some rest.

"Hi, Vanessa. How was your day?"

"Fine. Laurel's at the library. I stayed here because there's something I need to say to you."

"That sounds serious. Let me get my coat off and we can talk." Lilly hung up her coat and took her shoes off, then sat across from Vanessa. "What's on your mind?"

Vanessa took a deep breath and blew it out. "You know my situation. I'm pregnant, the father of the baby has left me, my parents will have nothing to do with me, I dropped out of college, and the list goes on."

Lilly nodded, waiting for Vanessa to continue.

"I've given this a lot of thought and I know it's going to come as a shock, but I need you to hear me out."

Lilly frowned, wondering what was coming.

"I'd like you to adopt my baby."

CHAPTER 48

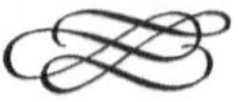

illy's mouth dropped open and she stared at Vanessa. She was incapable of forming a single word.

"Mrs. Carlsen? Are you all right?"

Lilly swallowed. What could Vanessa possibly be thinking?

"Say something, Mrs. Carlsen. You're worrying me."

Finally Lilly spoke. "I … I don't know what to say, Vanessa."

"Are you angry?"

"No. I'm just surprised. Well, no. 'Surprised' doesn't even come close to how I'm feeling right now."

"I feel like I've done this all wrong." Vanessa put her hands over her face.

"No, Vanessa. Don't feel that way. I just … of all the things you could have said to me, that wasn't what I expected." Lilly paused while Vanessa looked up. She searched Vanessa's face. "Why me? Why do you want me to raise the baby?"

"I've been thinking about it for a long time. I just can't do it myself. I don't have any money, there's no one to help me raise a child—"

"We'll help you. We told you that."

"Am I supposed to live with you forever? What about when

Laurel leaves? She'll move out and get married someday, I'm sure, and you want it to be just me and you and the baby?"

"You'll be back on your feet long before then. You can go to school, get a job, do whatever you want. It'll just take you a little longer."

"I can't. I'm not ready to be a mother." Vanessa shook her head.

"Suppose you do give the baby up for adoption. Are you going back to your parents' house? After what they've put you through?"

"No. I want nothing to do with them."

"So even if you do give the baby up, you'll still need somewhere to live, right?"

Vanessa nodded.

"And I assume you'll be living here, right?"

A shrug.

"I'm right. How hard would it be for you to live here if the baby wasn't yours anymore?"

Another shrug.

"Do you know what you want to name him?"

Vanessa let out a bitter laugh. "Definitely not Cyrus. Other than that, I haven't thought of names because I haven't allowed myself to." She held out her hands in a pleading gesture. "Please, Mrs. Carlsen. Please do this. At least think about it. Will you? I am not ready to be a mother. I know that in my heart. I would not be a good mother to a baby." She sighed and tears came to her eyes. "I resent him."

"Cyrus?"

"No. The baby. I resent him because of everything he's taken away from me."

"It's not the baby's fault," Lilly said gently.

"I know."

"Is this something you've discussed with Cyrus?"

"Yes."

"And what does he say?"

"He thinks it's a good idea. He never wanted the baby in the first place."

This is one of the saddest conversations I've ever had, thought Lilly.

"So will you? Adopt the baby?"

"Vanessa, I think you need to give this a lot more thought. Talk it over with your doctor, the nurse. Do you want to see a therapist? We could get you in to see a therapist if you want."

Vanessa shook her head. "I've made my decision. I'm giving the baby up for adoption. The only question is where he'll go once he's born." She swallowed hard.

"Okay. We'll talk about this again. I think you need to get some sleep."

Vanessa pushed her chair back and went upstairs.

Lilly put her head in her hands. Poor Vanessa. Between the pregnancy and the breakup with Cyrus and the estrangement from her parents and moving out of her home and dropping out of school, Vanessa's whole world had turned upside-down in a very short span of time.

She poured herself a large glass of wine and took it to the living room, where the dogs joined her on the sofa, one on each side of her. She stroked their ears while she thought about Vanessa's predicament. Was it possible she really didn't want her baby?

Laurel came home a few minutes later. She poked her head in the living room. "Hi, Mom. What's wrong?"

"Is it that obvious?" Lilly asked with a wan smile.

"You look so sad."

"Come on in. Have a seat." Lilly gestured to the other end of the sofa, where there was just enough room for Laurel to squeeze next to Barney.

"What's wrong? You're making me nervous," Laurel said.

"Nothing's wrong. At least, not with me."

Laurel frowned.

"Did you know Vanessa was going to ask me to adopt her baby?"

Laurel stared at Lilly. "What? Are you kidding?"

"No. I'm definitely not kidding. She asked me tonight."

Laurel's face slowly broke into a wide grin. "That's awesome!"

"What's awesome about it?" Lilly could not believe her ears.

"Seriously? Literally everything would be awesome if we adopted her baby! It solves all her problems."

"Um, Laur, it creates a few, too."

"Why?"

"You don't just adopt a baby on a whim. There's work involved. *Years* of work. A parent is a parent, no matter how old their kids are."

"But I could have a baby brother! Think of how great that would be! I would help take care of him and everything."

"He's not a puppy, honey. He's a person. A very needy little person."

"There's nothing you can say that will make me think this is a bad idea, Mom. You should think about it. I'm going to go talk to Vanessa about it."

Laurel had spun around and was darting up the stairs when Lilly called out, "Wait, Laur."

Laurel turned around. "What?"

"Please don't discuss this with Vanessa unless she brings it up. I don't want her to get her hopes up."

Laurel grimaced. "All right. But if she says anything, I'm going to talk about it."

CHAPTER 49

*L*illy took a big swig of wine and leaned her head back against the sofa. She closed her eyes. *A baby?*

Her cell phone rang. She glanced at the caller ID—it was Hassan. She answered it with a weary voice.

"Hi there."

"Hello, love. You sound tired."

"I am. It's been such a night."

"What happened?"

"I met Mirren for drinks after work because she was upset about her father. As we talked, it became apparent that the real reason she's upset has to do with her husband, who is trying to get her to leave Finley behind and move to Chicago. Mirren refuses to do that. Basil just won't let up."

"That must be frustrating for her."

"It is. So frustrating, in fact, that she drank way too much and I had to take her home to a decidedly ticked-off Basil."

"Uh-oh. Did he know he was the reason she was drunk?"

"I don't know, but given her state of mind, it wouldn't surprise me if she told him off. There was nothing I could do, so I just came home."

"Well, that is exhausting."

"Wait! There's more."

"There's more?"

"I had no sooner come in the door than Vanessa said she had something to say."

"That doesn't sound good. What was it?"

"She wants me to adopt her baby."

There was silence—what Lilly could only assume was stunned silence—on the other end of the line.

"Hello?" she asked.

"I'm still here. I can't believe it. I thought she was going to keep her baby."

"So did I. But she says she's made up her mind to give him up for adoption."

"What did you tell her?" he asked.

"I told her she needed to give it some more thought and that we would talk about it again. But she needs sleep. She looks like she hasn't slept in days."

"Making a decision like that would cause anyone to lose sleep."

"I know. Poor thing."

"Are you going to consider adopting the baby?"

Lilly sighed. "How could I have another baby? I'm forty-four years old. I'm not exactly a young mom anymore."

"But you could give that baby a life that Vanessa probably couldn't as a single mom, and a very young one at that."

"Whose side are you on?"

Hassan chuckled. "I'm on the baby's side."

Those five words, 'I'm on the baby's side,' hit Lilly like a punch to the gut. She could feel her face flush with shame.

"See?" she asked. "That right there is why you're a much better person than I am."

"What do you mean?"

"I mean, I've been thinking of me. And only me. I've been

focused on how much work it would be and how old I am and how hard it would be for *me*."

"Does that mean you're going to think about it?"

"I don't know. It's a huge decision."

"Did you ever think of having more kids?"

"Sure, fifteen years ago." Lilly smiled, remembering Tighe and Laurel as preschoolers.

"There are plenty of women who have kids at forty-four."

"Hmm. I don't know, Hassan. I thought that part of my life was in the rear-view window ... aaand I'm back to thinking about myself again."

"You're allowed to think about yourself, you know."

"I know. It seems I can't help it. What do you think I should do?"

"I don't know, love. It *is* a huge decision."

"I think the first thing I should do is get some sleep. I just want to clear my head."

"Get some sleep, Lil. I'll talk to you in the morning."

But after a night of tossing, turning, and envisioning every possible worst-case-scenario for Vanessa, for the baby, and for the small Carlsen family, Lilly awoke not with a clear head, but with gray bags under her eyes, a tension kink in her neck, and a case of nausea.

She shut off her alarm with a groan, waking both dogs as she did so. They stared at her sleepily. "I know, guys. I feel the same way." She texted Hassan to tell him she would call him later and that she was in no mood to talk about anything like a grown-up.

The weight of Vanessa's request became part of everything Lilly did that day. It was a Sunday—cleaning was harder, grocery shopping was harder, visiting Bev was harder. Lilly left Larkspur Manor with tears in her eyes and a lump in her throat. As she left, she met Mirren coming in. Lilly suppressed a tortured sigh. She hadn't wanted to run into anyone she knew.

"Hi, Lilly."

"Hi, Mirren. How are you feeling?"

Mirren blushed every shade of pink. "I'm so sorry about last night. I was going to call you when I got home from visiting Dad."

"There's nothing to be sorry for. You obviously needed to let off some steam."

Mirren laughed. "I sure did. Boy, was Basil mad."

"I could tell when I dropped you off."

"Was he rude? I have very little memory of it."

Lilly smiled. "Not really rude, just exasperated, I think."

"Well, I appreciate you listening to me talk. It means a lot."

"No problem at all, Mirren. Call me anytime."

Lilly headed home. She was just about to turn down her street when she decided to take a detour to Bill and Noley's house.

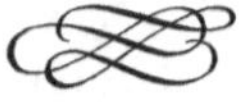

CHAPTER 50

*N*oley opened the front door and looked at Lilly in surprise. "What's up? You look terrible."

Lilly laughed aloud. It felt good. "Thanks."

"You know what I mean. I'm worried about you. What's going on?"

Noley stepped back into the foyer and Lilly closed the door behind her. She turned to see Bill standing behind Noley. "Hi. What's up?"

"Do you have any wine? I could use a glass. Sorry about the drop-in, but I didn't think you'd mind," Lilly said.

"Of course we don't mind," Noley said. "Come on in." She led the way to the living room while Bill went to the kitchen, appearing a moment later with a glass of white wine. Lilly accepted it gratefully and sat down while Bill and Noley sat across from her, concern written all over their faces.

"I came here because I need advice."

"Advice for what?" Bill asked.

"Let me ask you something. If it's too personal, I'll understand."

Bill and Noley exchanged glances, then looked back at Lilly.

"Are you two thinking of having kids?"

"I thought you were going to ask something much harder," Bill said with a chuckle. Noley nodded her agreement.

Lilly waited for them to answer.

Noley spoke up first. "We are not. We talked about it before we got married. We're not having children because we're both so happy with our careers and we don't want to slow down. Kids are not a priority for us. At least, not our own kids. We've always felt like honorary parents to your kids because we're so close to them, and we're both really happy with that. Forty-three is too old for me to be thinking about kids, anyway."

Lilly took a sip of wine with one hand and sat on the other so they wouldn't see her hands shaking.

"Why are you asking?" Bill asked.

Noley's eyes started to widen. She covered her mouth with her hands and squealed. "You're pregnant!?"

"No. No way." Lilly shook her head like it was a maraca.

"Then why are you asking?"

Lilly took a deep breath. "Vanessa wants me to adopt her baby."

Bill and Noley stared at her. Bill opened his mouth several times like he was going to say something, but each time he shut it again, speechless.

Lilly laughed. "I had the same reaction."

Finally Noley spoke. "I can't believe it. What did you tell her?"

"That she needed sleep."

"Is she serious?" Bill asked.

"I don't think anyone would joke about something like that," Lilly said.

"No, I know. I mean, has she thought this through? Giving up a baby. Man, that would be so hard."

"I think she actually has thought it through. She seems very determined. She said she's made her decision."

"What are you going to tell her?" Noley asked.

"If you had asked me last night, I would have said that's a big, fat 'no.' But then I talked to Hassan, and he got me thinking about more than just how a new baby would affect me—he got me thinking about the baby, too, and what might be in the baby's best interests."

"So have you changed your mind?"

"I wouldn't say that, but it's no longer a big, fat 'no,' either."

"You know we would help you in every way we could. Forever." Bill stood up and moved to sit next to Lilly. He put his arm around her and her tears finally started flowing.

"I just can't imagine the stress Vanessa must be under right now. This is incredibly stressful for me, and I'm not the one giving up a baby." Lilly covered her face with her hands. When she looked up again, Noley was sitting next to her and had her hand on Lilly's back.

"Honey, you have a whole team of people who are ready to help you. Have you talked to the kids about this?"

Lilly managed a smile through the tears. "Laurel thinks it would be the greatest thing in the world."

Bill chuckled. "Of course she does. How about Tighe?"

"I haven't talked to him yet."

"What about Hassan?" Noley asked.

"He agreed that it's a big decision." Lilly scoffed. "That's not much help."

Noley smiled gently. "Vanessa didn't ask him, though. She asked you. He's not in a position to tell you what to do. All he can do is give you his opinion. And if you sprang this on him the way you did to us, it wouldn't surprise me if he hadn't formed an opinion yet."

"I know. I just want someone to steer me in the right direction."

"Only you can do that," Bill said. "I wish we could be more

help, but it's a very personal decision. You know we'll support you, no matter what."

Lilly nodded and squeezed her eyes shut, then wiped them with the tissue Noley handed her. "I know. Thank you. I should get going. The girls are going to wonder what happened to me."

She stood up, followed by Bill and Noley. Noley gave her a hug at the front door. "You call me if you want to talk. Anytime. It doesn't matter, day or night. You know that."

Lilly smiled. "I know. Thank you."

By the time Lilly got home her tears had dried. She even managed a wide smile for Laurel and Vanessa, who were in the kitchen putting the finishing touches on dinner.

"We thought you got lost," Laurel said in greeting.

"I stopped at Bill and Noley's on the way home."

Vanessa gave Lilly a look out of the corner of her eye, as if she had guessed why Lilly made that stop after work. Lilly smiled at her and asked, "What's for dinner? It smells delicious."

"Roast chicken, mashed potatoes, and peas," Laurel said. "We figured some comfort food would do us all good."

"I agree completely," Lilly said. She set the table as Laurel took the chicken out of the oven.

They sat down at the table. No sooner had Lilly taken her first bite than Laurel spoke up. "Mom, Vanessa told me what she asked you. Are we going to talk about it, or ignore it and pretend we're not all thinking about it?"

CHAPTER 51

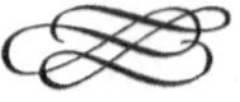

*L*eave it to Laurel to say exactly what was on her mind.

Lilly put her fork down slowly and wiped her mouth with her napkin while she gathered her thoughts. She looked from one girl to the other while she spoke.

"I am so very flattered that Vanessa has asked me to adopt her baby. But you both must realize that this is not a decision I can make lightly. It's life changing."

Vanessa gave a somber nod.

"That doesn't necessarily mean I'm going to say 'no.' I'm giving it serious thought. Laurel, I know you think a baby brother would be the greatest thing in the world, but there's more to a baby brother than cute clothes and photo opportunities."

Laurel grimaced. "I know that."

Vanessa spoke up. "I just thought you would make a wonderful mother for him." She swallowed and her lower lip quivered a little.

Lilly put her hand on Vanessa's. "And I am humbled and honored. I'm in awe of your strength. But I have to think very hard about it before I can make a decision. Do you understand that?"

Vanessa nodded. "I didn't expect you to answer me right away. I know it's a lot to ask."

You have no idea what kind of an ask it is, thought Lilly.

After the dishes were done and the girls were upstairs, Lilly called Tighe, who picked up on the first ring.

"Hi, Mom."

"Hi, honey. I haven't talked to you in a while. How's school going?"

"It's going fine. Are you calling me because of the baby?"

"What—? Oh. You talked to Laurel."

She could hear the grin in his voice. "Yeah, she called me and told me. What are you going to do?"

"I don't know. Have you given it any thought?"

"Is this, like, a change of life baby?"

"Honey, a baby is not a sports car. It also wasn't my idea."

"Yeah, I guess. Sorry."

"Anyway, what do you think?"

"Why do you want to know what I think?"

"You've answered pretty much all my questions with one of your own. I'd like to know what you think because I value your opinion."

"I think it would be cool."

"Cool how?"

"Cool because it would be cool to have a little brother. I think you'd be a good mom."

"Thank you. I'm not fishing for compliments, but I'd like to think I already am one."

Tighe chuckled. "You know what I mean. Of course you're already a good mom. You'd still be a good mom if you had a little baby."

This conversation was not as cerebral as Lilly had expected it to be. Her son, the engineering student, was not approaching the issue with the logic she had been hoping for. They talked about school for a few minutes before Lilly asked about Sally Anne.

"She's great."

"Is that it? She's great?"

"Yeah. She's great. It's great."

Lilly rolled her eyes. She thought about all the times she'd heard that boys' brains don't fully develop until age twenty-five. *I can believe it after a conversation like this one*, she thought.

"Well, it was good to talk to you, honey. Give me a call in a couple days."

"I will. Adopt the baby, Mom."

"I'll let you know. Love you."

"Love you."

She hung up and shook her head. It looked like she would be making this decision on her own.

CHAPTER 52

At lunchtime the next day she decided to surprise Noley with a sandwich from Armand's French bistro. She knew Bill was at work, so she and Noley could enjoy a girls' lunch. She had to make a phone call first, then she hurried over to the bistro and ordered one of Noley's favorites, a *jambon beurre,* and a brie and pear baguette for herself, placing them in a reusable cloth bag she kept in her car. She texted Noley to tell her not to make lunch, then hopped into the car and drove to her house. Just as she pulled up out front, Noley replied to her text.

"Had to run to the store. Back in a few minutes. Door's unlocked. Go on in."

Chelsea's car was out front. Lilly let herself in quietly so she wouldn't bother Chelsea's work. She placed her bag of food on the counter and sat down at the kitchen table to wait for Noley.

"Don't start with me. I came here for you!"

Lilly jerked her head toward the strident voice with a start. It was Chelsea talking—that much she knew. She didn't know whether she should stay quiet and listen or to cough or do something to let Chelsea know she wasn't alone in the house.

She decided on the former. Luckily the cloth lunch bag hadn't crinkled when she brought it into the house, so Chelsea probably didn't know she was there. This was a great opportunity to learn more about the young woman. A pity it involved snooping, but Lilly figured desperate times called for desperate measures. Maybe she could learn more about what Chelsea had been doing at Xavier's house the night he was killed. She wished she could hear who Chelsea was talking to, but it was obviously someone on the phone.

"If you hadn't dumped me, I wouldn't have gone out with him!" Chelsea shrieked.

There was silence while Chelsea listened to the person on the other end.

"Really, Tim? Are you sure you want to say that? Aaarrgh! I could just kill you!"

The next sound Lilly heard was something hitting something else. Maybe Chelsea had thrown her phone? Maybe she had punched her desk? Lilly didn't make a peep. She didn't want to deal with Chelsea in such a rage. She hoped the irate young woman would not come into the kitchen to find her.

But when had Lilly ever been so lucky?

Not ten seconds later, Chelsea stalked into the kitchen. She stopped short when she saw Lilly.

"How long have you been here?"

If that had been Laurel, Lilly would have wasted no time telling her to be polite. But she was beginning to wonder how highly strung Chelsea was and didn't think a manners lesson would go over very well at that moment.

"Long enough," Lilly said.

"Were you listening to my conversation?"

"It was impossible to ignore, Chelsea."

"I trust you won't tell Noley. I was on my break and what I do on my break is no one's business but mine."

"Unless you're damaging property that belongs to Noley or Bill."

"Oh, that? I threw my phone on the floor. No damage done."

Lilly nodded. "Okay."

"If you must know, my ex-boyfriend has been bothering me."

"I didn't ask for any details. Like you said, what you do on your break is your business."

"I just thought you might like an explanation." Chelsea's voice was descending from the stratosphere and Lilly wondered what kind of self-control the young woman was exerting to remain calm. One thing was certain: Lilly did not want to be on the receiving end of that kind of temper.

"I don't need an explanation."

Chelsea fixed herself a cup of coffee without another word to Lilly, then left the room. Lilly remained at the table, waiting for Noley to come back, reflecting on just how unpleasant Chelsea had been. Chelsea had seemed so friendly at Thanksgiving.

Lilly wondered what had happened since then to make her so antagonistic. The stress of committing a murder, perhaps?

Noley rushed into the house just a couple minutes later, her arms laden with bags of groceries. "This is all for something I've decided to make this afternoon," she said with a laugh. Lilly jumped up to help while Noley called for Chelsea. Chelsea came into the kitchen wearing a wide smile and offered to help organize the foodstuffs to make Noley's job a little easier after lunch. Noley accepted the help and Chelsea gave Lilly a warning glance.

After the groceries were set away, Lilly and Noley sat down to eat lunch while Chelsea said she had to duck out for a few minutes. Noley gave her a cheery wave goodbye while Lilly wrestled with whether to tell Noley about Chelsea's phone call.

She decided not to say anything yet.

CHAPTER 53

It was late that evening when Bill phoned Lilly.

"Another five minutes and I would have been sound asleep," Lilly said.

"Sorry for the late call, but I just got home from work and I wanted to let you know about something I learned."

Lilly's ears perked up. "What is it?"

"Before I tell you, remember: this is public information, available to anyone who wants to spend the time to go digging for it. You didn't hear it from me."

"Okay, okay. What is it?"

"Apparently our pal Isabelle Montrose was the realtor who brokered the sale of the herb shop to Phoebe."

"Huh. I didn't know that."

"That's not the interesting part."

"I figured that."

"The interesting part is that Phoebe filed an ethics complaint against Isabelle after the sale went through. The complaint alleges that Isabelle shared Phoebe's personal financial information with outside parties."

"Who are the outside parties?"

"We don't know yet."

"You're right. That is interesting. Very interesting. I wonder if Isabelle was so mad about the complaint that she killed Phoebe. She takes a lot of pride in that job."

The words left a sour taste in Lilly's mouth. Isabelle might bluster and bray, but Lilly didn't think she would ever stoop to killing someone.

Would she?

"If that's true, she has a lot more to worry about than just an ethics complaint," Bill said.

"She mentioned that she was moving away from Juniper Junction," Lilly said.

"Really? I don't know if Perez is aware of that."

"Don't tell her I told you. Isabelle will be furious."

"Isabelle won't know. I'll tell Perez to be casual about it, don't worry.

"Yeah. Casual like a tornado."

Bill chuckled. "I've got to get some sleep. Speaking of Isabelle, have you heard anything from her about Mom's house?"

"Not in the past few days. Someone looked at the house a second time, I know that. I'll call her tomorrow and ask her. In fact, let me call her before you tell Perez about Isabelle moving. That way I don't have to answer any of Isabelle's questions."

"Got it. Let me know what she says about the house."

When Lilly had a break at work the next morning she called Isabelle, who picked up on the first ring.

"I was just going to call you, Lilly."

"Oh? What's up?"

"I think I have a buyer for your mother's house."

Lilly's eyes widened. "Already?"

"I'm not known as the best realtor in Juniper Junction for no reason, Lilly."

"I know. Believe me, I appreciate it. I wasn't implying—"

Isabelle interrupted with a cackle. "I'm just joshin' you!"

Lilly was at a loss for words for a second. "Well … um … does that mean you don't have a buyer or that—"

"Hah! It means I was just joshin' you about not knowing I'm the best realtor in Juniper Junction. I really do think I have a buyer for your mom's house."

Lilly breathed a sigh of relief. "That's great, Isabelle. Who is it?"

"Woman by the name of Mary Balfer or something like that."

That couldn't be Mirren Balfour. Could it?

"Could her first name be Mirren?"

"Come to think of it, that is her name."

Lilly was speechless. *Mirren* wanted to buy Bev's house?

"Lilly? Earth to Lilly?"

Lilly rolled her eyes. She hated it when people said that. "I'm here. I'm just thinking. Okay, so what is the next step?"

"We wait for a formal offer, then I'll be in touch."

Lilly was preoccupied that morning, but not because of anything Isabelle had said. Harry tried to talk to her, but he eventually gave up when she couldn't hold up her end of a conversation. At lunchtime she hurried out of the shop and onto Main Street. She had chosen a place she didn't normally frequent for lunch because she didn't want to run into a lot of people she knew. She had arranged to have a private conversation and she wanted to keep it that way.

She sat toward the back of the dimly lit restaurant and waited for her companion to join her. The restaurant had mostly high-backed booths, so even the people sitting right near her weren't likely to be too nosy. Lilly positioned herself at the end of the booth so she could see anyone coming into the restaurant.

Presently someone entered, looked around blinking as if to adjust to the dimness, and asked a server a question. The server pointed toward the rear of the room. A moment later the woman slid into the seat across from Lilly.

"How are you, Lilly?"

"I'm fine. Thank you for meeting me here today."

The woman waved a hand. "No problem. I have to eat, too, right?"

Lilly smiled. "I know what I'm going to order. Take a look at the menu and once we've ordered I'll tell you why I've asked you here."

The woman picked up the menu and perused it, then set it aside. "I've eaten here several times before. I know what I want."

The server came over and Lilly gestured for her companion to go first. She ordered a French dip sandwich. Lilly ordered a turkey club.

When the server had left, the woman looked at Lilly intently. "I was surprised to hear from you. I know you didn't ask me here to shoot the breeze, so why don't we discuss why I'm here?"

Lilly folded her hands on the table in front of her to keep them from shaking. "You're right. I didn't ask you to meet for lunch so we could chat."

Her lawyer, Gretchen, raised her eyebrows, inviting Lilly to continue.

"I want to know what I would have to do to adopt a baby."

CHAPTER 54

Gretchen's face broke into a broad smile. "You're thinking of adopting?"

Lilly nodded. "It's a long story. My daughter's best friend is pregnant, about eight months along, and she has asked me to adopt the baby."

Gretchen's smile quickly turned upside-down. "She's due in a month? That doesn't leave us much time. I don't know much about adoptions, but I do know adoptions like this can take a *minimum* of three months to complete, and almost always longer. I have a colleague who would be perfect to work with you. Maybe she could pull some strings to get things done a little faster."

"The thing is, I haven't even decided for sure whether I'm going to adopt the baby."

"I don't want to put any pressure on you, Lilly, but you need to make that decision as soon as you can. Otherwise you risk all kinds of delays and issues with mother-baby bonding."

"I assumed as long as the mother wants me to adopt, and as long as I agree to it, it would be a quick process."

Gretchen shook her head. "There's a whole home inspection

process that needs to be completed before an adoption can be approved. The inspection takes a while. Listen. Let me call my friend and ask her. Do you mind?"

"No. That's fine." Lilly's stomach clenched and the reaction startled her. It was like some part of her mind had already decided to adopt the baby and the thought of a delay or a failure to bond properly with the baby was causing a physical response.

She had expected Gretchen to call her colleague after lunch, but Gretchen pulled out her phone immediately and only moments later was explaining Lilly's issue to someone. She handed the phone to Lilly.

"Is this Lilly?" a woman's voice asked.

"Yes. Thank you for talking to me."

"My pleasure. I'm Angie Haviland. I handle adoptions. From what I understand, you need to expedite a home inspection protocol."

"Well, um, I guess. I—to tell you the truth, I haven't even decided if I'm going to adopt the baby."

"Oh. I assumed you had made that decision. Are you planning on reaching a decision soon?"

"Yes. As soon as possible."

"Good. It doesn't make much sense for me to talk to you about procedure when you haven't even decided yet, but as soon as you're ready to move forward, call me. Tell my assistant that you're Gretchen's friend and that you've talked to me on the phone already. She'll put you at the top of my list for a call back."

"I will. Thank you."

"And Lilly? This is a big decision, so I don't want to rush you. But you're dealing with significant time constraints even now, so the sooner you decide, the better it will be for everyone."

"Okay. Thanks."

Lilly disconnected the call and handed the phone back to Gretchen with a dazed expression.

"I didn't mean to put you on the spot like that, Lilly, but time is of the essence. Angie is no-nonsense, as you may have guessed. If there's anyone who can guide you through this process quickly, it's her."

"I appreciate it."

Gretchen seemed to sense Lilly's bewilderment as they ate, so she steered the conversation to various topics having nothing to do with babies, pregnancy, adoption, or middle-aged moms. Instead, they talked about world events. That was depressing, too, thought Lilly, but better than dwelling on her own problems for a while.

After Lilly had paid the bill for their lunch, she and Gretchen stood in front of the restaurant before going their separate ways.

"Thank you so much for putting me in touch with Angie," Lilly said.

"You're welcome. Hey, let me know what you decide. I think it's pretty awesome that you're even considering adopting a baby. I'm thirty-seven and I would never be able to do it."

Lilly waved goodbye and when she arrived at the jewelry shop ten minutes later, she didn't even remember the walk back.

"Boss, you okay? You look a little pale. Can I get you anything?" Harry looked at Lilly with concern.

"Thanks, Harry. I'm fine. I think what I need is a month-long vacation in Europe."

"Sounds good. Alice and I'll join you." He grinned.

Lilly and Harry busied themselves waiting on customers during the afternoon. Lilly was grateful for the surge because it kept her mind busy and away from other, more overwhelming, topics.

But her subconscious was working all afternoon, too, and by the time Lilly walked in the door at home that evening, she had made up her mind.

Both girls were preparing dinner in the kitchen.

"Girls, put that stuff away. We're going out tonight."

Laurel looked at Lilly in surprise. "Why? What's the occasion?"

"We're celebrating. I'm going to adopt Vanessa's baby."

CHAPTER 55

*L*aurel dropped the spoon she had been holding as Vanessa covered her face with her hands and burst into tears.

"Vanessa, are you okay? If you've decided to keep the baby, that's fine. Don't worry about a thing." Lilly stood paralyzed while she stared at Vanessa.

Laurel didn't seem to know what to do, either. She looked from Lilly to Vanessa and back again in befuddlement.

"Vanessa?" she asked.

Vanessa looked up and made an unsuccessful attempt to blink the tears away. She smiled. "I just can't believe all the decisions have been made and this is really happening."

"Have you changed your mind?" Lilly asked in a gentle voice.

Vanessa shook her head vehemently. "No. You're going to make such a great mom, Mrs. Carlsen." She started crying afresh. "This baby is so lucky."

Laurel hugged Vanessa and beckoned Lilly to join them. By the time the three of them untangled, everyone was crying.

Lilly laughed as she hiccupped. "I need to call Tighe and Hassan and Bill and Noley. Then we'll go out, okay?"

Laurel and Vanessa nodded and put away the things they had gotten out to make dinner while Lilly went into the living room to make her calls. She called Tighe first.

"Hi, Mom."

"Hi. I won't keep you because I have other calls to make, but I wanted you to know that you're going to be a big brother again."

"You're preg—wait! You're going to adopt Vanessa's baby?"

"Yes." Lilly didn't trust herself to say more than that without more tears.

"Wow." His voice was soft and that's all he said.

"Are you still there?" Lilly asked.

"Yeah. I just can't believe it. I didn't really think you'd go through with it. I mean, I'm really happy, though. I just can't believe it," he repeated. "Wait 'til I tell Sally Anne."

"Well, it's not a secret, so you can tell her anytime. I have to submit to a home inspection, but the lawyer I talked to today seemed to think everything would be fine."

"You'll be a cinch for that."

"Thanks, honey. I'm taking the girls out to dinner to celebrate, but I wanted you to be among the first to know."

"Thanks, Mom. Congratulations, right?"

"Yes. Definitely congratulations. To all of us."

Next she called Hassan.

"I'm taking Laurel and Vanessa out to dinner. Care to join us?"

"Sure. What's the occasion?"

"I've decided to adopt Vanessa's baby."

There was silence on the other end of the phone while Lilly's throat felt like it was closing. She had assumed Hassan would be thrilled for her.

"Hassan?"

"I'm here. You have no idea how happy and proud this makes me." His voice broke.

"Are you crying?"

He sniffled and paused again before speaking. "Believe me, these are happy tears. And of course I'll go to dinner with you ladies. My treat. I'll leave now and swing by to pick you up."

"That's perfect. It'll give me enough time to call Bill and Noley to tell them the news."

"You haven't told them yet?"

"No. I told the girls, of course, then I just got off the phone with Tighe. You were next because you really rate." She laughed.

"You are amazing, love. I'll see you in a few minutes."

Lilly hung up and got that warm feeling all over that only Hassan could bring. She was thrilled that he was thrilled.

Finally she called Bill and Noley. When Bill answered, she asked him to put her on speakerphone so she could talk to them together. When she broke the news, Noley squealed and Bill let out a whoop of glee.

"I *knew* it!" Noley gushed. "I knew you'd say yes! I am so excited!"

They talked about babies and due dates and adoption procedures until Hassan knocked on the back door. Lilly finally got off the phone and found the girls talking to Hassan in the kitchen. He picked her up and swung her around when she came in, a wide smile on her face.

"I'm so happy for you, Lil. And for your kids and Vanessa, too." Hassan glanced at Vanessa, who nodded as if giving him permission to voice his feelings.

"Let's go eat," Vanessa said.

CHAPTER 56

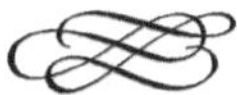

*D*inner was fun, though Lilly worried a bit that the celebration might be hard on Vanessa. Apparently she wasn't the only one who was worrying—just after everyone ordered dessert, Lilly excused herself to use the restroom. A moment later Laurel followed her through the door.

"Mom, do you think all this is bad for Vanessa?"

"I wondered about that myself. But it deserves celebrating, I think. Maybe we should talk about other things until we go home?"

"I think we should."

When Lilly sat down again she was just opening her mouth to say something decidedly not baby-related when her phone rang. It was Bill.

"What's up?" she asked in greeting.

"I've got news. You still at dinner?"

"Yes. Is it important?"

"It might be. Call me as soon as dinner is over." He hung up before Lilly could protest.

She frowned, and Hassan gave her a questioning look. "That

was Bill," she explained. "He said it's something that might be important." Everyone looked at her with concern.

"I wonder what that's all about," Laurel said.

"As soon as we finish dessert and pay the bill, we'll head out," Hassan said. The table was silent while the four ate their desserts in haste, then Hassan signaled for the bill, paid it, and they left.

When they got back to Lilly's house, she hurried inside to call Bill. She was worried something was wrong. Vanessa went into the house with her, already suffering from heartburn because of her dinner, while Hassan and Laurel stayed outside chatting.

"What's the news you have? Is everything okay?" Lilly asked in a rush when Bill answered the phone.

"Everything is okay so far, I guess. It's about Chelsea. Now, listen—"

"I know, I know. I can't tell anyone where I heard this."

"Are you going to interrupt me, or shall I continue?"

"Sorry. Go ahead."

"What I learned is actually public information. Like I've said before, it's available to anyone who wants to bother enough to go looking for it."

"Okay. What is it?" She wondered what public information there was about Chelsea that was potentially worrisome.

"After Noley hired her but before she started work, I did a little digging into her background in Seattle. When I didn't find anything, I assumed it was because she was firmly on the straight and narrow.

"At the time, I thought it was odd that she didn't even have any social media accounts. But I didn't pursue it because everything was working out all right. But then Xavier was killed and you saw Chelsea going into his house shortly before the murder and I started to worry, so I dug a little deeper. I'm embarrassed to say I never even thought of asking Noley to see

Chelsea's W-9 tax form. Turns out she's only been using the name Chelsea since coming to Juniper Junction. That's her middle name. Her real first name is Beatrice and she called herself Trixie before coming here. Noley didn't know it because she just took the papers and forwarded them to the accountant."

"Oh, my gosh."

"I found out that Chelsea has a record in Washington. And not parking violations, either. She's been arrested and charged with criminal harassment and assault of her ex-boyfriend, along with unlawful possession of a firearm."

The hairs on Lilly's neck prickled. "You're kidding."

"Would I kid about having someone like that in my own house, working with my wife?

"It's a figure of speech, Bill. So what are you going to do about it? And more importantly, do you think she had anything to do with Xavier's death?"

"To answer both questions, I don't know."

"Have you told Noley?"

"Of course. I called her first."

"And what did she say? Wait, let me guess. She told you she is not in any danger from Chelsea. She also insists that Chelsea continue working for her and that you stop worrying."

"You think you're so smart."

"Am I right?"

"Yes."

Lilly chuckled. "I've known Noley even longer than you have. I assume she thinks Chelsea has turned over a new leaf and is trying to start fresh in a new place."

"Her words almost exactly."

"Do you agree with her?"

"I'm a cop. I don't trust Chelsea anymore and I'm not comfortable having her in the house with Noley when I'm not there."

"Can you and Noley arrange it so Chelsea only works when you're home?"

"That's not very practical. Besides, my schedule isn't always predictable."

"You're right."

Lilly thought of the irate conversation she had overheard at Bill's house between Chelsea and Tim. Should she tell Bill about it? It would only upset him. "How about installing cameras in the house? You know, like the ones that can hide in teddy bear eyes or fake flowers or something."

"If Chelsea is going to hurt Noley while I'm at work, having cameras won't prevent that. It would only make arresting her easier."

"Yeah, I guess you're right. Well, we'll think of something." A gnawing feeling of guilt was whipping itself into a frenzy in Lilly's stomach. She had to tell Bill what she had overheard. "I probably should have mentioned this before, but—"

"Mentioned what before?" Bill asked quickly.

Lilly sniffed. "If you wouldn't interrupt me, you'd know already."

"Sorry."

"I was at your house the other day to have lunch with Noley. She had run out to the grocery store, but told me to go inside and wait for her. Chelsea was in there and I heard her talking on the phone. She was very angry."

"Who was she talking to? What were they talking about?"

"She was talking to a guy named Tim. She told him that if he hadn't dumped her, she wouldn't have gone out with someone else. She said she could kill him."

"That does it. She's out of my house. Why didn't you mention this before now?" Lilly cringed at his exasperation.

"I'm sorry, Bill. I've had so much on my mind lately and ..." She trailed off. "I'm sorry."

"Did you say the guy's name is Tim?"

"Yes."

"The man she was accused of assaulting in Seattle was named Tim. You don't know his last name, do you?"

"No. But I know she followed a boyfriend to Juniper Junction."

"Sounds to me like she's a stalker. It's got to be the same guy. And you don't know what, specifically, they were fighting about?"

"No."

"Does Chelsea know you heard the argument?"

"Yes. She came into the kitchen just after she hung up the phone. She had thrown something or hit something, so I knew she was angry. She told me that she was on a break and what she did on her breaks was her own business."

"All right. I'm going to deal with this right now. Noley is just going to have to find another assistant." Bill's voice was grim.

"What are you going to do?"

"I'm going to fire Chelsea."

CHAPTER 57

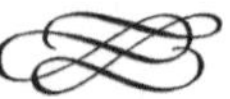

"Shouldn't you leave the firing to Noley? If Hassan went into my shop and fired Harry, I'd be pretty angry."

"But what if he did it to save your life? I bet you'd be pretty thankful," Bill countered.

"Well, maybe. But to say Chelsea is going to kill Noley is a pretty big assumption. At least discuss it with Noley first. Tell her how worried you are. Let her make the decision for herself. Trust me, Bill. This is the way to go."

Bill sighed. "All right. I'll talk to her. But if she says she's not going to fire Chelsea, I'll go ahead and do it myself."

"You can tell her how you feel, but I'm telling you, she's not going to appreciate being told what to do. The decision needs to be hers or I wouldn't blame her for holding it against you forever."

"All right, okay. I'll make her think the decision is her idea."

"Good luck. If you find out anything else about Chelsea, let me know."

"If I can, I will."

As soon as she hung up with Bill, Lilly called Noley.

"I just talked to Bill," Lilly said. "I'm just giving you a heads-up that he wants you to fire Chelsea."

"I can't fire Chelsea."

"He knows that's what you're going to say. What's your reasoning?"

"Well, I don't know, I only just hired her recently. It wouldn't be right. Besides, she's good at her job."

"Bill told me what he found out about her, and I know he's told you, too. She does sound like kind of a loose cannon, Nol. Bill is really, really worried about her being in the house with you."

"Bill worries too much."

"It's his job. He can't help it. Besides, it's better than not caring, right? I just wanted you to be thinking about it. Just remember, there are other people out there who are good at social media."

"I know. I get your point." She sighed. "If getting rid of Chelsea is going to make life easier for Bill, then I don't have much choice, do I? I hate to let her go, but I can't keep her around at the expense of Bill's peace of mind."

"He'll be relieved to hear that. I didn't tell you this before, but I just told Bill. I overheard Chelsea talking to some guy named Tim on the phone the other day when I was waiting for you to come home for lunch. She was pretty angry. Angry enough to throw something."

"Tim's the boyfriend she followed here from Washington," Noley confirmed.

"Bill thinks he's the one she assaulted in Washington."

"Poor guy. Chelsea seems so nice—I can't believe she's a stalker and an abuser. Oh, Bill's calling on the other line, so I need to take it. I'll call you tomorrow."

Lilly hung up and went to the kitchen, where Hassan was waiting for her.

"Everything okay?" he asked.

She relayed her phone calls with Bill and Noley. "I'm so glad Harry is so sweet and reliable. I couldn't handle work drama on top of all the normal drama," she said.

"I should get going," Hassan said. "I need to prepare for a call with the folks in Afghanistan. It's at two a.m. local time."

"Will you be talking about making the trip over there?" Lilly asked with a frown.

"Erm, yes."

"It's a good thing I love you so much."

CHAPTER 58

The next morning Lilly waited until the decent hour of nine o'clock before phoning Angie, the adoption lawyer. Angie promised to get the paperwork started that day. Lilly agreed to visit Angie's office at lunchtime to provide as much information as she could for the forms that needed to be filled out first. As soon as she hung up with Angie, she texted Noley.

Any news about Chelsea?

Noley texted back quickly. I fired her an hour ago.

How did it go? Lilly texted back.

She wasn't happy, but I think she realizes Bill would never have trusted her after he found out about her record in Washington.

I'll keep my ears open for a new assistant for you. Lilly added a crossed fingers emoji.

Her meeting with Angie was exhausting, and it ended up taking two hours. She hadn't thought so hard about her medical history, her milestones, and other major life events in ages. She left with a list of original documents she needed to provide Angie before the paperwork could be filed.

That evening after Harry had gone home, Lilly stood at her

desk, her coat on and her car keys in hand, rifling through the mail that had arrived earlier in the day. She wheeled around, startled, when there was a brisk knock on the back door of the shop.

She opened the door expecting to find Harry there, but instead it was Chelsea who stood in the alley, glaring at Lilly with a scowl.

Lilly took a step backward in surprise. "Chelsea. Hi. What are you doing here?" A frisson of unease snaked up her back.

Chelsea didn't move from where she stood, for which Lilly was grateful. "As if you didn't know. What did you tell Noley and Bill?"

"I told her I heard you talking to someone on the phone and that you were angry. It was the truth."

"Thanks a lot." Chelsea scoffed and shook her head in disgust. "Why couldn't you just mind your own business?"

Lilly stopped herself from blurting out something about Chelsea having a record in Washington, mainly because it occurred to her that angering Chelsea further might not be the smartest thing to do.

"Chelsea, I'm sorry about all this. But Bill's main concern is for Noley's safety and he was worried. Noley mentioned to me how good you are at social media, so I bet you'll find a new job in no time."

Chelsea didn't seem to have a reply to that, so she glowered at Lilly for several more seconds and disappeared on foot into the darkness of the alley. Lilly thought about going back into her office, but decided the safer course might be to get into her car immediately and drive home. She didn't want to take a chance that Chelsea would be waiting for her in the dark alley if she stayed in her office any longer. She locked the shop door behind her and hurried to her car.

When she got home she called Noley.

"Chelsea paid me a visit tonight," she said when Noley answered.

"She did? What did she say?"

"She met me at the back door of the shop and accused me of getting her fired because I told you and Bill about the phone call I overheard."

"I'm so sorry. Are you all right?"

"I'm totally fine. She didn't even come into the office. She stayed outside in the alley while we talked. She's pretty angry."

"You know, I think I'm glad I let her go. The more I know about her, the more I worry that she's going to become unhinged."

"I'll admit, I was a little nervous when I saw her standing there. You should have seen the look she gave me—it sent chills up my spine."

"I'm glad you're okay. I'm glad you and Bill talked me into letting her go. I hated to do it, but maybe she really hasn't changed much since she left Seattle."

"It seems not. It makes me wonder if she really did kill Xavier."

Noley took a moment before responding. "Anything's possible, but I don't know. I assume they were still dating at the time of his death. Why would she kill him, especially if she thought they might be getting married?"

"Maybe he told her he had no intention of getting married."

"You might have something there. Given her history with her ex-boyfriend, if Xavier had told her something like that the night he was killed, I bet she didn't take that very well."

"Can you think of anything she told you about their relationship after Xavier died?" Lilly asked.

"I don't remember anything. I didn't want her to think I was prying, so I never asked about him. I just figured she'd bring it up at some point. She's not exactly shy."

"Well, I think she needs to take the top spot on our list of potential killers," Lilly said. "The only person we *know* didn't kill Xavier was Phoebe, because she was already dead."

"Who else is on the list?"

"Besides Chelsea, I would have to say Isabelle needs to be there, as well as Mimi."

"Do you really think either one of them killed him?"

"I have no idea," Lilly said.

"Anyone else?"

"It could be anyone. A patient, someone he angered that we don't even know about, or a random stranger. Honestly, the random stranger scenario is the scariest one to me."

"Me, too. You need to be a lot more careful if you're going anywhere by yourself. You should always have someone with you. Same with Laurel and Vanessa. Make sure they stick together."

"The only places I really go are to Larkspur Manor, Hassan's house, and the shop. I think I'm relatively safe going to those places. And when I'm home, I'm with the girls. And if they're not home, the dogs are always here."

"Lilly, I question how much help Barney and Fred would be in an emergency."

Lilly laughed. "I know what you mean. But someone trying to get into the house might not know that."

"Well, you've had one murder on your block. Let's do everything we can to keep it that way, huh?"

"Don't even say that!"

"Just be careful, okay?"

<h1 style="text-align:center">CHAPTER 59</h1>

illy called Hassan before she went to bed that night. She told him about Chelsea's appearance in the alley behind the jewelry shop.

"I don't like the sound of that," he said. "Maybe I should come over there at closing time and make sure you get home okay from now on."

"I don't think you need to do that. I'll just leave when Harry does."

"That's fine, as long as you actually do that. If you don't, make sure you call me and I'll come over so you don't have to be by yourself."

"I will. How did the phone call go last night?"

"Pretty well. We're going to set up another one in a couple days. A few other people are going to join the Afghans on the call."

"Should I even ask when you're going over there?"

"You can ask, but I don't have an answer yet."

"Good. The longer you can put it off, the better."

Hassan let out a low chuckle. "There's no sense in worrying about something that may not happen. Let's talk about something else. How about coming over for dinner tomorrow night?"

"Sounds great. I'm going to stop and see Mom right after work, but I'll be over after that."

"See you tomorrow, love."

Lilly fell asleep smiling.

When Lilly left for work in the morning, she saw Mimi carting a big box out of Xavier's house. She took the box to her car, which was parked at the curb, and opened the hatchback door. Lilly pulled up alongside her.

"Good morning, Mimi. How are you doing?"

"I'm okay, I guess. I decided to start cleaning out Xavier's office. I'm just going to take this stuff back to my house in Cheyenne and go through it there. That way there's no pressure on me to do it on anyone's time frame but my own."

"Is the lawyer after you to get things cleaned out?" Lilly asked in a sympathetic voice.

"No. The lawyer wants the loose ends tied up as far as the business is concerned, but since I'm Xavier's beneficiary, I can take my time doing everything else. I'm going to put the house on the market as soon as possible, though, so that's why I need to clean it out."

"Well, good luck. Text me if you need any help."

"Thanks, Lilly. I might just take you up on that offer."

At lunchtime Lilly hurried to the bank. All the documents Angie had requested were in her safe deposit box, so she left with the originals. She handed them to Angie several minutes later and Angie promised to finish the necessary paperwork as soon as possible.

~

After work Lilly hurried over to Larkspur Manor. She wasn't surprised to find Bev in her darkened room, looking out the window.

"Hi, Mom."

Bev turned slightly to see who was standing there. She gave Lilly a blank look and turned back to the window. Lilly took her coat off and pulled a chair to sit near her mom.

"How was your day?" she asked.

Bev said nothing. Lilly willed herself to keep smiling, refusing to take it personally. She told Bev about her own day, about some of the customers who came in and what she had for lunch. Bev smiled in places, but otherwise was still and silent.

"How's Finley?" Lilly finally said. She had hesitated to bring up Finley because she so badly wanted her mother to talk about something besides him. In the end, though, she decided that hearing Bev talk about Finley was better than not hearing her talk at all.

"He's fine, thank you," Bev said primly.

"Has he been in here to sing?"

Bev shook her head. Lilly wondered if his depression was keeping him from singing.

Just then Greg appeared in the doorway. "Good evening, Bev," he said with a wide smile. "Hello, Lilly. Bev, I've brought your meds."

Bev looked up at him and held out her hand. Greg poured the pills from the white paper cup into her palm and handed her a plastic glass of water. Bev swallowed the pills and smiled at Greg.

"What's new, Bev?" he asked.

"Nothing. I was just watching the snow fall," she said.

Lilly wished she had been able to draw those few words from Bev, and she tried not to be jealous of Greg. She ground her teeth and pasted on a big smile like nothing was wrong. When

Greg left a few moments later, after engaging Bev in a short conversation about her dinner, Lilly could feel her face relax. She hated the feelings of sadness and jealousy and spite and anger that overwhelmed her every time she visited Bev now. She resented Bev for not recognizing her, yet being able to identify Greg, whom she had only recently met. She resented Greg for getting to spend more time with Bev than she did. She was angry with herself for not doing a good job of loving her mom through this experience the way she and Mirren had talked about.

Nothing was going right.

CHAPTER 60

She drove to Hassan's house and knocked once before letting herself inside.

"I'm in here!" Hassan called from the back of the house.

Whatever he was cooking smelled divine. Lilly put her coat and handbag on the bench in the foyer and went straight back to the kitchen. Hassan turned to her from where he stood over the stove, waving a wooden spoon and grinning.

"Hi, love. I'm making linguine Bolognese. I hope you're hungry."

"I'm starved. It smells delicious. What can I do?"

"Nothing. Everything's ready." He set the spoon down and took up two potholders. There was a large steaming pot of linguine next to him. He took the pot by the handles and poured the contents into a colander in the sink. He spooned linguine into two pasta bowls, then ladled the sauce over it. He carried the bowls into the dining room, telling Lilly to follow him.

"Come on. You sit and I'll get the garlic bread out of the oven."

"Garlic bread, too? You went all out! This is wonderful." Lilly breathed in the aroma of Bolognese sauce and sat down. Hassan placed the bowls on the table and hurried into the kitchen. A moment later he was back with garlic bread, already sliced and arranged on a wooden cutting board. He set it on the table.

He sat down next to Lilly and took her hand. "I couldn't wait to see you tonight."

"Wow. I feel like a princess."

"Before we eat, a toast." Hassan picked up his wine glass and Lilly picked up hers.

"Are these new?" she asked. She had never seen wine glasses like these—they shimmered and appeared to be made of mercury glass.

"Yes. I found them at an antique store and thought they were perfect." Hassan raised his glass. "To us."

"To us." Lilly clinked her glass against his and smiled at him. The glass was filled with red wine. She didn't like red wine because it often gave her a headache, but Hassan had been so nice to invite her over and cook dinner for her that she didn't want to say anything to spoil the atmosphere. She took a sip, then set it down and started eating.

"Don't you want more of the wine?" Hassan asked. "You must be thirsty."

"I'm fine."

"Have some more," he insisted.

"Okay." She took another sip and set the glass down.

"That was a baby sip if I ever saw one."

"I'm really not thirsty."

"I know red wine isn't your favorite, but I thought this might be okay for you. It has no added sulfites."

"Thank you." She took another sip as he watched. "Are you okay?" she asked.

"I'm fine." He took a bite of linguine and followed that with another large glug of wine. And another.

"Hassan, are you sure you're okay?"

"Of course. What makes you ask that?"

"I don't know. I'm getting a weird vibe tonight."

"You need to relax a little. You're imagining things. Have some more wine. I have a special dessert in the kitchen."

"It's like you're trying to get me drunk," Lilly said with a touch of annoyance.

"I'm not trying to get you drunk, love. I'm trying to get you to relax."

"All right. If you say so." Lilly took another sip of wine and continued eating.

"More garlic bread?" Hassan pointed to the cutting board.

"Sure. Thanks." She took another piece.

"It's pretty dry, if you ask me," Hassan said.

"I don't think so. I think it's delicious."

Hassan poured himself another glass of wine. "I'd offer you more, but you have to finish what you've got."

Lilly couldn't stand it any longer. "My God, Hassan. You're pushing this wine on me like you're a crack dealer. Fine. I'll drink the wine."

She raised the glass to her lips and in one long, unbecoming slurp, drank the wine that was left.

She had just enough time to register the hurt look on Hassan's face before she started coughing. She tried saying something, but couldn't get any words out. She couldn't get any air. She started to panic.

She made straining noises and let out one big cough. Something shot out of her mouth and onto the dining room floor. She still struggled to get air, and pointed to her throat.

Hassan watched the scene unfold with eyes bulging. Suddenly he leapt out of his chair and started pounding on her back. "Lilly! Breathe!" He pounded harder.

Something else shot out of her mouth and across the floor. With that, she slumped back in her chair and took a heaving breath.

"Are you all right?" Hassan said. He put his hands on her shoulders.

"I think so." Lilly's eyes widened. "I think I broke a tooth!" She spit something into her hand and let out a squeal when she saw it was green. "What the—"

Hassan had come around to face her. He knelt on the floor. He looked at the palm of her hand, where the object sat, covered with saliva, and took it from her.

"Lilly, this didn't go at all the way I had planned it."

"What are you talking about? What did you put in the wine? Are you trying to kill me?"

He laughed and took her hand in his. "No. I'm trying to ask you to marry me."

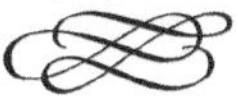

Lilly stared at him, barely comprehending what was happening. Her mouth hung open. "What?"

He squeezed her hands in his. "I'm trying to ask you to marry me," he repeated. "I had this great idea of putting three emeralds in your wine glass. When you got to the bottom, you were supposed to see them. I want you to choose the one you like best and I'll have it made into a proper engagement ring. You weren't meant to choke on the emeralds."

Lilly covered her mouth with one hand. "Then you're serious? You're proposing?"

He laughed. "I am. Are you going to leave me here kneeling all night?"

"No! Of course not! I mean, of course I won't leave you kneeling there all night! Yes! Of course I'll marry you!" She laughed. "I can't believe this!"

Hassan stood and pulled her to her feet, then kissed her. "I'm so happy, Lilly. I've been planning this surprise for a long time."

"And I ruined it by trying to swallow the emeralds. Oh, my gosh! The emeralds! Where are they? I can't believe I spat two jewels across the room!"

Hassan waved his hand dismissively. "We'll find them after dinner. They can't have gone far. Let's finish eating so I can bring out the dessert I made for you."

They sat down. Lilly could only stare at Hassan, and after several moments her tears started to fall.

"What's wrong?" Hassan asked in alarm.

"Nothing. Nothing at all. These are happy tears."

"As long as you're sure."

"I'm completely sure. I can't wait to tell the kids!"

"I've spoken to both of them and they've given us their blessing. I didn't want to ask you until I knew both kids were happy with the idea. The only thing they didn't know is when I was going to ask you officially."

"You're so wonderful to include them. Thank you."

"It'll be wonderful to be their stepdad. And speaking of children …"

"Vanessa's baby! You'll be a father!" Lilly hadn't even thought of the baby until Hassan mentioned children.

"Do you think she'll want me to adopt the baby, too?"

"Of course she will! She thinks the world of you. And how incredible that she's going to have a baby who will look just like the two of us. I can't believe how perfectly this is all working out."

"We have so much to talk about. A wedding date, where we're going to live, a honeymoon, the new baby, everything."

"I can hardly wait." Lilly picked up the emerald which Hassan had placed in front of her on the table. "I love the idea of choosing the stone for my engagement ring. Let's wait and have dessert after we find the two I spit out."

Hassan laughed. "All right." He turned around in his chair. "If I had to guess, I would say they flew right into the living room."

Lilly could feel her face flushing. "I will never live this down."

It took some time, but they found the two emeralds Lilly had choked on: one was under the sofa and another landed right next to a heat register. When she held the stones in her hand, she was mesmerized by their sparkling, deep green facets.

She knew immediately which one she wanted. "It's an emerald, so it has to be the one with the emerald cut. I love it."

"I had a feeling you would choose that one, but I wanted to give you the choice."

"It's just gorgeous. I can't wait to start wearing it."

"I'll have it made into a ring and you'll have it in no time."

They talked of wedding things until it was time for Lilly to go home. "I hate to leave," she said ruefully. "But I guess I have to get back to my house and reality."

Hassan grinned and cupped her chin in his hand. "Don't fret. Before long we'll be living in the same house and we'll see a lot more of each other."

"I can't wait."

When Lilly got home the girls were already in bed. Laurel had left a note on the kitchen counter saying she had let the dogs out at the regular time, but Lilly decided to let them out again before she went to bed,

She descended the back steps behind the dogs and stood in the backyard waiting for them, lost in her thoughts of something old, something new, something borrowed, and something blue. Presently Barney headed toward the fence along the side of the yard and Lilly could hear him snuffling noisily around on the ground. Whatever he was doing piqued Fred's interest, too, because he joined Barney. Lilly went after them, hoping they hadn't caught some kind of vermin.

But the object of their interest wasn't an animal—it was just a piece of paper. And as Lilly's eyes adjusted to the darkness, she noticed more paper. Lots of pieces of paper, all scrunched up under the bottom of the fence.

Seeing the papers brought her out of her wedding reverie. "Litter," she said in a disgusted voice.

She bent down and gathered all the pieces of paper she could see. There were dozens. "Come on, guys," she said to the dogs. They lost interest and scampered off to do their business once she had removed the papers.

She set the papers on the counter before going to bed. She didn't want to throw them away before checking them to make sure they didn't contain any sensitive information. She could shred them in the morning once she had taken a look at them.

CHAPTER 62

The next morning Lilly went downstairs to find Laurel and Vanessa already up and making breakfast.

"You guys are up early."

"I found a job opening yesterday at the college. The English department is looking for an administrative assistant. I texted Vanessa, she called them, and they want to interview her first thing this morning. Normally they're not at the school on weekends, but there's some kind of meeting this morning."

"That's great!" Lilly beamed.

"I hope I get the job," Vanessa said.

"So do I," said Lilly. "Actually, I have good news, too."

"What is it?" Laurel and Vanessa looked at Lilly expectantly. Laurel raised her eyebrows and Lilly wondered if her daughter had a hunch about what she was going to tell them.

"Hassan and I are getting married."

The girls let out whoops of joy and hugged Lilly fiercely.

"I knew it! I knew that's what you were going to say!" Laurel exclaimed. "I'm so happy! Did Hassan tell you he talked to me and Tighe about it?"

Lilly nodded, smiling. "He did tell me that. I was so thrilled to hear it."

"I just didn't know when he was going to ask you. I've been dying to tell you." Laurel grinned.

"Tell us everything. How did he ask you?" Vanessa wanted to know.

Lilly told them the story and Laurel and Vanessa laughed until the tears streamed from their eyes.

"Mom, only you would choke to death on the emeralds meant for your engagement ring. You're lucky to be alive. And you guys are lucky the one didn't roll right down into Hassan's furnace."

"But it'll be a great story to tell," Vanessa said.

"I don't know how many people need to hear what a nitwit I am," Lilly said. "I need to call Tighe, then Bill and Noley, before work. Good luck at your interview, Vanessa."

Tighe said he had been waiting for her call. "I'm really happy for you, Mom. Hassan is a great guy."

"I agree. It was wonderful of him to get your blessing before he asked me."

Next she called Bill and Noley. For the second time in recent memory, she asked Bill to put her on speakerphone so she could share her news with both of them at the same time. Like Laurel and Vanessa, they let out whoops of happiness.

Finally, something was going right.

The girls left and Lilly made a quick breakfast for herself. While she stood at the counter eating, she glanced through the papers she had found the night before.

There were copies of invoices, receipts, and some personal correspondence, but nothing to suggest whose papers they were. She had almost reached the bottom of the stack. She was gathering them up to put them in the shredder when she thumbed through the last two pieces of paper.

They were handwritten notes on lined paper that could have

been ripped out of any notebook. The handwriting was neat, but not elegant. The writer of the note could have been a man or a woman. Lilly's eyes widened as she read the words on the first paper.

Dear Dr. Gordon,

I know your secret. It would be a shame if your patients were to find out, so for $10,000 I'll keep it to myself.

For now.

Wire the money to the following account and don't bother trying to trace it:

There the letter ended, as the bottom of the paper had been torn off. There was no date on it. Lilly reread the letter, unable to believe her eyes. Someone had been blackmailing Xavier? This shed a whole new light on his murder.

But who had been blackmailing him, and why? What was the secret the letter writer knew? And why would it matter to Xavier's patients?

Lilly hastily read the last paper in the pile, letting out an involuntary gasp.

Dear Dr. Gordon,

Alas, $10,000 does not go very far these days. Another $10,000 ought to be enough.

For now.

In case you've forgotten, here's where to send it:

Like the first note, the bottom of this one had been torn off. Lilly picked up the phone and dialed Bill's number.

"Hi. What's up?" he asked in greeting.

"You are not going to believe what I found." Lilly proceeded to tell him about the papers that had found their way into her yard. She read the letters to him and he let out a low whistle.

"I'll need to come over and collect those," he said. "I can be there in twenty minutes. Don't tell me you touched them with your bare hands."

Lilly froze. "Yes, I did. I didn't have any reason to think they were important when I picked them up last night. And I was just leafing through them this morning."

"I'm sure your fingerprints will be on them, then. Can you come over to the station sometime today and give a statement and your fingerprints? That way there'll be some documentation about why your prints are all over a piece of evidence."

"I can come over during lunch."

"Okay, good. I'll be over in a little while." He hung up and Lilly gulped down the rest of her coffee. She also donned a pair of gloves and ran upstairs to her office with the blackmail letters in her hand. She had made photocopies of the letters and was ready to go by the time Bill got there. He pulled on blue latex gloves after he closed the kitchen door behind him. "All right. Let me see what you've got here."

Lilly pointed to the notes she had separated from the rest of the papers. Bill examined them quickly, then put them in evidence bags. He placed the rest of the papers in a separate bag. "I'll get all this to the officer in charge of the investigation as soon as I get to work. I'll see you at lunchtime. Before I go, I want to have a look around to see if there are any more papers on the ground."

CHAPTER 63

*L*illy's phone buzzed with a text almost immediately upon Bill's departure from her house. Lilly groaned when she saw who it was. Mimi.

I saw a cop at your house. Is everything ok?

Everything good, Lilly texted back. She hoped Mimi would drop the subject.

Her phone buzzed again. Was he looking for something?

Lilly decided to lie. I don't know.

As if Mimi's going to believe that. Good one, Lilly, she thought.

You don't know what a cop is doing at your house?

He's my brother. He was just looking around. Thought I heard someone in the yard last night.

Mimi texted back with a bug-eyed emoji, but didn't ask any more questions. Lilly heaved a sigh of relief when Bill came back into the house to tell her there were no more papers outside.

"I wonder how those papers got there," she said. "They had to have come from Xavier's house, right?"

"I assume so."

"In that case, Mimi must know something about them."

"I'm sure the officer in charge of Xavier's file will want to talk to her. I have to get going. See you later."

At lunchtime Lilly drove over to the police station to give a formal statement about finding the papers in her yard. She also submitted to fingerprinting so her prints could be accounted for when the papers were analyzed. As she was leaving the police station to go back to the shop, she caught a glimpse of Chelsea going into one of the rooms down the hallway where Lilly had written out her statement. She made a mental note to ask Bill what Chelsea was doing there.

About an hour after Lilly got back to work, she got a text from Laurel.

Where do we keep the ACE bandages?

Lilly gave a start, wondering who was hurt and how badly. Her fingers flew as she texted Laurel. What happened? Who's hurt?

Mimi. She fell down the front steps of Xavier's house. Vanessa and I saw her and we were able to help her back into the house. Her ankle is huge and purple. But Xavier's first aid stuff is all boxed up so I told Mimi I would get a bandage from our house.

Lilly heaved a sigh of relief that neither Laurel nor Vanessa was hurt. She told Laurel where to find the bandages and asked her to tell Mimi that she would stop by to check on her after work.

Thanks. Will do, Laurel replied.

Lilly had no sooner set the phone on the counter than Isabelle Montrose walked into the shop. She buzzed right past the engagement rings and walked up to Lilly.

"I have good news, Lilly," she said in her characteristically loud voice.

"What is that?"

"Can't you guess?"

"I'm assuming you've got a formal offer on Mom's house?" *Rats,* she thought. *I haven't even had time to talk to Mirren about it.*

"That's right." Isabelle blew on her fingernails and pretended to buff them on her jacket lapel. "And the potential buyer is willing to pay what you're asking."

"That's good."

"Is that all you can say? 'That's good'?" Isabelle cast her gaze around the store. Two customers came in, one right after the other, and one approached Harry. Lilly held up a finger to the other customer and faced Isabelle.

"It's great news, actually. Thanks for dropping in to tell me, Isabelle, though you didn't have to make a special trip. Is there anything else I can do for you?" Lilly wanted Isabelle to be on her way before she said something obnoxious, but Isabelle looked around conspiratorially.

"Can I talk to you? In private?"

"Um, sure. Can you give me a few minutes to help this woman?" Lilly nodded toward the customer waiting for her.

"Okay." Isabelle moved to the front door and stood there like a sentry.

Lilly turned to the woman, who wanted to see men's watches. She took photos of the ones she liked and left with a promise to return after she decided which one she wanted to buy for her husband. Lilly scowled at the woman's back as she walked out. She wouldn't be the first person to take a picture of what she wanted, then go home to find it for a lower price online.

Lilly beckoned Isabelle to follow her to the office in the back. She sat down at her desk and motioned for Isabelle to take the chair opposite her.

"What's up?" she asked.

Isabelle leaned closer, as if someone might be listening. "I think Xavier's ex-wife killed him."

Lilly didn't know what she had expected Isabelle to say, but that wasn't it. She sat back in her chair with eyes wide.

"What makes you think that?"

"Means, motive, opportunity." Isabelle jabbed her index finger toward Lilly with each word.

"How do you know?"

"Okay, means. It said in the paper that Xavier was stabbed. You don't have to watch a lot of tv to know that's an intimate way to kill someone. Lots of times it's a spouse or an ex-spouse that does such a thing."

Or a violent girlfriend, thought Lilly. *Or a crazy one.* She nodded, not saying anything.

"Well, obviously Mimi knew where the knives were kept." Isabelle said this like there was no possibility that anyone else could have known the knives were in the kitchen.

"I don't know, Isa—"

"Okay, motive. I think Mimi wanted Xavier back, and I think she killed him because if she couldn't have him, she wanted to make sure nobody else could, either."

"But—"

"Okay, opportunity. Mimi was in his house that night. She even *found* his body. Everyone knows that the person who finds the body is often the killer."

Lilly said nothing, waiting to be sure Isabelle was done talking.

Finally Isabelle raised her eyebrows and leaned her head forward. "Well?"

"Well what?"

"Do you agree?"

"I don't think so, no."

"So you think I'm wrong."

"I just don't believe Mimi killed him, that's all."

Isabelle gave an unbecoming snort. "You obviously don't know Mimi."

"Do *you* know Mimi?"

"Well, no, but I know *of* her. Xavier told me about her."

"I actually do know Mimi, and I spoke to her the night of

Xavier's death. She was beyond distraught. I can't imagine she was faking that emotion."

"She was probably sorry for what she had done."

"I just don't think she killed Xavier."

"What about the knife?"

"Everyone knows that knives are kept in kitchens. That's not something only Mimi could know."

"All right, I suppose you have a point. But it doesn't mean she didn't stab him."

"Plus," Lilly continued, "I don't think she was planning or intending or even hoping to get back together with Xavier. She told me they were good friends; better friends than spouses, in fact. What makes you so sure she wanted to get back together with him?"

"Who wouldn't? Look at him. He's a handsome doctor. Any woman would be foolish to give him up."

"It's an interesting theory, Isabelle, but I think Mimi is innocent. Call it a gut feeling." She stood up and hoped Isabelle would take the hint. "Is there anything else I can help you with?"

Isabelle rose reluctantly and shook her head. "I may go to the police with my theory. Maybe they need a jump start."

"Maybe, but I don't think so." Lilly had walked into the shop and Isabelle trailed behind her. She didn't want to discuss Xavier's murder where any customers could hear. She held the door open for Isabelle.

That night after work, Lilly stopped to see Bev before going to Xavier's house. As usual, Bev was staring out the window in her darkened room. Finley was there, holding her hand and looking out the window, too. Lilly sat down for a few minutes, but she could only stammer the occasional question or comment before she realized neither one of them cared whether she was there or not. They were lost in their own thoughts and did not speak to Lilly once. Dejected and sad, she left.

CHAPTER 64

At Xavier's house, Lilly knocked on the front door.

"Who's there?" Mimi called from inside.

"It's Lilly!"

"Hold on a sec!"

Lilly waited a full minute before she could see Mimi's form limping into view through the door's frosted glass. Mimi opened the door and smiled at Lilly. It looked more like a grimace.

"Thank you for coming over, Lilly. I'm sorry it took me so long to get to the door. My ankle is killing me."

Indeed, she was having trouble walking. Lilly helped her into the living room and propped her ankle on a small pile of throw pillows.

Do you have any pain reliever?"

"Yes, but I just took it an hour ago."

Lilly looked at Mimi's face. Mimi had obviously been crying —her face was red and puffy, her eyes tired-looking and bloodshot.

"Are you okay, Mimi?"

Mimi shook her head. "My ankle hurts, but I'm crying

because I miss Xavier." Her face crumpled and tears flowed afresh.

Lilly sat down in the uncomfortable acrylic chair near Mimi. "Of course you do. He was an important part of your life."

"I feel like I should get back to Cheyenne, but I just don't trust myself to drive that far alone. I'm afraid I would lose control and start sobbing and die in a car accident or something."

"Is there someone helping out at your flower shop?"

Mimi shook her head. "It's just me. I had a neighbor hang a temporary 'closed' sign on the front door, changed my voice-mail message to explain that I'm dealing with a family emergency, and changed my website to say the same thing."

"So you don't have to hurry back yet, right?"

"I have to go back eventually if I'm ever going to make a success of that shop."

"But this is more important, isn't it? Your ankle needs to heal before you go traveling, and it's totally normal, and okay, to be sad. It would be weird if you *weren't* sad."

"I know. It might be better for me to work, though. You know, to keep my mind off Xavier."

"Maybe, but you shouldn't expect too much of yourself at this point. Xavier's absence is still very raw for you."

Several stray tears slipped down Mimi's cheeks. "I just miss him. He said he would always take care of me. How many ex-wives can say that about their former husbands? I never thought he would be gone so soon." She used the damp tissue she was holding to blow her nose loudly.

"I didn't really know him, but he seemed like a very nice man," Lilly said. She didn't quite know what else to say.

"I appreciate you stopping by, Lilly. Don't feel like you need to look in on me. I don't want to be a burden on you."

Lilly waved her hand dismissively. "Oh, don't worry about

that. I'm happy to stop by. Do you need me to get you anything while I'm here?"

"No, thank you, though. I'll be fine. I'm just going to try to get some sleep."

"All right. But you really need to be icing that ankle, and I want to you to avoid walking as much as you can. I'll get you an ice pack before I go." She stood and turned toward the kitchen.

"Xavier doesn't have any ice packs."

"That's no big deal. We'll improvise."

"Really, Lilly, I'm fine."

"You need to ice that ankle."

"I don't want an ice pack."

"That's ridiculous."

"Lilly, no!"

Lilly was taken aback by Mimi's refusal to use an ice pack, but it was foolish of her to decline it, because there was nothing as good as ice for bringing swelling down. She ignored Mimi's plea and marched into the kitchen. There was a tea towel hanging from the oven door handle, so she grabbed that and opened the freezer. Mimi was right—there was no ice pack in there. But there was a bag of frozen peas, and that would do the trick nicely. Lilly wrapped the bag in the tea towel.

She was about to head back into the living room when she saw movement in the doorway.

"You should be lying down, Mimi. Look, I found a bag of frozen peas for your ankle. They're good because they're not a solid, hard mass of ice. They'll mold to the shape of your ankle."

"Fine. I think it's time for you to go, Lilly."

Lilly was a little hurt by Mimi's tone of voice. It wasn't very nice, especially considering Lilly didn't *have* to help her and was just trying to be a good neighbor. Besides, this woman was grieving. The last thing she needed was a sprained ankle.

"Okay. I'm leaving. I'm sorry to intrude. I just thought—"

"I know. I'm sorry, too. I just didn't want you to see what a mess it is in here." Mimi tried to smile.

"Don't worry about that." Lilly cast a glance around the kitchen, which was indeed quite messy. If she could just find a bottle of pain reliever, she would leave that in the living room for Mimi, too. The poor woman needed to rest that ankle. But there was no pain reliever in sight. Dishes were piled in the sink, a mortar and pestle sat on the counter, plastic bags littered the entire space, and boxes were piled haphazardly against one wall, waiting to be filled with kitchen supplies.

"If you need help packing up the kitchen, let me know. Don't be a hero and try to do it yourself," Lilly said as they returned to the living room.

"I won't." Mimi accepted the ice pack with a grateful look and Lilly let herself out the front door.

illy couldn't wait to get her shoes off and her pajamas on. Once she had changed and gotten comfortable, she joined Laurel and Vanessa for dinner. Before she could even take her first bite of food, Vanessa announced that she had gotten the job in the English department.

"That's wonderful!" Lilly cried. "When do you start?"

"At the beginning of the January term." Vanessa wore a broad smile. "They seemed concerned that I'm so pregnant, but I told them I'm giving the baby up for adoption. So I'll just need a few days off to recover from the birth and then I can get right back to work."

Lilly wondered what to say next, but Vanessa put her at ease.

"This is a good thing, Mrs. C. Don't worry about me."

Lilly gave Vanessa a warm smile. "I can't promise that I'm not going to worry about you, but if you say this is a good thing, it's a good thing."

Conversation turned to Vanessa's doctor appointment, scheduled for Monday.

"Mrs. C, maybe you should go with me, since you're going to be the baby's mother," Vanessa said.

Lilly's stomach did a funny little lurch. "Oh, I don't think your doctor will want me in the room, Vanessa. I trust him and you to make the right decisions about the baby."

"If you say so. But the invitation is open, just so you know."

Lilly smiled at Vanessa. She was thinking how hard it must be for Vanessa to go to doctor visits, knowing someone else would be raising the baby. "Thanks, honey. But I'll let you handle the appointments. Laurel can go with you if you'd like, if she's available."

Laurel nodded, her mouth full, then swallowed. "I can go with you if you'd like."

Vanessa smiled tremulously. "Yeah, I think I'd like that."

Which, of course, made Lilly feel like a heel. Should she have accepted Vanessa's invitation? She didn't know how adoption etiquette worked. Anyway, it was too late now. Laurel would tell her all about the appointment.

After dinner the three of them sat down to play a board game. The girls wanted to talk about the wedding while they played. Lilly worried that such talk might upset Vanessa, but as they chatted, Vanessa became more and more animated.

"Where do you think you'll have the ceremony?" she asked.

"Oh, gosh. I haven't even thought about it," Lilly said. "It would be nice to have it outdoors, I think."

"Then you'll have to wait for warm weather." Laurel picked up a game piece, then set it down again with a frown.

"You're right. I don't know that we should wait that long," Lilly said.

"Why not?"

"Because of the home inspections that have to take place before the adoption can proceed." Lilly glanced at Vanessa to gauge whether taking the conversation in this direction would be okay. Vanessa continued to look over her game pieces, but she nodded her agreement.

"I didn't even think of that," Laurel said.

"I would imagine there's a better chance of getting through the inspections quickly if there's a mother and a father in the household," Lilly said.

"I'm sure you're right." Vanessa tapped her finger on the table. "Your turn, Laur."

Laurel moved her game piece. "All right, so the wedding venue is in question. What are you going to wear, Mom?"

Lilly chuckled. "I haven't thought about that, either."

"What *have* you thought about?" Laurel asked.

"Nothing, really. Since this is my second wedding, I prefer something really low-key. But it's Hassan's first marriage, so he and I need to talk about what he wants. Maybe he'll want something big and fancy, though I doubt it. We'll have to talk to his parents, too. They might want some input."

"But they're not the ones getting married," Laurel said.

"I know, but I want to include them."

"You and Hassan should start making plans, Mom."

"We will. Don't worry."

But Lilly did start to worry. That night as she brushed her teeth, she could feel her heart start to beat a little faster. She knew the cause of it was her conversation with the girls about her wedding. *Maybe we should get married as soon as possible. Will that make it easier to adopt the baby?*

She brought it up to Hassan as soon as she called him to say goodnight.

"What do you think we should do?" she asked when she had explained the dilemma.

"I think we should make it official as soon as we can. If by getting married we increase our chances of being able to adopt Vanessa's baby as soon as he's born, let's do it yesterday."

Lilly hadn't realized she had been holding her breath. "So you're okay without a big wedding and all the trimmings?"

"Lil, all that stuff is just window dressing. The important thing is that we get married so that baby has two parents when he arrives. And frankly, the sooner I'm your husband, the happier I'll be."

Lilly almost burst into happy tears when she heard those words, but she managed to take a deep breath and remain calm. "Then what do you say we get to work on it?"

"Sounds good to me. I'll call the courthouse Monday morning and see about getting a license and scheduling the ceremony. "

"I can hardly believe this is happening," Lilly said.

"I can't, either."

Lilly fell asleep with a smile on her face.

CHAPTER 66

First thing the next morning, Lilly called Bill. "Do you know what Chelsea Fortune was doing at the police station yesterday?" she asked when he picked up his phone.

"Hello to you, too. Actually, I do know—"

"Why was she there?"

"If you'd let me talk, I'd tell you."

"Sorry."

"She was there to answer more questions about what she was doing at Xavier's house the night he was killed."

"And what did she say?"

"That, I can't tell you."

"Bill."

"It's strictly confidential, and besides, I don't even know what she said."

"Can you ask someone and then give me a hint?"

"Why do you need to know? The police are on top of this and frankly, we don't need your help."

"That hurts."

"But it's true. Just let us do our jobs. You'll see—we're quite capable of figuring out who killed Xavier."

"I didn't say you weren't. But I am in a position to potentially glean a lot of information because I'm the only friend Mimi seems to have around here."

"We're also capable of talking to Mimi."

"But you can't be sure she's telling you the truth. Don't you think she's more likely to tell *me* the truth? I'm far less threatening than a cop."

Lilly didn't have to see Bill's face to know he was rolling his eyes. "That depends on who you ask," he said.

"You're hilarious. Okay, if you won't tell me what Chelsea said, can you tell me what they found out from those papers in my yard?"

"Forensics still has the papers. It's not like a television show where you get all the answers overnight. It takes some time. Why do you need to know any of this information?"

"Are you dumb? Because he's my next-door neighbor, or at least he was. I'd like to know if a blackmailer killed him. If it was a blackmailer, there's less likely to be someone out there picking off the people on my street."

"Lil, if someone was doing that, Xavier wouldn't be the only dead one."

"Not if the killer is biding his time, waiting for his chance."

Bill sighed. "I have to get back to work. When I hear anything about the papers in your yard, I'll let you know. How does that sound?"

"Fine," Lilly grumbled. "I wish those blackmail letters had had a signature."

"You and me both."

Customers came into the shop in a steady stream on Monday. Lilly and Harry were run off their feet waiting on people. It wasn't until early afternoon that Lilly remembered Vanessa's OB/GYN appointment that day. Her stomach lurched and she stood still for a moment, waiting for the queasy feeling to pass. How was Vanessa doing? What was the doctor saying? Was everything normal? Was the baby growing and did he have all the parts he was supposed to have? Lilly's physical response to the thought of Vanessa's appointment stopped her in her tracks.

She was already scarily attached to this baby.

She couldn't bear it if anything happened to him. *My son. My youngest.* She smiled to herself. The overwhelming weight of responsibility and love for a baby she hadn't met yet forced Lilly to sit down hard on the stool behind the counter.

"You okay, boss?"

"Yeah. Thanks, Harry."

"Are you sure? You don't look too good." The grim line of Harry's mouth betrayed his concern for her.

She thought for a moment. "Can you keep a secret?" she asked him.

"Sure. What's wrong?"

"I'm planning to adopt Vanessa's baby."

Harry took a step backward, staring at her. "Wait. Are you serious?"

She laughed. "Yes."

He shook his head and started to laugh. "Wow! I have to tell Alice. She won't believe it. I'm so happy for you!"

"Thank you."

"So what's wrong? What made you sit down so fast with that look on your face?"

"I guess I was just overwhelmed all of a sudden, that's all. Vanessa has an appointment with her OB today, and I got thinking about how nervous I already am about it. It's like I'm having the appointment myself. And the adoption process has only just begun. I already feel like the baby is part of my family, and I don't want to think about what'll happen if I don't meet the requirements. Maybe I'm too old."

"Listen. Everything will work out. Of course you're not too old. What do the kids have to say about it?"

"Laurel is thrilled. I think Tighe's excited, but he's not as ebullient as Laurel."

"How about Hassan?"

"He's thrilled. And speaking of Hassan, I actually have another piece of news."

Harry's eyes widened. "More news? What is it?"

"Hassan and I are getting married." Lilly grinned broadly.

Harry let out a whoop. "I can't wait to tell Alice this, too! Congratulations! This is great news."

"Thank you. We're very excited."

"So am I. When's the big day?"

"We don't know yet."

"I'm so happy for you both. For the whole family."

"Thanks, Harry."

It was mid-afternoon when Vanessa texted Lilly to tell her everything had gone well at her doctor's appointment. Lilly heaved a long sigh of relief upon receiving the text. With all the issues going on in her life, she needed this one thing to proceed without any problems.

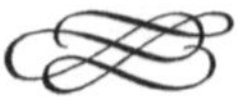

CHAPTER 67

It was late that night when Angie phoned Lilly.

"Hi, Angie." There was a feeling of dread in Lilly's chest. She wondered why her lawyer was calling so late.

"Hi, Lilly. Before you ask, nothing's wrong."

Lilly let out a half sigh of relief-half laugh and Angie continued. "I'm just calling to let you know I filed the first set of papers this morning. Now we just wait for the court to take action. I didn't realize you're unmarried. Is there a partner in the picture?"

"Actually, yes. And he just asked me to marry him."

"Congratulations!"

"Thank you."

"I'm happy for you, of course, but I'm also happy because that might make the paperwork go a little faster. When's the wedding?"

"We haven't decided."

"Well, it probably goes without saying, but the sooner the better as far as the adoption is concerned. Courts like to know that a baby or a child is being placed in a stable home. Of course single people adopt all the time, but it goes a bit more quickly if there are two parents."

"Okay. I'm sure we can speed up the process. Let me talk to Hassan and we'll see what we can do."

"All right. Let me know what happens and I'll amend the paperwork as necessary. And listen—because the holidays are coming up, we may not hear anything about the paperwork right away. I don't want you to get nervous if we don't hear anything. With that being said, though, you should know that it will be almost impossible for an adoption to be finalized at the time of the baby's birth."

"Oh." Lilly's heart sank.

"But the solution is relatively simple. You and your partner would apply to be foster parents of the baby. That would likely be decided very quickly, since the home inspection would probably be done by then and there's a lower threshold for foster parents than for adoptive parents."

"Okay. Thanks for letting me know, Angie."

She hung up with Angie and called Hassan. She told him what Angie had said.

"Everything's going to work out, Lil. I feel it. And if we have to be foster parents, that's okay. The baby would still live with us while the process sorts itself out."

Talking to Hassan, with his level-headed optimism, made Lilly feel much better.

"Did you talk to anyone at the courthouse today?" she asked.

"Sure did. We're getting married next Tuesday afternoon."

Lilly swallowed. She didn't know what to say. Everything was happening so fast.

"You okay, love? Is that all right?"

She let out a self-conscious laugh. "It's great. I can't believe we'll be married so soon."

"I'm over the moon."

"I am, too. I guess I'd better get to work, huh?"

"Get to work doing what?"

"I want to get a new dress, for one thing. And we'll need to invite a few people—the kids, Bill and Noley, your parents and sister, Mom, and Harry and Alice. And then we should probably take guests out to dinner, right?"

"I'll take care of inviting my side of the family. Should we do dinner at the Water Wheel after the ceremony?"

"Perfect. You call your mom and dad and sister, and I'll handle everything else. I love you."

"I love you, too."

CHAPTER 68

$\mathcal{A}$fter work the next day Lilly went to Larkspur Manor to see Bev. She found her sitting in the lobby with Finley and a few other residents.

"Hi, Mom," Lilly said. She wondered if it startled her mother when Lilly said "Mom," since Bev didn't recognize Lilly as a daughter anymore, but it was a hard habit to break. She sat down on the sofa next to Bev and took Bev's hand in hers.

"I have good news," Lilly said.

Bev looked at her with a question in her eyes. Lilly didn't know if the question was "What's your news?" or "Who are you and why are you holding my hand?" but she forged ahead.

"Hassan and I are getting married."

Bev looked at her blankly and Lilly wondered if Bev had understood what she had said. "Do you remember Hassan?"

Bev shook her head slightly.

"Well, never mind. But we'd like you to be there, and to come out to dinner with us afterward. Would you like that?"

"Can Finley come?"

Lilly didn't hesitate. "Sure." Of course Finley could be there if Bev would be more comfortable that way.

"Okay." Bev smiled. Lilly could almost hear a long-ago snatch of what Bev's laugh had sounded like and knew the old Bev would have been thrilled that her daughter was getting remarried.

And speaking of being remarried ... Lilly thought about Beau for the first time since Hassan had proposed. She wondered with an inward grimace if she should invite Beau and Nikki to the wedding. It was probably the right thing to do, since she and Hassan had been invited to his wedding to Nikki. Maybe they would decline the invitation.

When Lilly got home she and the girls got to work planning the tiny ceremony. Laurel pulled out the laptop and Lilly chose flowers that would make a beautiful bouquet. Laurel wrote them down so Lilly could order them from the florist. Lilly called to make a reservation at the Water Wheel, including Beau and Nikki just in case, and then all three of them made plans to meet the next day at lunchtime to help Lilly find a dress.

Noley called while they were discussing which bakery would be best to call for a last-minute wedding cake to serve at the Water Wheel.

"What's up?" Lilly asked.

"I thought you'd be interested to know that I had to talk to Chelsea today because I needed the login information for one of the accounts she created."

Lilly didn't say anything, assuming Noley had something important to say. She wouldn't have called just to chat about her login details.

"She apologized for not being upfront about her legal problems in Washington."

"And what did you say?"

"I said that I was sorry, too. I also told her I would give her a good recommendation to anyone who asked me for one."

Lilly didn't know if she agreed with that or not. It wasn't

important—she wasn't the one giving or asking for the recommendation.

Noley continued. "Then she started to talk about why she moved to Juniper Junction. I felt sorry for her. She said she wanted to start a new life, away from everything that had happened in Washington."

"I guess that rings a little hollow, since she came here to pursue the guy who had accused her of domestic violence in Washington."

"I know. I guess what I meant was, I feel sorry for the whole situation, not her specifically. I feel sorry that she can't get her act together."

"I would agree with that."

"She seemed eager to talk, which I thought was strange. She wanted to talk about Xavier."

Lilly's ears perked up. "What did she say?"

"She said that she enjoyed spending time with him. She tried not to mind that he went on dates with other women." Noley paused. "But here's the most interesting part: she said she went to Xavier's house the night he died because she was going to break up with him."

"Really? Did she say why she was breaking up with him?"

"She said their relationship had happened too fast. She decided she needed to learn to be comfortable with herself before she could be comfortable in a relationship."

"So did she actually break up with him that night?"

"She says she did, and that he was alive and well when she left."

"That's interesting. Do you believe her?"

"I don't know. Why would she talk to me out of the blue like that if she didn't want to unburden herself?"

"Did you know she was questioned at the police station yesterday?"

"No." Noley sounded surprised. "Bill didn't mention it."

"Apparently Chelsea is not off the hook for Xavier's murder, or they wouldn't have called her in for questioning. She may have figured if she talked to you and told you the same story she told the police, they might be more likely to believe her."

Noley exhaled loudly. "You're probably right. Now I don't know whether she's telling the truth or not. My problem is that I'm inclined to believe everything I'm told."

Lilly could hear Bill talking in the background. Lilly could hear Noley say "you should tell her." A moment later Bill came on the phone.

"I found out something today I thought you might want to hear."

CHAPTER 69

"Really? What is it?"

"Perez told me that when she talked to Chelsea yesterday, Chelsea mentioned visiting Phoebe Detweiler's herb store several times."

Lilly gasped. "Does Perez think *Chelsea* had something to do with Phoebe's murder?"

"I can't discuss that. I'm only telling you about this because it's technically public information. Anyone could have seen Chelsea walking into Phoebe's shop and simply told you about it. So it's not a big deal if you hear it from me instead. Just the same, don't go around telling people I'm the one who told you."

"I won't. Why did Chelsea visit the herb shop? Did she say?"

"Apparently Phoebe was concocting a love potion or something like that." Bill snickered.

"For Chelsea?"

"Yup."

"And what was Chelsea going to do with it? Do you take a love potion yourself or do you give it to the object of your affection and have them take it?"

"I have no idea and I didn't ask. I only know about it because

Perez was laughing about it and everyone was talking at the station."

"This is interesting. It means there's a possible connection between Phoebe's death and Xavier's death. Does Perez have any ideas?"

"If she does, she's not discussing them with me."

"Can you ask her?"

"Not without raising suspicions that I'm going to blab my information to you."

"Hey, speaking of Phoebe, do you know what happens to her shop now that she's gone?"

"No. You could probably figure that out for yourself by going to the county clerk's office."

"I could, but it would be faster and easier if you knew the answer."

"I don't. What do you think? Someone killed Phoebe so the killer could take over her lease or get her inventory? Seems far-fetched. Why would anyone do that?"

"It's just a thought."

"Not only that, but she just opened it, right? So she probably had a lot of time left on the lease when she died. Anyone who wants that shop would have to take over the lease."

"I suppose so. I do know that she didn't have any close living relatives, so she might not have left the contents of the store to anyone in her will. If there even was a will. Which leads me to another question. Who gets what's left of her estate?"

"You're asking the wrong person. Perez might know, but you're the last person she's going to tell. You could probably go to the courthouse and see if anyone has filed her will."

"I might do that, but I really don't have a lot of time on my hands to do Perez's job for her."

"Then I have an idea. Let Perez do her own job," Bill warned. "She does it well."

"Fine." Lilly huffed.

Noley got back on the phone a moment later.

"Any news on a wedding date?"

"Yes. We got caught up talking about Chelsea and I forgot to tell you. It's next Tuesday at two o'clock at the courthouse."

"What?!" Noley shouted. Lilly could hear Bill asking questions in the background. "Hold on a sec," Noley said to him. Then she spoke to Lilly again. "So soon? How can that even happen?"

"Hassan has made the arrangements. Next Tuesday was open and he doesn't have any particular dream of a fancy wedding, so we decided to go for it. And the sooner it happens, the better it is for the adoption process."

"That makes sense. I'll tell Bill to clear his calendar next Tuesday afternoon. Do you think your mom will be able to come?"

"She's coming, even though she doesn't know me or Hassan—"

"She doesn't know me or Bill, either," Noley cut in. Lilly was secretly relieved to hear it. She didn't know if she could bear it if Bev still recognized Bill and not Lilly.

"Well, it'll be good for her to get out and go to a fancy restaurant for dinner. We've made reservations at the Water Wheel."

"This is so exciting!"

CHAPTER 70

Isabelle called on Tuesday morning. "I wanted to let you know that the woman who wants to buy your mom's house is going to sign the contract this week. This is just a courtesy call."

Rats. Lilly had completely forgotten about the house with everything else going on. She needed to talk to Mirren.

"That's great, Isabelle. Thanks for the heads-up. Any particular reason you had to call at six-thirty to let me know?"

At lunchtime that afternoon, Lilly glanced at her watch and told Harry he could go to lunch. As soon as he returned, she asked him to mind the store while she met Laurel and Vanessa to go dress shopping. She met them at Ruby Red's, the nicest dress shop in town. Also the most expensive. The girls were standing out front of the store when Lilly joined them.

"Laurel, I can find a nice dress for less money somewhere else." Lilly was whispering, though there was no way Ruby could hear her.

"Mom, it's your *wedding*. You deserve to get a dress from the best shop in town. Come on, this is where we're shopping."

Laurel tugged on Lilly's arm and led the way into the beautiful little shop.

An hour later, Lilly emerged with a shopping bag. It contained a long, pale pink chiffon skirt, a crisp white silk blouse, and nude suede pumps. Laurel and Vanessa chattered excitedly about the jewelry she could borrow from the shop for the big day.

"A thick gold chain with a pink pendant of some kind would be perfect," Laurel said.

"And a matching bracelet," Vanessa added.

"I've got just the set." Lilly smiled, mentally going through her inventory. She had a gorgeous morganite necklace, earring, and bracelet set with round-cut morganite nestled in simple gold settings. It would match her outfit beautifully.

Before going back into her shop, she pulled out her phone and sent a text to Mirren. She had pondered how to broach the subject of Bev's house, and in the end she decided to just blurt it out.

Guess what? The house you're about to put an offer on is my mom's!

Mirren responded almost immediately. No way! I should explain. Can you meet me for dinner tonight?

Sure. How about the place just up the road from Larkspur Manor? I'd like to stop in and see Mom afterward.

Sounds good. 6:30?

See you then.

As soon as the jewelry had been placed in the vault overnight, Lilly drove the short distance to the restaurant just a quarter mile from Larkspur Manor. Mirren was waiting for her in the small, tasteful foyer.

"It was a nice surprise to get your text," Mirren said in greeting. "And by the way, I promise not to drink anything tonight." She winked and Lilly laughed.

They ordered dinner and Lilly leaned toward Mirren. "So

tell me. Why are you looking for a new house? Yours is gorgeous."

Mirren took a deep breath. "I'm leaving Basil."

Lilly nodded. "I had a feeling that would be your answer."

"I just can't leave my father and I have no intention of moving to Chicago. I don't even *like* Basil anymore."

"Well, I was worried that you might not want to buy the house once you found out Bill and I are selling it on Mom's behalf."

"Why would that bother me?"

"I—" Lilly shrugged. "I was just worried, that's all."

"Now that you and I are going to be stepsisters, I say let's keep the house in the family!"

Lilly looked at Mirren, bewildered. "What do you mean?"

Mirren inhaled sharply and covered her mouth with her hand. "You don't know?"

"Know what?"

"Your mom and my dad are getting married."

Lilly could only stare at Mirren, her mouth agape. "What? Are you sure?"

"Dad told me they're getting married. Bev was happy about it when I spoke to her."

Lilly shook her head. "I can't believe this. She hasn't said a word."

"I probably shouldn't have told you."

"No, no—I'm glad you did. Mom barely talks to me anymore. I'm a stranger to her."

Mirren frowned. "I'm sorry. I know how much that hurts."

Lilly nodded. Her mind was racing. When was this supposed wedding going to take place? Were they going to continue living in separate rooms? And Bill needed to know about this!

"You okay, Lilly?"

"Yes. I'm sorry. I'm trying to digest all this."

"I'm so happy for them."

"So am I." Lilly's face clouded. "I'm sorry it's coming at the same time you've decided to divorce Basil."

"I'm not sorry. It's time for us to go our separate ways. Him to Chicago, me to my new house. If you're going to sell it to me, that is."

"Of course we will. This is exciting, isn't it?"

Mirren grinned. "It sure is."

Lilly didn't visit her mom that night. The news of Bev's impending marriage had her reeling. She drove home lost in thought and called Bill as soon as she was inside. "Mirren told me Mom and Finley are getting married."

There was silence—what Lilly could only assume was shocked silence. Eventually Bill spoke. "You're kidding."

"I'm not kidding. I haven't talked to Mom or Finley about it, but Mirren obviously has."

"What did she say?"

"I've told you everything I know."

"I can't believe this. Should we say something?"

"Say something to whom?"

"Mom." Bill sounded like he couldn't believe how dumb Lilly was.

"And what are we going to say?"

"I don't know."

"All we can do is confirm it. They're adults—they're free to do whatever they want."

Bill sighed. "I guess you're right. What do we know about this Finley?"

"He worked in construction his whole life and he loves to sing. And he loves Mom."

"I guess that's all that really counts."

"I guess it is."

"Thanks for letting me know. I'll tell Noley. She's not going to believe it." Bill chuckled. "Who would have thought this would happen when we first moved her into Larkspur Manor?"

"Not me," Lilly said with a laugh.

"I'll talk to you later, Lil."

Lilly called Hassan before going to sleep that night. He was as incredulous as she and Bill had been. But he was happy for Bev, which made Lilly love him even more. As she drifted off to sleep, still lost in her own thoughts, there was something bothering her. She couldn't put her finger on it. She knew it had nothing to do with Bev and Finley's nuptials, but beyond that she was having a hard time grasping the thought. It was dancing around the periphery of her consciousness, just out of reach.

CHAPTER 71

*M*imi texted Lilly the next day. I hate to bother you, but could you stop over here tonight? I need some help with a couple things.

No problem. I'll be over after dinner, if that's ok.

Sounds good. Thanks.

Lilly stopped to see Bev before going home that night. She had promised herself not to say anything about Bev marrying Finley, but as soon as she saw Bev that promise flew right out the window.

"I hear you and Finley are getting married," she said when they were seated, as they had so often recently, in Bev's darkened room. They were watching the snow fall lightly outside.

Bev's smile lit up her whole face. "We are getting married, yes."

"I'm very happy for you," Lilly said. She touched Bev's hand and Bev didn't pull away. "Maybe I could come and see you get married?"

Bev glanced at Lilly out of the corner of her eye. "I suppose so."

"Thank you. I would like that."

Before leaving Larkspur Manor, Lilly stopped at the nurse's station to talk to Greg. "Did you know my mother and Finley are getting married?"

"Yes," he answered, smiling. "It happens more often than you'd think."

"When is the wedding? I would ask her, but I wasn't sure she'd remember the date."

"A judge is coming here to marry them Tuesday."

Lilly and her mother were getting married on the same day.

Lilly gasped and Greg gave her an odd look. "You knew about the wedding, right?"

"Not until yesterday. I've had a day to get used to the idea, and I'm happy for them. Will they move into another apartment?"

"I assume so. That's something the families will have to work out."

LILLY CHANGED her clothes after work, grabbed a quick dinner with the girls, and headed over to see Mimi. She hoped Mimi's ankle had improved.

Mimi opened the door just a few seconds after Lilly knocked.

"How's your ankle?" Lilly asked.

"Much better, thanks. That ice pack really helped. Come on in."

"Sorry I couldn't get here any earlier. What do you need help with?" Lilly asked.

"Just lifting a couple boxes in the living room."

"I'm happy to help."

Mimi turned off the porch light and locked the front door,

which Lilly thought was a little odd—but then again, there *had* been a murder in the house. Mimi led Lilly into the living room, limping slightly. Lilly was pleased to see how much her ankle had improved in just twenty-four hours. There were several boxes piled up against one wall and Mimi pointed to them. "Right there."

"Okay. Where do you want me to put them?"

"Just in the office."

Lilly hoisted the top box onto her hip and left the living room. She was passing the doorway to the kitchen on her way to the office when she realized what had been bothering her the previous night.

The mortar and pestle. On the counter in Xavier's kitchen.

And Mimi wasn't a cook—she had said so herself and Xavier had agreed.

The mortar and pestle were just like the ones that had been on the back counter in Phoebe's herbery. Lilly recalled seeing only the cash register on the counter the night Phoebe died.

Lilly knew with sudden certainty who had killed Phoebe.

She had to get back to the house immediately and call Bill. Or Perez. Or anyone else who could help.

Mimi was right behind her. Too close behind her, in fact. Lilly stumbled and the box fell on the floor.

"Something wrong, Lilly?" Mimi asked. Lilly turned to her and was startled to see her dark, glittering eyes.

"Um, no. I just remembered something, though. I left a pot of soup on the stove and I need to get back home before it catches fire."

Mimi reached for Lilly's arm, but Lilly yanked it out of her reach and sprinted for the door. She struggled for just a second with the lock, then flung the door open and tripped onto the porch. She clattered down the front steps as Mimi reached the front door.

"Lilly! Come back!"

Lilly didn't bother to turn around. An instant later, a bright beam of light illuminated Lilly and she could hear footsteps pounding irregularly the ground behind her. Mimi was surprisingly fast for someone with a sprained ankle.

"Lilly, come back here!" Mimi shouted. It was a command, not a suggestion. Lilly ran faster.

She had almost reached the gate to her backyard when something went whizzing past her head and smashed into the fence with a loud *thud*. The noise startled her enough to stop running for just a moment, but it was long enough for Mimi to come flying at her and tackle her to the ground.

"Mimi! Stop!" Lilly shouted. She could hear the dogs inside her own house, barking frantically. They must have heard the commotion outdoors.

"You saw, didn't you? I know you saw!" Mimi screeched. She landed a punch in Lilly's gut.

With the wind knocked out of her, Lilly could only wheeze feebly, hoping Mimi would get off and let her try to catch her breath. And Mimi did get up. As Lilly was struggling to her knees, though, Mimi reached out to grab the thing that had hit the fence.

It was the pestle. The one that had no doubt killed Phoebe.

A tsunami of fear coursed over Lilly, stunning her into paralysis, but it only lasted a second. She scrambled to her feet, still fighting for breath, as Mimi returned her attention to Lilly. She raised the pestle above her head and swung.

Lilly just managed to dodge out of the way, but she could feel the rush of air as the pestle almost grazed her cheek. Mimi hadn't let go of the weapon; she raised her fist again and swung.

As Lilly ducked and charged toward Mimi, the gate from Lilly's backyard flung open and two furry bodies flung themselves at Mimi's legs, causing her to slam onto the ground. Her hand went limp and the pestle fell onto the grass. The dogs set up a cacophony of barking and growling as Laurel and Vanessa came hurrying through the gate.

"Who's there?" shouted Laurel.

"It's me, Laur," Lilly squeaked.

"Mom! What happened? Are you all right?"

"I think so." Lilly stood up from where she had fallen to the grass, finally feeling the tightness in her chest starting to loosen. She took a shaky breath and limped over to where the pestle was lying on the ground next to Mimi's outstretched hand. She kicked the weapon out of Mimi's reach.

She looked down at Mimi, who was groaning. Her eyes were closed, but she was conscious. Barney had one of her arms in his mouth, closed just tightly enough so as not to break her skin—unless it became necessary.

"Laurel, I need you to dial 9-1-1, then call Uncle Bill. Tell him to get over here as fast as he can. Then I want you to go inside. Vanessa, you go with her. I don't want you staying out here. It's too dangerous."

Laurel whipped her phone out of her pocket and was talking to the dispatcher just a moment later. She explained what she needed in a calm voice that impressed Lilly. Then she hung up and called Bill. As soon as she started talking to him, she burst into tears trying to explain what had happened.

"Okay," she said, heaving a loud sob. She ended the call. "He'll be right over, Mom. Are you sure you're okay? Are you hurt? What happened?"

"I'll explain everything once we get Mimi squared away. Bill can take care of her as soon as he gets here."

"I'm staying with you until he gets here," Laurel said.

"Me, too," Vanessa said with a nod.

Mimi tried raising her head off the ground, but ended up letting it fall back onto the grass. Lilly, the girls, and Barney stood watch over her until they heard a car screech to a stop in front of their house. A door slammed and Bill's voice called out, "Lilly?"

As if he knew everything would be okay now that Bill had arrived, Fred sauntered over to Mimi's limp body, raised his leg, and piddled on her sprained ankle.

CHAPTER 72

*I*n the chaos that ensued, Bill told Lilly, Laurel, and Vanessa to go back to the house and to take the dogs with them, which they all declined to do. Two other officers arrived just a couple moments later, and they were soon followed by Officers Perez and Nutley. Lilly wondered how Nutley would ever be able to write down everything she was going to have to say.

Bill, who had been standing over Mimi to make sure she didn't try to get away, relinquished control of the scene to the newly arrived officers and while they placed Mimi under arrest for assaulting Lilly and waited for the ambulance, Bill, Perez, and Nutley accompanied all the women and the dogs back into the house.

Laurel prepared coffee while Perez and Nutley bombarded Lilly with questions about what had happened, what she saw at Xavier's house, and how well she knew Mimi. Bill stayed in the kitchen until the questioning was over, then he took a tray of coffee into the living room for everyone. He sat down and pulled out his phone, saying to Lilly, "Noley made me promise to tell her what was going on as soon as I could. I'm sure she's a mess by now."

Indeed, Lilly could hear Noley crying with relief when she heard Bill's voice and learned that everyone at Lilly's house was okay. Hearing that, Lilly started to cry, too. Laurel came over to put her arms around Lilly. Bill, who was sitting next to Lilly on the couch, took her hand in his.

"I'm okay," she sniffed. "It's just, you know, it's a shock when things like that happen and it takes me a little while to realize it."

Perez and Nutley stood up. "We'll be in touch, Mrs. Carlsen. Goodnight, Bill." Bill told them goodnight while Lilly sat on the sofa, staring straight ahead.

She took a sip of her coffee, then squinted. "Wait a minute. Why are they going to be in touch? They don't need to talk to me ever again now that they know Mimi killed Phoebe."

"But they don't know that. Mimi had the weapon, yes, but it was in Xavier's house. It's entirely possible Xavier killed Phoebe."

"I didn't think of that." She slumped back with a groan. "Why do they need to talk to me again, though?" She knew she sounded whiny, but she couldn't help it. And besides, she deserved to be a little whiny after all that had happened.

There was a knock at the back door. Bill went to answer it and came back into the living room with an EMT in tow.

"Lilly, he wants to check you out to make sure you're okay."

Lilly submitted to the man's brief examination while trying to tell him and Bill and the girls that she wasn't hurt, just stunned. Presently the EMT pronounced her fine, told her to get some rest, and left.

"I need to call Hassan," Lilly said. She glanced at her watch and was stunned to see that it wasn't even time for bed. It felt like the evening had lasted for weeks.

Bill left for home after making Lilly, Laurel, and Vanessa

promise they would stay inside for the rest of the night. They promised. Lilly couldn't remember the last time she had felt so tired. She had no intention of going anywhere.

She called Hassan and told him what had happened. He was shocked, as she had known he would be. He insisted on coming over to satisfy himself that she was all right, and was at the house just ten minutes later.

He hugged her as soon as he saw her, then held her away from himself while he looked her up and down. "Are you sure you're okay?"

"I'm sure. And you're sure you want to marry into this family?"

He laughed and Lilly smiled for the first time all evening.

"I'm sure."

The next morning Bill called at an obscene hour.

"I'm sorry if I woke you," he said.

"It's okay. What's up? Have you heard anything?"

Bill's voice was grim. "Mimi is pinning Phoebe's murder on Xavier. She admits the pestle was the murder weapon, but insists Xavier is the one who wielded it. She says she was in Lupine at the time of the murder."

Lilly frowned. "That makes it convenient for her, since Xavier is dead. Why would Xavier have killed Phoebe? What does Perez think?"

"Mimi didn't explain why Xavier killed Phoebe, and now we can't ask her again because she lawyered up. As for Perez, she obviously has more work to do."

"I trust it doesn't involve me?"

"Hopefully not. The first thing she has to do is confirm that the blood on the pestle is Phoebe's, and that will take some time. If it is Phoebe's blood, we know it's the murder weapon. But we obviously can't take Mimi's word for it that Xavier killed Phoebe."

"Where is Mimi right now?"

"They kept her overnight at the station. She'll be arraigned on an assault charge first thing this morning."

"What do you think will happen?"

"She'll plead not guilty. She'll probably be released on bail because she's not considered a flight risk, believe it or not. She's also being charged with simple assault."

"Can't she just stay in jail?"

"Unfortunately, no. But don't worry. If she's released, we'll be keeping a close eye on her pending trial."

"I hope so."

"Be vigilant and keep the doors locked."

"Trust me, I will."

Lilly was at the shop early that morning, since she couldn't go back to sleep after talking to Bill. She was working on some sketches when Mirren called her cell.

"I hope I'm not calling too early," she said.

"Not at all. I'm at work already."

"I just wanted to let you know that I dropped off the contract with your realtor this morning. It's really happening! I'm so happy."

"Me, too. I'll let you know when I've heard from Isabelle."

By mid-morning she hadn't heard from Isabelle. She kept looking at her watch, wondering when Isabelle would call. The shop was empty of customers and Lilly was cleaning the glass tops of the display cases when Harry interrupted her.

"Don't look now, but there's a creep in the window," he said, inclining his head toward the front window.

Lilly shifted her gaze to try to look unobtrusively out the window, but gave a start when she realized it was Mimi. She was skulking slowly past the store, an ugly glare in her eyes.

"Creepy, huh?" asked Harry.

"More than that, I'm afraid." Lilly hadn't taken her eyes off Mimi.

"What do you mean?"

"She assaulted me last night. She was arrested, but Bill told me she'd probably be free on bail today. I guess he was right. He also said they'd be keeping a close eye on her. I guess he was wrong."

"She assaulted you?" Harry's voice went up half an octave. "Were you hurt? Are you okay? What are you doing here?"

Mimi was now standing still outside the window, her eyes locked on Lilly's.

"She threw something at me. I'm fine, and I'm here because there was no reason for me to stay home today."

"She looks familiar. But I can't think where I've met her," Harry said. By now Mimi was walking away without another glance at Lilly.

"She's the ex-wife of my next-door neighbor, the one who was killed," Lilly said. "I'm sure she's mad because she had to spend last night in the clink."

"What happened, exactly?"

Lilly told Harry the story, ending with "Until last night, I thought she and I were friends."

"With friends like that, who needs enemies?"

Lilly chuckled, hoping the image of Mimi staring at her through the window of the jewelry shop would soon fade.

CHAPTER 73

After she returned from lunch, Lilly got the phone call she had been waiting for.

"I received the contract from Mirren Balfour this morning, Lilly," Isabelle said. Her voice sounded nasal and stuffy. "She wants to move in as soon as possible."

"Are you sick?" Lilly asked.

"No, I'm okay. Sorry I didn't call you earlier. Your friend said she would call you and tell you the good news. What do you think?"

"I think it's great. Bill and I will happily sell the house to her."

Isabelle sniffed loudly. "Okay. I'll put everything in motion. I'll be in touch when I have a list of dates for you. You know, for inspections and stuff like that."

"Okay. Are you sure you're okay, Isabelle?"

"Yeah. I'm okay." Isabelle ended the call.

Lilly stared at the phone in her hand for a moment before setting it down. A familiar feeling of guilt rose in her chest as she thought about Isabelle, probably sitting at home without anyone to talk to. The poor woman needed friends. Lilly would call her again tomorrow and invite her to lunch or coffee or something.

Lilly texted Bill to tell him the good news.

HASSAN JOINED Lilly and the girls for dinner that evening. Laurel and Vanessa offered to do the dishes while Hassan and Lilly retired to the living room. They had things to discuss.

Like putting another house on the market.

It wasn't urgent, but they would need to put at least one of their houses on the market. Before they could do that, they had to decide where they wanted to live once they were married.

"We can either live in my house or live in your house or sell both houses and move into a new one," Hassan said, leaning back against the sofa. He put his arm around Lilly's shoulders.

"Do you really want to go through the hassle of selling two houses and moving everything we have into a new house?" Lilly asked. Just the thought of that amount of aggravation threatened to give her hives.

"I really don't. I just thought I'd put it out there as an option. But it sounds like we agree on that. So now we just have to choose which house to keep."

After much discussion of home prices, locations, and the baby on the way, they decided to make their home together at Lilly's house. Hassan was thrilled because he had made so many wonderful memories at her house, and Lilly was thrilled because she didn't want to move into a house with a pool as long as there was going to be a little one to worry about. And while they were at it, they decided to wait to take a honeymoon. Lilly couldn't close the shop for more than a day or two on short notice, and there was too much to do with the baby coming.

It was after midnight when the phone rang. Lilly fumbled for it in a haze of sleep, then punched several places on the screen before landing on the "talk" button.

"Hello?" she mumbled.

"Lilly? It's Harry. I'm sorry to call so late, but I couldn't sleep."

Lilly sat up in bed. "Harry? Are you okay? Is Alice okay?"

"We're fine. But I was thinking and I realized something and I had to call you."

"What is it?"

"I figured out where I know that woman from. The one who was staring at you through the shop window today."

CHAPTER 74

*L*illy's pulse quickened. "Mimi? Where do you know her from?"

"She was the one looking in the window of the herb shop the night Phoebe was murdered."

"Are you sure?"

"I'm positive."

"If she was looking in Phoebe's shop window just before the murder, then that means she was lying about being in Lupine at that time. Harry, I'm going to call Bill. I'm sure Officer Perez is going to want to talk to you."

"That's fine. I expected it. Do you want me to call the station?"

"No, that's okay. I'll call Bill directly and he can probably get Perez on this faster."

"Are you going to call him now?"

"I'll text him first to see if he's up. If he is, I'll call him. If not, I'll wait until early in the morning. Thanks for calling me to let me know."

"No problem. I'm glad I realized who she is. See you in the morning, Lilly."

Lilly texted Bill, but after fifteen minutes hadn't received a reply. She would call him first thing in the morning. It took her a while to fall asleep. Her mind swirled with scenarios in which Mimi or Xavier killed Phoebe. If what Harry said was true, that Mimi was in Juniper Junction around the time of Phoebe's murder, was it possible she helped Xavier? Was it possible she committed the murder herself, instead of Xavier?

But why would either of them have a reason to kill Phoebe?

Lilly called Bill as soon as she awoke the next morning and told him about the call from Harry. Bill let out a low whistle. "I'll text Perez right now. She's going to want to talk to Harry. Will he be at your shop today?"

"Yes."

"Perez will probably stop in this morning to talk to him."

"Thanks, Bill." Lilly dithered for a moment about telling Bill that Mimi had walked by the shop the day before, but decided against it. She wasn't a sissy, for heaven's sake.

To Lilly's surprise, Perez was waiting at the back door of the shop when she arrived for work. The officer looked somehow more pleasant without her sidekick, Nutley.

"Good morning, Officer Perez," she said, alighting from the car.

"Good morning. I talked to your brother earlier and he said your employee had some information for me about the night of Phoebe Detweiler's murder."

"He does. He called me late last night to tell me he realized who it was looking into the window of Phoebe's shop the night she was murdered."

"And it was...?"

"Mimi Gordon."

Perez nodded. "When does Harry get in?"

Lilly glanced at her watch. "Any minute. You're welcome to wait inside the store if you'd like." She was feeling particularly generous now that it seemed less likely Perez would accuse her of committing murder.

"Thanks." Perez followed Lilly into the back of the shop and sat down in the chair Lilly indicated with a wave of her hand.

Lilly went through to the front of the shop to turn on the lights and Harry had arrived by the time she returned to the office. Perez had vacated her chair and Harry sat there instead. Lilly ducked quickly back into the shop to give them privacy to discuss what Harry had seen. She sat down on a stool and put her elbow on the counter, her hand in her chin.

Suppose Mimi had killed Phoebe. What reason could she have had to want Phoebe dead? Was it possible that Xavier had actually dated Phoebe? Maybe they had dated long ago, and that's why Phoebe was surprised to see him at Thanksgiving. Maybe Mimi was incensed at the idea of Phoebe and Xavier together. But no, thought Lilly, Mimi really did seem to enjoy being good friends with Xavier instead of being his wife. They had agreed their divorce was not a bitter one, so there was no reason to think she would carry around a deep-seated rage that could have propelled her to kill Phoebe.

There was something here that Lilly wasn't seeing. The police were obviously not seeing it, either, because no one was in custody for killing either Phoebe or Xavier.

And that was another thing ... could Mimi have killed Xavier? Lilly had been opposed to taking that train of thought because she couldn't reconcile the Normal Mimi she knew with the Scary Mimi she had glimpsed when Mimi threw the pestle at her. Now, she wasn't so sure. She had seen the look in Mimi's eyes and realized there was definitely the capacity to commit violence, as she later became all too aware.

But why would Mimi have killed Xavier? Perhaps for the reason Isabelle had put forth: if she couldn't have him, no one could have him. But again, Lilly was firmly convinced that Mimi was perfectly happy being the ex-wife.

CHAPTER 75

*L*illy's wedding was only two days away. So was Bev's. Lilly and Mirren had arranged for Bev and Finley to be married by the same judge as Lilly and Hassan, and since they were going to be at the courthouse for Lilly's wedding, it was decided that they would get married at the same time, too.

Laurel and Vanessa had found dresses to wear to the ceremony. Tighe had promised to come home from school for the occasion, and, at Lilly's request, did not plan to bring Sally Anne with him. As much as Lilly liked Sally Anne, she didn't feel the young woman belonged at the wedding, since it was only for family. Tighe had explained it to Sally Anne, and she had accepted Lilly and Hassan's decision with grace.

Vanessa was another matter, of course. While she wasn't technically family, she was giving birth to the boy who would become Lilly and Hassan's son, so there was never any question of her attendance.

Beau and Nikki had declined, saying they had other plans. Lilly thought it was probably a fib, but she didn't mind. The two places she had reserved for them at The Water Wheel were now being taken by Mirren and her sister, who would be there to watch their father marry Bev.

Lilly, Hassan, and Laurel spent hours on Sunday clearing space in Lilly's large closet for Hassan's things. They also made a couple trips to Hassan's house to take small items of furniture and décor back to Lilly's house. The couple had decided to keep much of Hassan's furniture, since it was in nicer condition, and to sell Lilly's stuff. Vanessa's job, because she was just a little over a month away from giving birth, was to avoid exerting herself. She was putting Lilly's furniture up for sale online.

That afternoon, Isabelle called Lilly.

"Hi, Isabelle. What's up?"

"I just called to see if you're available this evening to meet me at your mother's house to go over a few issues for the inspection."

"Actually, tonight's not a good time, Isabelle. Hassan and I are getting married on Tuesday and we're all pretty busy. Can we meet next week?"

"Well, I thought you wanted to get this done sooner rather than later. Here I am offering to work on a Saturday night and you're not even willing to meet me halfway."

Lilly's hand clenched the phone a little more tightly as she counted to ten. "I really appreciate your willingness to work tonight, Isabelle, but I'm afraid I just can't spare the time right now. I can meet you as early as Wednesday if you'd like."

"The inspection is first thing Monday, Lilly. There are some things we need to discuss. Now, either I cancel the inspection and there's no telling when the guy will be able to get to it, or you just meet me for a few minutes to go over the last-minute stuff in the house."

Lilly's patience was nearing the breaking point. She spoke a little more harshly than she had meant to. "Fine. I'll be there in fifteen minutes. She smashed the "end call" button with her finger, letting out an exasperated "Ugh!"

"What's wrong, Mom?"

"It's that woman! She is going to drive me right around the bend."

"The realtor?" Laurel asked.

"Yes. She's insisting that I meet her at Gran's house to go over some things that the inspector is going to look at on Monday. I don't know what I can possibly do this weekend if there's anything that needs fixing. I certainly can't do it myself because I have no idea what I'm doing, and I'm fairly sure Bill is working the next two days, so he can't help."

"I can go with you," Hassan offered.

His kindness took the wind out of Lilly's indignant sails and she smiled at him. "That's okay. You and the girls can keep doing what you're doing."

"Yes, ma'am." He saluted her with a grin.

"I'll be back in a little bit." Lilly stood up from where she had been sorting through ancient household documents. "Vanessa, if you want to give your eyes a break from the computer screen, you can start scanning these papers. Once you've scanned them, they can be shredded."

Vanessa grinned and said she would get right to it.

Lilly left with instructions for them to call the Juniper Junction Diner with their dinner orders and she would pick up the food after she met with Isabelle.

When she arrived at Bev's house, Isabelle wasn't there yet. Lilly let herself into the house with her set of keys and turned on the living room lights to wait. She was fidgety, so she sat cross-legged on the floor in front of one of the built-in bookcases next to Bev's fireplace and started pulling out books and objects Bev had displayed there. She stacked the books next to her and ran her fingers over the spines. Some of those books were decades old—Lilly could remember reading them as a teenager.

She would have to get a box and take the books home with

her after her meeting with Isabelle. She didn't want them littering the floor when Mirren and the home inspector were there.

The front door handle rattled and Isabelle blew in with a gust of icy wind.

CHAPTER 76

"Wow! It's cold out there!" she said in her unnaturally loud voice. Lilly cringed inwardly at the sound of it.

"Going through some of Bev's stuff?" Isabelle nodded to the pile of books at Lilly's feet. She looked ridiculous, Lilly thought, in an array of outerwear in every color of the rainbow.

"Yes. I'll put this stuff in a box and take it home with me tonight."

"Let's get started, shall we?" Isabelle said. "The first thing you need to see is in one of the bathrooms upstairs. The one in your mom's bedroom."

Lilly followed Isabelle up the stairs and into Bev's en suite bathroom. There was a hole in the drywall near the toilet. "What's this all about?" Isabelle asked.

"I don't know. I haven't been in this bathroom in a long time. I suspect Mom might have fallen against the wall in here before she was confined to the downstairs."

"Well, it'll have to be fixed. Obviously."

"Yes. Obviously." Lilly rolled her eyes. Had this really

required her presence at Bev's house? "Is there anything else I need to see before I go home?"

"Follow me."

Isabelle led the way into the guest room next to Bev's room. She pointed an accusing hot-pink-gloved finger at a broken pane of glass in the window overlooking the street. "This'll have to be fixed, too."

"Have you written these things down somewhere? I could just look at the list and get someone over here to fix everything."

"I always have the homeowner accompany me on a look-around before the inspection. That way the owner knows what blatant things need to be fixed."

"All right. What else is there?"

In the other upstairs bathroom, there was a loose floor tile. "You don't want the inspector or Mirren tripping on this," Isabelle scolded. "They could sue you and own this house without paying you a dime."

"Okay. What's next?"

Isabelle then proceeded to tell Lilly every little thing that she had found wrong with the house, from the poor water pressure in the kitchen sink right down to the calk that was peeling from around the back door. Lilly was finding it harder and harder to suppress her annoyance at this exercise. A written list of issues would have been sufficient for Lilly to get everything repaired.

"Isabelle, if that's all, I really need to get going. I have a thousand things to accomplish."

"Yes, yes, I'm well aware you have a wedding to plan, Lilly. You don't need to keep mentioning it."

Lilly was taken aback, unaware that she had mentioned it after her phone call with Isabelle earlier. She felt her cheeks bloom with embarrassment. She hadn't meant to make Isabelle feel bad.

"I'm sorry, Isabelle. That wasn't my intention. Is there anything else you think I should see?"

"Yes. It's in the basement. Come on." She beckoned and Lilly followed. She had hated the basement since she was a child. She found the dank, dark place terrifying, though she wasn't about to share that information with Isabelle.

Isabelle clicked on the light switch at the top of the stairs. Descending the steps with her hand on the rough-hewn banister, Lilly suppressed a shudder. She was grateful Isabelle was in the lead. She would gladly let the realtor handle any overgrown cobwebs or, worse, their inhabitants, before Lilly reached the bottom of the stairs.

At the bottom of the stairs, Isabelle turned to the right. There was an old ping-pong table in the dark corner, and the washer and dryer were back there, too. There were stacks of deck chairs and watering cans and boxes, old tools and a big trunk. Taken together, Lilly thought they looked like a great hulking demon waiting to pounce on her.

Isabelle moved forward toward the back wall, where the light barely reached. "Do you have a flashlight?" she asked. "I left my phone in the car."

Lilly fished her cell phone out of her pocket, clicked on the flashlight icon, and handed it to Isabelle. Isabelle swung the beam of light into the corner. "See that? It's a giant puddle. It's coming from somewhere, and you'd better hope it's an easy fix. The whole deal could collapse because of this."

"And you didn't think I needed to know about it until the Friday night before the home inspection?" Lilly frowned, her hands on her hips.

"I just found it myself earlier today."

"All right. I'll see about getting it fixed as soon as possible."

Isabelle turned to her, shining the light in Lilly's eyes.

"Isabelle, could you aim that somewhere else?"

"Oh, sorry. Sure." Isabelle clicked off the flashlight and slipped Lilly's phone into her pocket.

"That's my phone, Isabelle."

"I know. I want to talk to you about something."

Lilly felt a prickle race up her arms. "What do you want to talk about?"

"Xavier."

"What about him?"

"Why are you so interested in finding out who killed him?"

"Because he lived next door to me and if there's a lunatic running around loose in my neighborhood, I'd like to know about it."

Lilly took a tiny step backward in the direction of the staircase leading to the kitchen, hoping Isabelle wouldn't notice. Her palms were sweaty and she had the distinct feeling something was very wrong.

"Stay where you are, Lilly."

"Isabelle, what is wrong with you? You're making me uncomfortable and I'm leaving right now. And I will not hesitate to tell the police you stole my phone if you don't give it back to me."

With a speed Lilly wouldn't have thought possible, Isabelle leapt around Lilly, blocking her access to the cellar stairs. Lilly didn't want to take her eyes off Isabelle, but she let her gaze rove the basement for just an instant in search of something she could use as a weapon.

But Isabelle was more agile than Lilly had realized. The moment Lilly's gaze dropped away from Isabelle, Isabelle lunged forward and pushed Lilly onto the concrete floor.

The last thing Lilly heard before everything went black was the sound of Isabelle clattering up the stairs.

CHAPTER 77

$\mathcal{L}$illy lay face-down on the cold, damp floor. The earthy odor of mildew assaulted her nose as she opened her eyes, trying to focus on the objects nearby. Her head throbbed and she tasted blood. She couldn't remember where she was. She closed her eyes tightly, but that hurt too much. She felt them fluttering open again. As best she could without moving the rest of her body, which was stiff and sore, she groped around the floor for her phone. There was something about her phone...

It was the thought of her phone that provided Lilly with a glimmer of recollection. She had been at her mother's house, looking for problems that could crop up during the home inspection. Isabelle had been there, too, and for some reason she remembered Isabelle refusing to give Lilly her phone.

She closed her eyes, wishing she could go to sleep. Certainly rest would make her feel better. But as she lay there, images crowded inside her head. Isabelle had pushed her. She was sure of that. And Isabelle had left her here in this basement.

She was in the basement. Lilly let out a whimper of fear and pain. She needed to get out of there. Why had Isabelle done such a thing? She couldn't understand it. Then she remembered their odd conversation about Xavier and how ticked off Isabelle had seemed that Lilly was getting married soon.

Getting married! Where was Hassan? How long had she been in the basement? Long enough for him and the girls to start to worry about her?

Dragging herself forward, Lilly inched toward the bottom of the stairs. She ran her tongue over her lips, tasting blood. She must have split her lip when she fell. One slow step at a time, Lilly managed to get up the stairs until she came to the door to the kitchen. She reached for the light switch and flicked it, but the basement remained drowned in darkness.

She leaned her head against the door to catch her breath, then extended her hand to scrabble for the doorknob.

It was locked.

She was trapped in her mother's basement with no light and no phone. She rested her head on her knees and cried quiet tears of frustration.

After several minutes, though, frustration gave way to a slow burn of anger. Isabelle was responsible for this and she wasn't about to get away with it. Lilly knew it was only a matter of time before Hassan and the girls would come looking for her, and even if they didn't check Bev's house for some reason, the home inspector and Mirren would be going through the house Monday morning.

Monday morning?! Lilly couldn't wait that long.

By this time, her eyes had adjusted to the inky blackness of the basement and she could see the faintest light coming through the high windows. She figured it must be coming from a streetlamp. Her head pounding in protest, she gingerly made her way back down the stairs and stood under the window, trying to figure out how to open it.

The ping-pong table. She could drag that under the window and step on it to get out. She turned around and held her hands out in front of her as she walked in the direction of the ping-pong table. She rammed into it with a *thwack* as her thigh grazed the side of it.

Walking backward, she pulled the table to the wall underneath the closest window. She clambered cautiously onto the tabletop and felt the window for a clasp to unlock it. It took her only a few seconds to realize the window did not have a clasp. There must have been another way to open it, but Lilly wasn't about to waste a lot of time trying to figure it out.

She slid off the table and fumbled around until her hand closed around a broom handle. She took the broom back to the table and climbed up again. Without hesitation, she bashed the broom handle through the pane of glass in the window. *Another item on the list of things to fix*, she thought wryly.

A chill wind blew through the broken window and Lilly shivered with cold. And maybe a little bit of fear, too. She used the broom to smash off the remaining pieces of glass in the window frame and reached up, with the idea that she would hoist herself up to the window and crawl outside onto the ground.

After a few unsteady jumps, Lilly knew without doubt she would need something else to stand on to give her a boost. She got down and groped around again for something to stack on top of the ping-pong table. She tried dragging over the trunk she had seen earlier, but it was too heavy. Eventually she found two boxes of books that would likely stand up to her weight. She pushed them over to the table, hefted them up, and then climbed up again. She was panting by the time she got the two boxes stacked, but, she realized, at least she didn't feel as cold anymore. She climbed up the boxes carefully, then finally smiled as she poked her head out the window.

There was still quite a lot of glass in the frame, but she didn't want to cut up her hands trying to brush it away. Better to go through the window and let her clothing absorb the razor-sharp shards of glass, she thought.

Her body was half in the basement, half on the ground outside, when she saw the red and blue flashing lights. The police. Thank God.

She dragged herself fully onto the ground outside the basement window and lay on her back in the snow for a moment to catch her breath when she heard someone shout, "Don't move!"

CHAPTER 78

"Hands where I can see them!"

You have got to be kidding me, thought Lilly. She held her hands above her head. One officer ran over to her and clapped handcuffs on her wrists.

"You don't understand—" she began.

"Oh, I understand perfectly. Thought you'd free all the valuables from this house when the owners aren't home, huh?" The officer took Lilly's elbow and drew her to her feet.

"No, that's not it at all. Please, a woman locked me in here. Isabelle Montrose. She's a realtor and she's selling this house for me and my brother. It's our mother's house."

"Right."

"No, really. Bill Merriweather is my brother. Call him and check."

The officer hesitated for an instant, but he recovered quickly. "All right, I'll just do that." He called another officer over and asked her to stand guard over Lilly while he walked to the front yard to call Bill.

Moments later he returned. "She's telling the truth," he told the other officer. "Merriweather's on his way over." He turned to Lilly. "What the hell were you doing?"

"The realtor pushed me down and locked me in the basement. I have no idea why. She's responsible. She's the one you're looking for." Lilly paused. "What time is it?"

The officer looked at his watch. "A little after nine."

"Sunday night?"

The officer gave her an odd look. "Yes. Sunday night. I think we should call an ambulance. How long have you been here?"

"Just a few hours. I didn't know how long I was unconscious. Isabelle took my phone, so I couldn't call for help."

"You're lucky the next-door neighbor heard the sound of breaking glass and called us to tell us the owner isn't inside."

The other officer brought Lilly a blanket and she wrapped herself in it, shivering. "Can we go in the house?" Lilly asked. "I have the key in my pocket." She produced the key and led the way into the house.

It wasn't long before Bill pulled to a screeching halt by the curb. Lilly was seated by the living room window and she could see him dashing up the front walk, followed closely by Officer Perez. He crashed into the house. "Lilly?" he called.

"I'm in here."

The officers who had responded to the burglary call stood to greet Bill. He acknowledged them with a nod and covered the distance to Lilly's chair in two steps. "Are you all right? What happened?"

"I'll tell you everything, but you have to look for Isabelle. She did this. There's something really wrong with her."

Bill turned to the officers and instructed them to locate Isabelle Montrose. "Perez, you stay here with me for now." She nodded and stood behind Lilly's chair as the other officers left.

"Tell me everything," Bill directed.

Lilly told the story, beginning with Isabelle's insistence that Lilly meet her at Bev's house that evening and ending with how she had escaped from the basement. She had no sooner started speaking than she was interrupted by the arrival of the ambulance and two EMTs.

"We meet again, Mrs. Carlsen," the driver said. He was the one who had examined her the night of Mimi's assault.

"Yes, I'm afraid so," Lilly said ruefully. The EMTs checked her out, bandaging her cuts and scrapes and examining her head before recommending that she be taken to the hospital for an evaluation.

"I'm not going to the hospital," Lilly said. She looked up at the EMT standing next to her. "I promise I'll call my family doctor and have her look at me, okay?"

The EMTs agreed, had Lilly sign the form stating she was refusing a trip to the hospital, and left. Lilly turned to Bill and finished her story.

"We need to get Isabelle in for questioning," Bill said to Perez. "I don't like the sound of the questions she was asking about Xavier Gordon." Perez nodded tersely.

Bill's cell phone rang. "Yeah." Then he smiled and handed Lilly the phone. "Someone's looking for you."

When Lilly heard Hassan's voice, she started crying all over again.

CHAPTER 79

Upon getting home, everyone insisted that Lilly go straight to bed, but she refused. "I'm staying down here with the rest of you. I will not be talked into going upstairs." No one had the temerity to contradict her.

About an hour later, Perez called. Bill spoke to her for a couple minutes, then hung up and turned to Lilly, Hassan, and the girls, all of whom were gathered in Lilly's living room.

"They got her even before they could ping your cell phone, Lil. She ran her car off the road on the other side of Lupine. She's singing like a bird."

Laurel gave him a quizzical look.

Bill smiled. "It means she's confessed to some bad acts. Like killing Xavier Gordon."

Lilly had thought it was a possibility, but when she heard the news, her eyes bulged. "Really? Isabelle killed him?"

"Yeah. I guess they had two dates, neither of which went well, and he spurned her advances one too many times after that. The guy must have been a lothario. I mean, between Isabelle and Chelsea and who-knows-who-else, when did he have time to practice medicine?"

"We saw the end of one of those dates. It was ugly," Lilly said. Hassan nodded in agreement. "I wonder when the other date was."

"I think she said they had dinner the Saturday after Thanksgiving," Bill said. He exhaled loudly. "So that solves one murder, but we're still working on the Phoebe Detweiler case. I've got a feeling the two are connected."

"Do you think Isabelle killed Phoebe?" Lilly asked. "Or it could have been Chelsea, though the only connection is that love potion Phoebe was making for her."

"I don't know," Bill said. "Why would Mimi try to pin it on Xavier if someone other than her or Xavier killed Phoebe?"

"So it's down to the two of them," Lilly said.

"Yeah. Listen, I've got to get back to work. If you're okay, I'll head out. I want you to rest. You'll be in no shape to get married on Tuesday if you don't get some sleep." Lilly didn't mention it, but everything hurt and she was ready to go to bed.

Bill left and Lilly let Hassan lead her upstairs and into the bedroom. He made sure she was warm and almost asleep before he left the room.

"You're *sure* you want to marry into this family?" she asked drowsily as he leaned down to kiss her forehead.

"Of course I'm sure," he said with a chuckle. "Get some rest. I'll sleep on the sofa downstairs, so just call me if you need me."

Lilly slept soundly all night, but woke up with a start as the sky was just beginning to scatter its ribbons of gray morning light along the peaks of the nearby mountains. She was sore all over.

She had had an idea. Just before she awoke, she had been dreaming of the papers stuck under the fence in her backyard. A whorl of papers was fluttering around her and she couldn't see the sky or the ground. It caused her to sit up with a start. Her mind had immediately prodded her with the recollection of the blackmail letters that had been addressed to Xavier.

She went downstairs, being quiet so as not to wake Hassan, and walked straight to the sideboard in the dining room. That was where she always displayed birthday, holiday, and other notecards she received. She clicked on her phone's flashlight and reached immediately for the note Phoebe had written. She took the notecard upstairs and practically burst into her office. She rifled through the top desk drawer and located the copies she had made of the blackmail letters.

Sure enough, the two examples of handwriting matched perfectly.

Phoebe was Xavier's blackmailer.

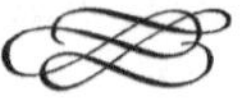

CHAPTER 80

"Hassan!" Lilly cried. "Come up here!"

She heard a loud *thud* downstairs and several seconds later Hassan was standing in the office doorway, a wild look in his eyes and his hair disheveled.

"What's wrong? Are you all right?" His words tumbled over each other.

"I'm fine, just achy. What happened down there?"

"I fell off the couch when I heard you yell. What's going on? Is everything okay?"

"I'm sorry about that. I wasn't thinking. I was just so excited. I figured out it was Phoebe sending the blackmail letters to Xavier."

"Phoebe? How do you know that?"

"I just compared the writing on the blackmail letters to the writing in the note she wrote thanking me for inviting her to Thanksgiving dinner. They're a perfect match."

Hassan let out a low whistle. "I can't believe it. She didn't seem the blackmailing type."

"I know. Blackmail and herbology don't really go hand-in-hand, do they?"

Hassan rubbed the stubble on his chin. "Why do you think she was blackmailing him?"

"I have no idea. I'm going to text Bill and tell him about the handwriting. I'm sure Perez will want to know about this."

"I'll make breakfast. Are you sure you're feeling okay?"

"I'm fine, really." She kissed him.

He grinned and went downstairs while Lilly pulled out her phone.

Are you up? she texted Bill.

Feeling ok? he replied.

I'm fine. Realized this morning that Phoebe was the one black-mailing Xavier.

She waited for him to reply, but he phoned her instead.

"How do you know that?" he demanded.

Lilly explained that she had compared two pieces of hand-writing. "It had to be Phoebe. The handwriting is exactly the same."

"I'll call Perez right away. She's going to need that notecard."

"Do you want me to drop it off at the station?"

"No. She can go to your house to get it. You're getting married Tuesday. I'm sure you don't need extra things to do today."

"Thanks."

Lilly had closed the jewelry shop Monday and Tuesday. She and Hassan spent the day before the wedding trying to sort some of the things he had brought from his house and those Lilly had brought from Bev's house. Laurel was in charge of steaming Lilly's wedding outfit and Vanessa was in charge of confirming the dinner reservation with The Water Wheel, making sure the florist knew where to drop off the flowers, and double-checking that the bakery would deliver the wedding cake to the restaurant. Tighe had arrived at home shortly after breakfast and jumped into the fray to help out with the mine-field in the living room.

Perez knocked on the door late in the morning and Lilly invited her inside. Since every available seat was taken up by piles of stuff, they stood in the foyer to talk.

"Bill told me about a note you have written by Phoebe Detweiler?"

"Yes. She sent me a thank-you note after Thanksgiving. I checked and the handwriting matches the blackmail letters."

"Well, we'll need it examined by our forensic team. Do you have the notecard?"

Lilly went upstairs to retrieve the note. Perez took it with gloved hands and looked carefully at it. "Thank you. We'll be in touch."

Before Lilly left the office, she received a text from Mirren.

Inspection went great. Full speed ahead!

Lilly replied with a thumbs-up and a heart, then returned to the living room. She leaned down to kiss the top of Hassan's head. "I feel like things are finally coming together."

CHAPTER 81

Tuesday morning was glorious. The sun was out, the air was brisk and clear, and there wasn't a cloud in the sky. Lilly skipped her coffee that day, figuring she didn't need anything that would make her even more jittery. She settled on herbal tea.

"Hi, Mom." Tighe walked into the kitchen, still wearing his pajamas. "You ready for today?"

Lilly took a deep breath. "I think so."

"It's going to be great. I mean, I'm sure the wedding will be great, but I think it'll be great for you to marry Hassan." Lilly smiled at up her son.

Tighe poured himself a glass of orange juice and sat across the table from her. "Are Uncle Bill and Noley going to pick up Gran?"

Lilly nodded. "I just hope she agrees to go with them. Mirren and her sister are going to drive Finley to the courthouse and meet us there."

"It'll be good to see Gran. And meet Finley. They haven't known each other for very long, have they?"

"No. She's going downhill, Tighe. Finley makes her happy."

Tighe studied his orange juice. "I miss the old Gran."

"So do I, honey." Lilly pushed herself away from the table. She didn't want to spend too much time thinking about Bev or she would fall apart. She, Noley, Laurel, and Vanessa had appointments to get their nails done and then she was visiting the hairdresser for an updo. She had paid for an employee of the nail salon to visit Larkspur Manor to do Bev's nails, too, and for Bev's old hairdresser to style Bev's hair.

Lilly felt like a princess when she returned home from her pampering. Noley had gone home to get ready for the wedding, so Lilly ate a quick lunch with the kids and Vanessa. Hassan had planned to spend the morning with his parents and sister, then they would all meet at the courthouse.

She was just about to leave the house when her cell phone rang. It was Perez. She thought about ignoring the call, but decided to answer it.

"You were right, Mrs. Carlsen," Perez said. Lilly shivered. She wouldn't be Mrs. Carlsen for long—she would be Mrs. Ashraf before the afternoon was out.

"About Phoebe's handwriting?"

"Yes, ma'am. A handwriting expert on staff confirmed it. I wanted to thank you for pointing us in the right direction."

Lilly hadn't exactly pointed them in the right direction—she had practically served up that piece of the puzzle on a silver platter. But she didn't want to seem petty. "You're welcome. I was happy to help."

"I think we can officially remove you from the suspect list now. Congratulations on your marriage this afternoon, ma'am."

It was the best wedding present Lilly could have gotten —so far.

CHAPTER 82

The weddings went off without a hitch.

"Well," said Harry at the celebration dinner that evening, "there were a couple hitches."

Everyone stared at him.

"Get it? Lilly and Hassan got hitched? Bev and Finley got hitched?"

Everyone groaned and Alice rolled her eyes. "See what I have to live with?" she joked.

The happy couples, along with the Ashraf family—Hassan's parents, Basra and Amir, and his sister, Ghada—Bill and Noley, Tighe, Laurel, Vanessa, Harry and Alice, and Mirren and her sister were seated in a private room at The Water Wheel.

Champagne was flowing for the adults and mocktails for the under-twenty-one set. Everyone wore a smile, and even Bev seemed happy. She hadn't recognized a single person at the wedding except for Finley and Mirren. Bev and Finley sat at the table, holding hands. Bev smiled benignly at everyone around her and Finley only had eyes for Bev.

Before dinner Bill pulled Lilly aside. "Perez called when I was on my way over here," he said. "She talked to Mimi and her lawyer. Mimi made the lawyer leave the room and she spilled her guts to Perez about everything. She killed Phoebe."

"I figured that was the only explanation for why she blamed Xavier for Phoebe's death. He couldn't defend himself and she assumed throwing him under the bus would get her off the hook. Why did she do it? Did she say? And why did she confess?"

"I'll answer the last question first. Perez told Mimi that the only fingerprints on the pestle, besides Phoebe's, were hers. At that point Mimi knew she was cornered. As for why she did it, that's simple. It all came down to money. Xavier set her up with a florist shop before they were divorced so she would have a way to earn an income, but it wasn't doing well."

"How could it, when she spent so much time here?"

"I don't think she has much of a head for business, to be honest. Anyway, he was still paying alimony, but apparently she was afraid he was going to lose his shirt if he continued to pay off Phoebe every time she demanded money. And you'll never guess why she was blackmailing him."

"You're not going to make me guess, are you?"

"According to the documentation on Phoebe's computer, which Perez just received yesterday, she had written a draft email to the district attorney revealing that Xavier Gordon was practicing medicine without a license. He had been caught practicing without a license years ago in Arizona and Phoebe knew about it because she had worked in a medical office in the same city. She ran a search on him after seeing him on Thanksgiving and found that he had been nabbed for the same thing in Wyoming, too. That's why he moved to Colorado. He used a slightly different version of his name each time he opened a new practice, so the states where he'd been caught never synced their information to figure out it was the same person in each case."

"And Phoebe was demanding money to keep his secret," Lilly

surmised. "She needed the money. She was paying rent and having a house built in addition to opening a new business."

"Exactly. And we already know from the letters that he paid the hush money at least once. Perez is going to get his bank records and Phoebe's bank records. Anyway, like I said, Mimi started getting nervous that Phoebe would continue blackmailing him and he would continue parting with his money to shut her up. If that happened, Mimi would suffer, too, because he wouldn't be able to pay her alimony. So she solved the problem by offing Phoebe."

"So how did the blackmail letters make it into my yard?"

"She dropped a box with a ton of papers in it. She didn't realize the blackmail letters were in the box. Otherwise she would have tried harder to retrieve them."

"I wonder why the police didn't find the papers in their search of Xavier's house."

"Because they only had the authority to search for clues that might point to the identity of the killer, not the whole house."

"That also explains why they didn't find the mortar and pestle, I guess. They were probably hidden where the police would have no reason to look."

Bill nodded.

Lilly shook her head. "Both Mimi and Phoebe seemed so nice. Who would have thought they were so devious? And— wait a minute."

"What?" Bill asked.

"I just realized something." Lilly hit her forehead with the heel of her hand. "Of course Xavier didn't kill Phoebe! I should have known that was a ploy by Mimi to throw suspicion away from her."

"What do you mean?"

"You told me that Isabelle and Xavier had a dinner date the Saturday after Thanksgiving. That's the night Phoebe was killed. I remember hearing Xavier on the phone making that date. I didn't know who he was talking to at the time, but he told her he would pick her up at six. That's about the time Phoebe was killed, because it had just happened when I got to her shop between six and six-thirty. So he was out with Isabelle at the time of Phoebe's murder. Who would have thought that Xavier's murderer would provide the alibi for him in another murder?"

"There's one more thing," Bill said.

"What's that?"

"Noley called Chelsea as soon as I got off the phone with Perez. She wanted to tell her she's off the hook."

"Oh?"

"Chelsea said she's leaving town and heading back to Seattle. Apparently this whole incident has taken the shine off Juniper Junction and she can't wait to get out. Can't say that I blame her. I'm glad she's leaving, though."

So it looked like Chelsea was heading back to Seattle. Lilly hoped she could straighten herself out and get help for her relationship issues.

Hassan came over and put his arm around Lilly's shoulders. "Everyone wants us to make a proper entrance with your mom and Finley."

She grinned and let him take her by the hand, which now sported, in addition to her wedding band, a beautiful ring with a white gold setting, her emerald in the center, and three small diamonds along each side of it. Hassan had slipped it on her finger just before the wedding ceremony saying, "I couldn't let you marry me without the engagement ring."

Hassan led Lilly to the vestibule outside the dining room. Lilly could feel her face glowing, and Hassan's broad smile meant the world to her. When the two happy couples reentered the dining room to applause and whoops from the small crowd of the people they loved most, Lilly had to blink back tears.

In a twist on tradition, the grooms stood to make the toasts.

Finley got up and thanked people for coming and told everyone how much he loved Bev. He surprised and delighted everyone when he sang a short song to her. When all the guests had wiped the tears from their eyes, Hassan thanked everyone for their love and support and for sharing the day with him and Lilly and with Bev and Finley. Then he turned to Lilly and held up his glass.

"To my wife, whom I love more with each passing day. Next year at this time if all goes according to plan, our family will include a new baby and we'll have even more to celebrate on Thanksgiving. Thank you for this journey we're about to take."

Lilly, wiping away tears for the umpteenth time that day, looked up at him and smiled. He sat down to applause and glasses clinking, and he kissed Lilly. As the conversation started up again all around them, he leaned toward her ear so only she could hear what he was saying.

"I wanted to give you something special for our wedding, and so I did the one thing I thought would make you happiest."

He pulled away and she looked at him in puzzlement. "What's that?"

"I cancelled my trip to see the lapis lazuli in Afghanistan."

It was even better than Perez's gift, and he was right. Nothing could have made Lilly happier.

〜

The End

CHICKEN DIVAN

2 10-oz. packages frozen broccoli spears
¼ c. butter
5 T. flour
2 c. chicken broth
¾ c. heavy cream
3 chicken breast halves, cooked
¼ c. grated Parmesan cheese, plus extra for sprinkling

Preheat oven to 350 degrees.

Cook broccoli according to package directions and set aside. In a medium saucepan, melt butter. Add flour, salt, a dash of pepper, and chicken broth. Cook, stirring constantly, until mixture thickens and is bubbly. Stir in cream.

Arrange broccoli in a 9x9" broiler-proof baking dish. Cover with ½ the sauce. Top with chicken breasts. Add Parmesan cheese to remaining sauce and pour mixture over chicken. Sprinkle with a little bit of extra Parmesan cheese.

Bake until heated through and bubbling, about 25-30 minutes. Turn on broiler and broil just until sauce is golden.

EASIER-THAN-IT-SOUNDS
FOCACCIA

1 envelope active dry yeast (not rapid-rise)

2 t. honey

2 ½ c. lukewarm water (use a thermometer! Water should be between 105 and 115 degrees Fahrenheit)

5 c. all-purpose flour

1 T. kosher salt (or you can use 5 t. Diamond Crystal salt)

6 T. extra-virgin olive oil (do not use regular olive oil), *divided*, plus more for hands

Flaky sea salt

Whisk the yeast, honey, and water in a medium bowl. Allow it to sit for about 5 minutes. It should get foamy or creamy. If it doesn't, you might need to use new yeast.

Add flour and salt and mix with a rubber spatula just until there are no more dry streaks. Your dough will be shaggy.

Pour 4 T. olive oil into a large bowl—one that will fit into the refrigerator. Place the dough in the bowl and turn it so it's coated in the oil. Cover the bowl tightly (with a lid, plastic wrap, or foil). Place in fridge and chill for 8-24 hours (the longer, the better).

Generously butter an 18x13" or similar-sized lipped baking sheet. Pour 1 t. olive oil onto the middle of the prepared sheet.

With the dough still in the bowl, take one fork in each hand and gather up the edge of the dough farthest from you. Lift it into the center of the dough. Give the bowl a ¼ turn and do it again, then repeat the process two more times. This deflates the dough and shapes it into a (very) rough ball.

Place the dough on the baking sheet and pour any oil remaining in the bowl over the dough. Turn the dough to coat it in oil.

Place the pan, uncovered, in a warm, dry place for 1 ½ to 4 hours (again, the longer the better), until it is doubled in size.

Place a rack in the middle of the oven and preheat oven to 450 degrees. Lightly oil your hands and, if necessary, stretch the dough to fill the baking sheet. Poke the dough hard all over, letting your fingers reach through to the baking sheet.

Drizzle dough with remaining 1 T. olive oil and sprinkle with the sea salt.

Bake for 20-30 minutes, or until bread is puffed and golden.

This makes a delicious pizza crust!

HASSAN'S BOLOGNESE SAUCE

2 T. olive oil
2 t. butter
2 oz. diced pancetta
½ lg. onion, chopped
1 med. carrot, peeled and chopped
1 celery stalk, chopped
½ lb. ground beef
½ c. dry red wine
1 ½ c. half-and-half (or less, according to how think you like your Bolognese)
1 14.5-oz. can chopped tomatoes, undrained

In a Dutch oven over medium heat, add oil, butter, and pancetta. Fry the pancetta for about 3 minutes, until it starts rendering its fat. Add the onion, carrot, and celery and sauté for about 5 minutes or until softened.

Reduce heat to medium-low and add beef. Break up beef and cook only until meat is no longer pink, about 3-5 minutes. Add wine, raise heat to medium, and simmer until wine evaporates, about 2-3 minutes. Add ¾ c. half-and-half and simmer until heated through.

Add tomatoes; season with salt. Bring to a simmer and cover partially. Set heat to low and cook, stirring occasionally, for about 4 hours. Sauce should be thick. Add water if needed to keep the sauce from sticking.

During the final 45 minutes of cooking, add the remaining half-and-half in three additions, stirring to combine well after each addition. If you like your sauce a little thicker, do not add all the half-and-half.

Serve over cooked pasta.

JOIN MY VIP GROUP

If you enjoyed *Fowl Play*, I invite you to join my VIP group by visiting www.amymreade.com.

VIP Group members are treated to exclusive content, behind-the-scenes views of my bookish life, news of upcoming releases, and free goodies in The Secret Room of my website.

ABOUT THE AUTHOR

Amy M. Reade is the *USA Today* and *Wall Street Journal* bestselling author of cozy, historical, and Gothic mysteries.

A former practicing attorney, Amy discovered a passion for fiction writing and has never looked back. She has so far penned three standalone Gothic mysteries, the Malice series of Gothic novels, the Juniper Junction Holiday Cozy Mystery series, the Libraries of the World Mystery Series, and the Cape May Historical Mystery Collection. In addition to writing, she loves to read, cook and travel. Amy lives in New Jersey and is a member of Mystery Writers of America and Sisters in Crime.

You can find out more on her website at www.amymreade.com.

www.ingramcontent.com/pod-product-compliance
Lightning Source LLC
Chambersburg PA
CBHW060516220726
48290CB00015B/1562